'No doubt what I am about to say will vex you, but on your father's death I became your legal guardian. It might seem strange to you, but he trusted me. I refused at first, for I did not wish to be burdened with finding you a spouse, but he persisted.'

'But I do not wish to marry,' Beth blurted out.

'So your father told me—and frankly I do not believe it,' said Gawain, with a shake of the head.

An angry sparkle lit her eyes. 'You are mistaken. I presume he will have left his business to me? There is naught preventing me from taking control of it when I return to London. I will be able to support myself financially, so I have no need of a husband.'

## DEDICATION:

To my fellow author, the prolific Anne Herries,
for all her encouragement over the years.
This one's for you!

**June Francis**'s interest in old wives' tales and folk
customs led her into a writing career. History has
always fascinated her, and her first novels were set in
Medieval times. She has also written sagas based in
Liverpool and Chester. Married with three grown-up
sons, she lives on Merseyside. On a clear day she can
see the sea and the distant Welsh hills from her house.
She enjoys swimming, fell-walking, music, lunching
with friends and smoochy dancing with her husband.
More information about June can be found at her
website: www.junefrancis.co.uk

**Previous novels by this author:**

ROWAN'S REVENGE
TAMED BY THE BARBARIAN
REBEL LADY, CONVENIENT WIFE
HIS RUNAWAY MAIDEN
PIRATE'S DAUGHTER, REBEL WIFE

**Did you know that some of these novels
are also available as eBooks?
Visit www.millsandboon.co.uk**

# THE UNCONVENTIONAL MAIDEN

June Francis

MILLS & BOON

All the characters in this book have no existence outside the imagination of the author, and have no relation whatsoever to anyone bearing the same name or names. They are not even distantly inspired by any individual known or unknown to the author, and all the incidents are pure invention.

First published in Great Britain 2011
Paperback edition 2012
by Mills & Boon, an imprint of Harlequin (UK) Limited.
Harlequin (UK) Limited, Eton House, 18-24 Paradise Road, Richmond, Surrey TW9 1SR

© June Francis 2011

ISBN: 978 0 263 89219 2

Harlequin (UK) policy is to use papers that are natural, renewable and recyclable products and made from wood grown in sustainable forests. The logging and manufacturing process conform to the legal environmental regulations of the country of origin.

Printed and bound in Spain
by Blackprint CPI, Barcelona

# AUTHOR NOTE

Perhaps it's because my husband was a printer and I'm a novelist that the early days of printing should hold a fascination for me. It was William Caxton who introduced the printing press into England, and his first book was printed in 1477. By the time of 1520, when this story is set, the handwritten book was being superseded by the printed one at a rate of knots.

At first most books were religious ones, and Henry VIII had a bestseller on his hands when he wrote a slender volume in defence of the seven sacraments of the faith in response to the writings of the German priest and professor of theology Martin Luther. It was illegal to print and distribute leaflets of the teachings by him, and could be punished by death. During the Tudor period printing really took off, and more people wanted to learn to read. Their interests were not only in religion, but in such subjects as the classical period of the Greeks and Romans, hawking and, of course, Chaucer's *Canterbury Tales*—the bestseller of its day. I have used a little poetic licence by having it printed before it actually was. Poetry itself was extremely popular.

There were, of course, those who considered it dangerous to make the printed word so readily available to so many people. *Goodness knows what would happen if more merchants, artisans and even the masses were ever to learn to read and to think for themselves! It could lead to revolution!*

Ladies in particular were considered by some to be too delicate and weak to cope with some of the material coming off the presses, never mind their actually writing for publication themselves. But of course there were women who wrote books—mostly religious, or to do with the organisation of one's household—and of course there were those men and women who kept journals and reported on great events of the day.

Printed books were expensive, and it was to be some time before the masses were to be taught to read and write, but as we all know it eventually happened and books are now read by millions. But that makes me think about the revolution in reading habits that is taking place now. Some of us believe there is nothing so aesthetically pleasing as to hold a brand-new hardback borrowed from the library, whilst some love to snuggle up in bed with a good paperback. Others much prefer to download a whole load of eBooks onto a reader—especially when they're going on holiday.

I'd like to finish by telling you about a small old book of almost six hundred pages that belongs to my husband. It gives me a special feel when I hold it. It was printed in 1824 and has a woodcut of William Caxton on one page. On another is the title *Typographia or the Printers' Instructions by J. Johnson, printer*. It includes an account of the origins of printing. What's so great about that? you might ask, but inside is printed a dedication to the Right Hon. Earl Spencer, KG, president of the Roxburghe Club and its members, who include the writer Sir Walter Scott. The Earl, of course, is an ancestor of Prince William—our future king.

*June Francis*

# Prologue

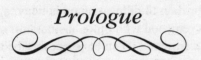

*London—May 1520*

'So what do you think of my Beth?' asked Master Llewellyn, handing a goblet of ruby-red wine to Sir Gawain Raventon. 'Would she not make the right man a wonderful wife? She has kept house for me since the death of her mother and she has proved to have a good head for figures and is thrifty, so I have allowed her to do my business accounts.'

'You have a husband in mind for her?' asked Gawain, who had met that young woman only a quarter of an hour ago and had found her extremely self-possessed.

Master Llewellyn shook his head. 'She is adamant that she will not marry. I tell her that she must get herself a husband. This whole matter concerning Jonathan has aged me and is keeping me awake nights.' He sighed heavily as he gazed into the strong handsome face of the man sitting opposite him.

'In the light of the evidence I uncovered I do believe your son Jonathan's death to be highly suspicious,' said Gawain. 'Do you have any notion of who might have wanted him dead?'

'A madman, for what sane person would want to kill my dear Jonathan?' said the old man huskily. 'He was well liked and did good business selling our services and wares. It is true that sometimes he would absent himself for days. I didn't know his whereabouts, but he always returned with more business for us.'

Gawain frowned. 'You have questioned these customers?'

A muscle in Master Llewellyn's cheek twitched. 'No, Jonathan dealt with them himself, although I did once meet... Now, I wonder...'

Gawain raised an interrogative dark eyebrow. 'You have thought of someone who might know something?'

Master Llewellyn pursed his lips and he looked unhappy. 'I could be mistaken and I do not wish to damage a man's reputation. I would rather not name names.'

'If you do not mind my saying so, remaining silent could prove a mistake if we are dealing with a possible murderer,' Gawain pointed out.

The old man remained stubbornly silent.

Gawain was exasperated. 'Does your daughter know aught about this person or anything that could help us?'

Master Llewellyn looked shocked. 'She believes that Jonathan's death was an accident and I want her to continue to do so. The truth might prove too much for her to bear. The fair sex are not as strong as us men,' he added, taking a hasty gulp of his wine.

Remembering the firmness of Mistress Llewellyn's chin, Gawain thought the other man underestimated his daughter's strength. 'You should tell someone,' he said firmly.

'When the time is ripe I will,' assured Master Llewellyn, downing the rest of his wine and banging down his goblet. 'But I would ask of you a boon, Sir Gawain. If I were to die before this matter is cleared up, would you be Beth's guardian and take on the task of choosing a husband for her? I must have a grandson,' he added fretfully.

Gawain could understand the old man's need for a male heir to carry on his line. He thought of his own son, who had died when he was only two years old, and the pain was as fresh to him now as it had been then. Indeed, it had intensified in the weeks since his wife, Mary, had disappeared with their daughters and he had feared the boy's death had caused her to lose her senses.

'I do not wish to gainsay you, Master Llewellyn,' he rasped. 'But I know more about timber and shipbuilding, and even what is happening at King Henry's court, than what kind of man would make a suitable and pleasing husband for your daughter.'

'I think you underestimate your judgement,' said Master Llewellyn persuasively. 'I believe you to be sound and I entreat you to grant me this boon. Women so often do not know their own minds and need a man to guide them in the right direction. You will not lose by it, I promise. I will bequeath you shares in my company and I cannot say fairer than that.'

'That is indeed generous of you,' said Gawain, taken aback. 'But surely you have a close friend to whom you can entrust this task?'

Master Llewellyn grimaced. 'At my age I have few friends left and they are enfeebled. I have appreciated the manner in which you took my suspicions seriously and investigated Jonathan's so-called boating accident.' His voice trembled. 'You have a strength of character I have seen in few men. Please, let me have your hand on it, so I can have my will rewritten before I leave for France next month.'

Gawain experienced a pang of pity for the old man; as he was to return to his home in Kent that afternoon, and had to make all speed to Dover Castle the next morning, he decided that the only way to terminate this conversation swiftly was by agreeing to do his best for Beth Llewellyn, if the need should arise. At least she would not be short of suitors—she would inherit her father's thriving printing and bookselling business and his aunt could chaperon her if need be. 'All right, I will do as you ask,' he said.

He was rewarded by Master Llewellyn's relieved smile and they shook hands.

Gawain drained his cup. 'I also am bound for France at King Henry's bidding. You go there on business?' he asked politely.

'Aye, I hope to meet an old friend in my line of business in Calais,' replied the older man, his rheumy eyes bright. 'Also, the king, who occasionally patronises my shop, has generously said I may attend some of the festivities on this occasion if I wish, so I have suggested to my daughter that she accompany me.'

'Then it is possible I might see you there,' said Gawain, taking his leave.

On the way out of the chamber he collided into Beth Llewellyn. He steadied her and was aware of the softness of her breasts pressed against the wall of his chest and the swell of her hip nestled against his thigh. For a moment her startled, luminous chestnut-brown eyes rested on his face with an expression in them that caused him to remain as if cast in marble whilst his heart thudded against his ribs. Then he snatched his hands away as if she was a hot brand. 'I beg your pardon, Mistress Llewellyn!' he said stiffly and hurried away before he gave way to the urge to taste lips the colour of raspberries that were parted as if she were holding her breath—no doubt fearing what he might do next.

# *Chapter One*

*France—June 1520*

A strong hot wind blew from the south and dust clung to Beth Llewellyn's perspiring face as she pushed her way through the crowd. She wondered what event it was this time that was being performed for the entertainment of those gathered in the place that some were already naming the Eighth Wonder of the World. Many from the surrounding district and further afield had flooded into the area to witness the glittering splendour of the kings of England and France.

Beth could hear the thud of feet on turf, wheezing of air in chests and whistling between teeth. A sudden roar from the throats of those who could see what was happening caused her to believe she might have missed the finale and she thrust herself forwards into the crowd. But no one was giving way, so she dropped to her knees and managed to worm her way between the forest of hose-clad legs, ignoring the curses and clouts that came her way.

At last she arrived at the front, only to find herself almost eyeball to eyeball with the black-browed, hard-mouthed Sir Gawain Raventon. She could scarcely believe it was him and her pulse raced. She prayed that he was far too occupied to notice her, never mind recognise her in her male attire!

He was obviously having difficulty breathing. Around his throat was a hairy, ham-size arm. His strong-boned, tanned face was tight with determination as his long sinewy fingers forced their way between that arm and his throat. The next moment he heaved up his body and threw off his opponent. She did not know how he managed it because it happened so swiftly: several moments later, he had the other man pinned to the ground. Then Sir Gawain sprang to his feet, eased a shoulder with a grimace before being declared the victor. His opponent stared at him sullenly as the Englishman was handed the winner's purse, which he tossed to a young man standing a few feet away.

Beth knew at this point that she should retreat or at the very least avert her eyes. It seemed odd that only now did she become fully aware that Sir Gawain was *half-naked* and, as it was the first time she had seen a man's unclothed body, she was transfixed. His muscular chest was coated with a sheen of sweat and dark hair curled downwards in a V to the waist of his snug-fitting hose. She remembered colliding into him the first day they had met and felt a similar sensation at the core of her being that sent heat darting through her. Having a need to cool off, Beth reached for the laces at the throat of her tunic. She should never have made that move because it drew Sir Gawain's attention to her. Hastily, she attempted to back away, but he was too swift for her and dragged her upright.

'Who have we here?' he growled, lifting her off her feet.

Beth gripped the opening at the throat of her tunic in an attempt to bring the two edges together, only to get her hand jammed between his chest and her breasts. She gasped with pain.

'That was a rather foolish move,' he said, loosening his grip slightly so her hand could slide free, his penetrating blue eyes scanning her face. His orbs turned into dark slits. 'We've met before.'

'No, we have not,' lied Beth, shaking her head vigorously.

That was her second mistake for the action dislodged her cap, freeing her bronze-coloured braids. 'By Saint George,' he muttered. 'It can't be!'

There came a sudden roar from behind him, causing her eyes to widen. 'Look out!' she cried.

Gawain dropped her and turned to face his disgruntled former opponent.

Beth scrambled to her feet, scooped up her cap and made her escape. She forced her way through the crowd, stuffing her hair beneath her cap as she went, praying that Sir Gawain had been unable to put a name to her face. Yesterday, she had watched him at the joust and he had been clad in armour from head to toe. She remembered imagining that beneath all that gilt-and-silver metal was a finely honed body.

But what was she thinking of, bothering her head with such thoughts? She must make haste to reach her father's tent, not only to change her garb, but also to write down what she had just seen whilst it was fresh in her mind. Hopefully, when she returned home, her words would be read in the news sheet for the rising merchant-and-artisan class back in London that she printed secretly. Her father had scanned its pages recently and shaken his hoary head as if in disbelief. If he had known she was now its author, he would have soon put a stop to it and forbidden her access to the print room. She despaired when she thought of his lack of foresight. Why could he not see that, since the invention of the printing press, the numbers of those learning to read had increased enormously? She remembered Jonathan saying that they were greedy for anything they could get their hands on and not all of it educational or religious. Beth was determined to continue to provide for that market, despite her half-brother's death, by writing about such events as this one and in the process making money for herself. She felt it was what Jonathan would have wanted.

Words buzzed in her head. *He was a giant of a man, six feet or more and broad in the shoulder. He held himself well, with a sort of easy, well-knit movement that spoke of training and perfect physical fitness.*

Beth relived that moment when Sir Gawain had flung his opponent to the ground. Never had she met a man who had made her so aware of the beauty of the male physique: its form, its strength, its grace. She had admired his skill with the lance and sword yesterday, but today he had used his body as a weapon in a way that had been utterly thrilling. She might have told her father that she did not wish to marry, but it was not because she had a dislike of men.

Her father would be horrified if it came to his ears that she had attended a wrestling match dressed in male attire. Jonathan would have pretended to be so, too, but in reality he'd have been amused because he'd secretly enjoyed cross-dressing himself. She had discovered that fact several years ago and mentioned it to her mother, but she had been hushed and told to keep it to herself. A sigh escaped her. Beth had been extremely fond of Jonathan despite his being their father's favourite. The son who was supposedly so much cleverer than her and who would have inherited the business if he had not died so unexpectedly. Poor Jonathan!

'Mistress Llewellyn!' called a voice that she recognised.

Beth's heart leapt and her step faltered, but then she put on a spurt, knowing it was best that she appeared not to own to that name. In her haste she did not see the guy rope of a nearby tent and was sent sprawling on the ground.

Before she could scramble to her feet, she was hauled upright. Her eyes were parallel with Sir Gawain's chest and she could not help but notice that his doublet was unfastened and the ties of his shirt hung loose, exposing his bare throat. She fought back a temptation to reach up and touch his bare skin and struggled in his grasp.

Before she could gather her wits and act as if she had never seen him before, he removed her cap, causing her braids to once more tumble down her back.

He smiled grimly. 'So I was right, it was you. By St George, what are you thinking of wearing such garb?'

Beth tilted her chin. 'Why did you have to come after me? Couldn't you have pretended that your eyes had deceived you?' she said heatedly. 'What I do is really none of your business, sir!'

'Is it not?' he said drily, grabbing hold of her plaits and stuffing them inside her cap. 'You are a disgrace to womanhood and I could no more ignore your behaviour than fly to the moon.'

The colour in her cheeks deepened. 'Do you not think that is rather an exaggeration? I have done naught wrong. I have hurt no one by my behaviour. But I do beg you not to mention this to my father. He has had enough to grieve him in the past few months.'

Gawain's eyes held hers. 'Perhaps I will do as you ask if you provide me with a worthwhile explanation. Otherwise, I must believe that the heat has affected your sanity.'

'You are insinuating that I am crazed just because I wished to pass unnoticed amongst the crowds!' She raised her eyebrows and gave him a look of disdain.

A short derisive laugh escaped him. 'You call crawling on your belly into a wrestling ring going unnoticed? You are crazed, woman!'

'I was simply curious!' she protested.

'Curiosity can get people into trouble.'

'Obviously, but I am not the only person here showing curiosity. Why should I satisfy yours, sir? What is important is whether my father really needs to know the truth about a matter that would cause him embarrassment and make him angry?'

'If you knew that, then why do what you did?' he asked.

Beth said scornfully, 'You wouldn't understand because you are not a daughter.'

'You forget your place,' he snapped. 'And that remark is a typical feminine excuse to avoid telling the truth.'

'Men are not always honest,' said Beth recklessly. 'Perhaps you would like to tell me why you were wrestling half-naked.'

'The heat?' he suggested, raising his eyebrows.

'Then you must have broiled alive in the armour you wore in the lists yesterday,' she said unthinkingly.

'Aye,' he said, holding her gaze. 'But I did not notice you there.'

'I was not amongst the ladies,' she countered, wishing he would not look at her so. There was something about this man that caused her to be hot and bothered and it was not due to her concern about his informing her father about her alter ego.

'You mean you were dressed as a youth then, too!' Gawain swore softly and thrust her away from him. 'I must be mad, but I will say naught about your disgraceful behaviour if you promise never to wear male garb again.'

'Of course, if that is the price I have to pay for your silence,' she said with a sudden meekness that he found unconvincing. 'Now, if you do not mind, Sir Gawain, I must be on my way.'

He frowned. 'You do realise that if you betrayed yourself as a woman in front of a priest, then he could have you clapped in prison. Your head would be shaved and you would be dragged through the streets in disgrace.'

Beth stiffened. 'I deem you are trying to frighten me, sir.'

'Not at all, Mistress Llewellyn. I am just pointing out to you the punishment that could be heaped on your lovely head if you don't do what I say,' said Gawain, exacerbated.

Hot words were on the tip of Beth's tongue, thinking how there was one rule for men and another for women, but she decided to hold them back. 'I've noted your warning, Sir Gawain, so may I now be on my way?' She gave him a limpid look and a honeyed smile.

He found himself once again comparing the colour of her lovely eyes with polished chestnuts and her lips with soft fruit. Would they yield to his tongue and teeth and release their sweetness? And what of her body? His thoughts shocked him. He was a married man despite having been informed that Mary had been seen arm in arm with another man in the next shire, information that had resulted in him lying through his teeth to the informer. Maybe it was due to the fact that he had not slept with a woman for six months that had resulted in him desiring Beth Llewellyn? If so, it had to stop!

Beth wasted no time hurrying away. She wondered what would be Sir Gawain's reaction if she told him that it was her mother, Marian, who had first put the idea in her head to don a disguise if need be to gather interesting little snippets of news. It was Beth's mother who had also encouraged her to jot down her thoughts and feelings about this and that. She had been a great admirer of the mystic, Dame Julian of Norwich, who was believed to have been the first woman to have written a book in the English language.

Sadly her mother had died four years ago when Beth was sixteen. If Marian had been alive today, then she would have insisted on her husband allowing their daughter to play an even greater part in running the business. Her father, on the other hand, was determined to marry her off to a man who would be his partner in the business, whilst she would be expected to keep house for them. It was why she had stubbornly refused to marry!

The thought infuriated her as she made her way into the next field, where thousands of tents of lesser splendour were pitched. Both Henry VIII and Francis I had determined to outshine the other, with tents, horses and costumes displaying accoutrements and jewels amidst much expensive fabric woven with silk-and-gold thread. The most elaborate arrangements had been made for the two monarchs and their queens, Katherine of Aragon and the pregnant Claude of Brittany. No doubt King Henry was wishing that it was his Katherine who was expecting a child, as he was desperate for a legitimate healthy son, according to rumour.

She hurried between the tents and, as she approached her father's tent, thought she caught sight of a whisk of a red skirt as it vanished behind the next tent. No doubt it belonged to one of those loose women she had seen disappearing into the gloom the other night. Cautiously she drew back the flap of her father's tent, praying that he was still talking business with his old friend in Calais.

Her prayer went unanswered.

Lying on the ground was her father with the jewelled hilt of a dagger sticking out of his back. Her heart began to pound in her chest and she felt sick as she fell on her knees beside his body. Her first instinct was to remove the dagger and see if he was breathing. But as she reached for it, there came a sound behind her. She whirled round, fearing that the murderer had returned, and saw Sir Gawain standing in the tent-opening.

For a moment she could not speak and then she cried, 'Help me!'

Scowling, he took her by the shoulders, hoisted her to her feet and set her aside. Then, gritting his teeth, he hunkered down beside the body and searched for a pulse before looking up at her. 'I am sorry, Mistress Llewellyn, but your father is dead.'

'But—but he can't be dead,' she stammered, scarcely able to believe his words nor her own eyes.

'Did you catch sight of anyone lurking outside as you approached?' asked Gawain.

'I—I thought I caught a glimpse of a woman's scarlet skirts, but I cannot believe my father would have been—' She fumbled for a camp stool and sat down. 'Who could have done this?' she asked in a bewildered voice.

Gawain remembered Master Llewellyn mentioning someone who might have wanted his son dead, but had refused to name names. Could he have confronted this person with his suspicions here in this tent and met his end at that villain's hand? 'Do you recognise this dagger at all?' he asked, getting to his feet.

Beth stared at the elaborately decorated weapon and shuddered. 'No, but I would wager that it is not the instrument of a hireling.'

Gawain agreed, frowning as he took a cloth from a pouch at his waist and wiped the blade. He wrapped the dagger in the cloth and placed it on the small table nearby. 'Whoever did this must have been in a hurry to leave such a distinctive weapon behind. Perhaps he heard you approaching and made his escape via the back of the tent.'

Beth glanced at the canvas wall that divided the living area from the sleeping quarters. She opened her mouth to speak, but already Gawain had walked over to the dividing canvas wall and stepped through the opening. She hurried after him.

He was kneeling by the billowing outer wall of the tent; at the sound of her entry, he glanced over his shoulder. 'The murderer most likely did make their escape this way. See how the bedding has been pushed aside and there are scuff marks on the ground and a couple of tent pegs have come loose. Perhaps the woman you caught sight of might have seen who it was and would recognise him again.'

Beth took a shaky breath. 'Should we try to find her?'

'Aye. Where are your servants?' he asked abruptly. 'You need someone with you.'

'They were given leave to see the sights and were to return this evening.' She swallowed the lump in her throat and added in a husky voice. 'Jane and Sam have been with our family for years and this will be a terrible shock to them.'

Gawain rasped his unshaven jaw with a finger and his dark lashes hooded his eyes as his gaze washed over her and the froth of feminine garments sprawled on her bedding. 'Perhaps someone tending a cooking fire nearby might have noticed whoever entered this tent. You will stay here and change your garments whilst I see if I can discover if that is so.'

She moistened her lips. 'What if the murderer returns for the weapon?'

Gawain hesitated, then said reassuringly, 'I will keep this tent in my sight, so I will see if anyone approaches it.'

She thanked him.

He brushed past her and vanished from her sight. For a moment she considered running after him, not wanting to be alone. Then she tilted her chin, knowing she must depend on herself for so many things from now on. With her father dead, she would now inherit his business. Even so it made sense to obey Sir Gawain's order and change her clothing. Swiftly she stripped and donned a cream-coloured high-necked chemise, stockings, garters and a long-sleeved dark blue gown that fastened at the waist to reveal the underskirt of the chemise. The front of the gown was cut to an arch over her bosom and the neckline was fashionably square. She searched for the shoes with buckles that her father had insisted on having made for her in London before they came away. He had never bothered much about her appearance and she guessed that he had only done so recently because he was determined that she should attract a suitor. Well, his plan would come to naught. She would not marry, but run his business herself and make her mother proud of her. God grant that she was in heaven and able to look down on her. Father, too, now, she added forlornly.

Who could have killed him and why? She wiped her face with a drying cloth and then, with a shiver of apprehension and praying that Sir Gawain was keeping his promise, hastily coiled her braids beneath her head-dress, the front of which was shaped like the gable of a house. Then from a box, inlaid with different kinds of woods, she took the simple cross of amethyst on a silver chain that had belonged to her mother and placed it about her neck. She smoothed down the conical-shaped skirts of her gown before picking up a blanket and leaving the sleeping quarters.

She gazed down at her father and then kissed his cheek. With trembling fingers she covered him with the blanket and then shot to her feet at the sound of footsteps outside. She gazed towards the tent opening with a racing heart and then sagged with relief as the flap lifted and Sir Gawain ducked his dark head and entered the tent.

'Thank God, it is you! Did you discover anything?' she asked.

'A woman was seen entering this tent,' he said curtly.

Beth was stunned. 'I—I don't believe it!'

Sir Gawain's frown deepened. 'She was wearing scarlet, so it seems likely that it was the woman of whom you caught a glimpse. Apparently she was tall for a female, so she could stand out in a crowd and be easily recognisable.'

'I—I still don't believe my father would entertain a woman alone in this tent,' she said fiercely. 'Maybe it was a man in disguise?'

'I suppose that is possible,' said Gawain slowly.

'It's also possible that it could have been just an opportunist thief who made the mistake of entering the tent, not realising Father was here.' She seized on that idea because it was less frightening. 'It could even have been an accident.'

Gawain did not look convinced and she guessed that he thought she was deceiving herself. 'You'll have to go through your possessions to see if aught is missing,' he said.

Beth reached for the cross at her throat. 'This was not taken.'

He stared at the lovely column of her neck and felt an unexpected urge to press kisses on her white skin and was stunned that he could feel such thoughts at such a moment. He had a need to clear his throat before saying, 'Whoever it was must be found. I have initiated a search, but the men are also seeking the youth that one saw enter this tent shortly before I did. They gave me your description,' said Gawain tersely.

'You—you mean they think I could be responsible?' gasped Beth.

'Hush, woman, keep your voice down,' growled Gawain. 'We do not want folk knowing that you dress up as a youth. I told them that he must have escaped by crawling beneath the back of the tent as soon as he heard me enter.'

She sank on to a stool and chewed on her lip. 'They will wonder why I did not see this youth and scream.'

'Most likely they will believe that you returned while they were elsewhere. I asked another man to find a physician.' He paused, 'You'll need to get rid of the male clothes you wore. Best give them to me to dispose of. Go, fetch them now.'

Beth hesitated.

He glowered at her. 'Mistress Llewellyn, if you still have it in mind to continue with this charade, then forget it. You will never again don that costume while I am responsible for you.'

Beth's head shot up. 'But I am not your responsibility.'

Gawain hesitated, uncertain why he felt so reluctant to tell her that her father had made him her legal guardian. 'Someone has to take care of you,' he muttered.

'I am able to bear the responsibility for myself,' said Beth, squaring her shoulders.

Gawain scrutinised her pale, tear-stained but proud face. 'I would not dispute that you are an extremely capable young woman. Having said that, I deem the circumstances in which you find yourself in right now would prove difficult for anyone. You will need my help to deal with the rigmarole involved in a suspicious death. This will have to be reported to the proper authorities and I will need to hand over the weapon. If fortune is with us, then someone will recognise it.'

They both looked towards the table where he had left the dagger wrapped in its cloth. It was not there! 'The murderer must have come in and taken it whilst I was changing and you were outside!' cried Beth.

Gawain frowned. 'They'd have to be invisible or hellish quick.'

'Of—of course,' stammered Beth. 'Perhaps it is on the ground!' She dropped to her knees and Gawain hunkered down beside her. They bumped heads, both winced and hastily drew back.

'Did I hurt you?' asked Gawain, reaching forwards and straightening her headdress.

'N-n-no!' She felt breathless. 'Did I hurt you?'

He smiled grimly. 'I have a hard head.'

'You'd need to have with all the fighting you do,' she said, without thinking.

'My fighting days are mostly over,' he muttered, getting to his feet.

'It must be here somewhere,' she said, continuing to search whilst wondering what he meant by his words.

'I'll have the servants make a thorough search.' He held a hand out to her and pulled her to her feet.

Beth saw him wince. 'What is it? Are you hurt?'

'It is nothing!' He was not about to explain that he was suffering for his foolish behaviour in accepting the challenge to wrestle earlier. Why did he feel this need to prove his manhood just because Mary had been seen with another man? Especially when he knew it could result in more than a few bruises and strained muscles? It was not the same sense of rightness and pride that had resulted in him resigning his position in Henry's Gentlemen of the Spears, whose duty it was to look to the king's safety on the field of battle, at court and on ceremonial occasions such as this one.

'I don't believe you,' blurted Beth. 'You are obviously in pain.'

'It is nothing,' he repeated through clenched teeth. 'I will need to report your father's murder to Cardinal Wolsey.'

'No! Father—' She paused to swallow the tightness in her throat. 'He—he did not like Cardinal Wolsey,' she added weakly. 'Could you not investigate my father's murder instead?'

Gawain hesitated. 'It wouldn't be right. I could be a suspect.'

'Why should you be?' She was aware of a sense of unreality and felt sick, then added faintly, 'I cannot believe this is all happening. It is as if I was taking part in a masque.'

'You're not about to swoon, are you?' he asked, taking her arm and lowering her on to the stool, praying that she would soon recover her composure. 'Come, you showed such strength earlier,' he said encouragingly. 'I did not mean that I really was a suspect. You can trust me.'

'Then why say what you did? You might as well say I could be a suspect, too. I have much to gain by my father's death,' said Beth, shivering.

He realised that what she said was true, but surely she would not have killed her own father? There came the sound of voices outside the tent. 'Go into your sleeping quarters and remain silent,' he hissed. 'I'd rather you left this to me.'

Beth hesitated, but then, still suffering from that sense of unreality, she decided she had to trust him and wasted no time in doing as he bid. She gathered together the clothes she had worn earlier and stuffed them inside her pallet of straw and lay down. She could hear the murmur of voices, but could not make out the words. She wished she could leave this tent now and never return. Yet somewhere outside lurked her father's killer.

Beth did not know how long she lay on her pallet, waiting for Sir Gawain to call her. It seemed an age before the voices trailed off and she heard him call her name. Then she rose and went out to him and saw that her father's body had been removed. 'Where have they taken him?' she asked.

'To the village church until he can buried in the morning,' said Gawain.

'So soon,' murmured Beth. Yet she understood that it was the only sensible action to take in such heat. 'I—I will go there later and speak to the priest about having masses said for his soul.'

'If that is what you wish, but in the meantime I must inform Wolsey what has happened.' Gawain's voice brooked no argument. 'He organised this whole event.

He would think there was something amiss if I did not
report the matter to him.'

'You know him well?'

'We are acquainted due to my having spent time at
court,' said Gawain.

The colour in Beth's cheeks ebbed and she thought
how there would definitely be an enquiry now by the
Cardinal. She hated the idea.

'Did your father not have a business meeting this
morning in Calais?' asked Gawain.

She hesitated. 'Aye, but what has that to do with this?
Monsieur Le Brun is but a master printer and he and
my father have done business together for as long as I
can remember. He would never hurt him.'

'Your father wouldn't have considered him a suitable husband for you?'

'What!' She stared at him incredulously. 'He is an
old man.Besides, he has a wife and three sons.'

Gawain was relieved. 'It was just a thought. Yet his
conversation with your father earlier today might provide some clue to his murderer. With his being an old
friend he might have spoken to him about matters he
would not have told others. Do you know his whereabouts in Calais?'

Beth mentioned the name of a street.

'Then I will go there,' said Gawain. 'But first I must
speak to Wolsey.'

He drew back the tent flap and ushered her outside.
Immediately the strong wind caught her and almost
blew her off her feet. She clung to his arm as her skirts
were whipped about her legs and she felt him stiffen.

Obviously he did not want her touching him, so she released her hold on him and was aware of curious glances as they made their way past the tents.

'I wish we had never come here,' she said in a low voice. 'But Father was adamant that I should see some of the places that he had visited with the king's father when he was a penniless fugitive.'

'Perhaps it will be worth mentioning the link between the Tudors and your family to Wolsey.'

'I do not doubt he already knows of it,' said Beth. 'My Welsh great-grandfather fought beside the king's great-grandfather, Owain ap Twydr, at Agincourt, but that did not mean much to Wolsey. He and Father met and they disagreed on matters of religion.'

'I see,' said Gawain, wondering if the Llewellyn menfolk had been involved in the printing of illegal religious tracts at any time and, if so, maybe that could have had something to do with their deaths? 'Anyway, I am hopeful that when I explain the situation to the Cardinal, he will speak with the king and he will allow me to escort you back to England as soon as possible.'

'Why should you want to do so?' asked Beth, surprised. 'Would you rather not stay here?'

'I deem it my duty to see you safely home,' he said firmly.

'I still do not understand why you should feel responsible for me,' said Beth. 'I have my servants to accompany me.'

Gawain frowned. 'Do not allow your pride to get in the way of common sense. Because of my position your passage will be more comfortable. Besides, you will be safer with me. Allow me to help you, Mistress Llewellyn.'

Beth did feel safer knowing that he was at her side, despite his overbearing and disapproving manner earlier. 'I will do so for now, Sir Gawain, but do not feel that I will acquiesce so easily another time,' she murmured.

'I am not such a fool that I have forgotten our earlier exchange, Mistress Llewellyn,' he said, then changed the subject. 'Now, tell me your opinion of our king's temporary palace.'

Beth saw that they were heading through the crowds to that edifice and could not help but marvel at what the old king's money had built here in Balinghem. The palace was in four blocks with a central courtyard. The only solid part was the brick base and above that were thirty-foot-high walls made of cloth on timber frames, painted to look like stone or brick. The slanting roof was made of grey oiled cloth and gave the illusion of slates. There were huge expanses of expensive glass windows.

'One cannot accuse our king of tightfistedness,' said Gawain drily.

'Do you like him?' asked Beth in a low voice.

'What is there not to like?' parried Gawain.

Beth would have argued that was not a proper answer, but Gawain had turned away now and was talking to one of the guards. Once inside, it struck her that he knew a lot of people as he spoke to several of those there. 'How will you find the Cardinal in this great edifice?' she asked, glancing about her at the luxurious fittings and the profusion of golden ornaments.

'A messenger has been sent to inform him that I seek an audience with him.'

'Then you know for certain that Wolsey is here,' she said, her fingers reaching for Gawain's sleeve as he led the way to a bench, flanked by flowering shrubs in pots.

'Aye, it is not unusual for him to work from dawn to dusk on the king's behalf whilst his Majesty and his court enjoy themselves.'

She nodded, having heard it was so from Jonathan, who'd had acquaintances at court.

Gawain was soon summoned to the Cardinal's presence. His dark blue eyes held Beth's for a moment. 'Do not fret. You are safer here than alone in your father's tent. Only a lackwit would risk harming you with so many witnesses present.'

Beth nodded, wondering why he should think anyone should want to harm her. She carefully arranged her skirts as she sat down and watched him cross the sunlit space with a loose-limbed stride until he was out of sight. Then she freed a pent-up breath and prepared for what she guessed could be a long wait.

The time passed slowly and she was seized again by that sense of unreality. She felt set apart from the folk who came and went in colourful costumes, like so many peacocks, jays and magpies, chattering and shrieking with laughter. Now and then she was aware of glances being cast her way and wished that Sir Gawain would return. There were questions she wanted to ask him, such as why he should have even mentioned his being considered a suspect? Could it be possible that he had cause to want her left all alone in the world so that she might depend on him? Well, he was mistaken if he thought that was so because she could look after herself. She rose and crossed to one of the windows and gazed out on the courtyard where the fountains of wine flowed freely. Some people had already imbibed too much and were staggering about and carousing in voices that made her wince.

'Mistress Llewellyn,' said a voice behind her.

She turned swiftly, surprised by the strength in the surge of relief she felt, collided into Sir Gawain and was knocked off balance.

'Careful,' he murmured, fighting against the sensations caused by the swell of her breasts against him. He found himself imagining their pale softness with their rosy peaks and forced himself to hold her off at arm's length. Beth Llewellyn's father had deemed him her protector; until he found her a husband, that meant he must keep faith, whatever temptation she put in his path.

## Chapter Two

'Let's get out of here,' said Gawain, seizing Beth's hand and hurrying her towards the outer door.

Beth thought he looked grim and her heart sank. 'What—what happened? Did the Cardinal suspect that I am responsible for my father's death and will not agree to my leaving France?'

'Why do you think I should have put such thoughts into his head?' said Gawain, glancing down at her pale face. 'Is it that you overheard my conversation with your father that day we met in London?'

'No!' she cried, tripping over her hem in an attempt to keep up with him. 'Please, of your courtesy, Sir Gawain, if you would just slow down! Your legs are so much longer than mine and I cannot keep up with you.'

Gawain begged her pardon and attempted to set his pace to match hers. It was not easy and he was impatient to reach his tent, hoping he would find his man, Tom Cobtree, there. He must not be alone with her.

'Why do you ask about your conversation with my father and where are you taking me?' she demanded.

'To my tent. If fortune is with me, then my man will have returned and we will have something to eat and drink.'

'What of my servants?' asked Beth. 'And will you tell me exactly what passed between you and the Cardinal, as well as my father?'

'I told the Cardinal the facts and deemed it necessary to inform him of my suspicions concerning your brother's so-called accident.'

Beth took a deep breath. 'My brother's so-called accident! Are you saying that Jonathan's accident was no accident?'

'Did your father not speak of it to you? Despite his reluctance to do so, I had hoped that he might have done,' said Gawain.

Beth stopped in her tracks. 'He has not spoken of it to me. Are you telling me now that my brother was murdered?'

'I suspect it was so,' said Gawain.

'I don't understand,' she cried. 'And how is it that my father should have involved you in the matter?'

'If you'll allow me to answer one question at a time, Mistress Llewellyn, instead of throwing them at me like spears, I will endeavour to do so.'

'Likening my questions to spears is an odd way of referring to two simple questions,' she retorted.

'I felt you were suddenly beginning to regard me as your enemy. Your voice was getting shrill.'

'My voice is not shrill,' she denied.

A smile eased up the corners of his mouth. 'It was certainly not dovelike, but let us not quarrel, Mistress Llewellyn.'

That unexpected smile did strange things to her and she found herself answering it with one of her own. 'All right, I will calm down, but you must understand how difficult all this is for me.'

'Of course I understand,' said Gawain, his smile fading. 'I will answer your first question. I had the boat your brother purchased raised and dragged ashore at low tide. Holes had been drilled into the hull.'

'What!' She was aghast. 'Who would do this and how did Jonathan not spot the damage?'

'I can only believe that the plugs were loosely put back into place; once it was afloat, the water forced them out. I had recently taken charge of the yard where the boat was built and your father came to me in great distress, searching for answers to why a newly made boat should sink.'

Beth was hurt that her father had kept such important information from her. When he had introduced her to Sir Gawain back in London, she had believed him to be just a new customer. 'So you are a boat builder, as well as a knight,' she said.

'I am no boat builder. I own land in Kent where I rear sheep, as well as a whole swathe of forest on the Weald. I supply timber to several ship- and boat-building yards at Smallhythe and Greenwich.'

'Does the king not have a palace at Greenwich?'

'Aye. He takes a great interest in shipbuilding, as did his father. He is building a navy and that is how I came to Henry's notice,' said Gawain. 'But we are digressing. Your brother…' He paused.

'I don't understand. Why should a boat builder hold a grudge against Jonathan?' Her voice shook.

Gawain raised an eyebrow. 'We have no reason to suspect that the craftsman who built the boat killed your brother. Anyone with a knowledge of boats would be quite capable of drilling holes in the bottom. Maybe your brother wronged a shipwright's wife and he was intent on revenge.'

'Jonathan could be very cavalier in his treatment of my sex, but he would not seduce another man's wife,' she said firmly.

Gawain stared at her thoughtfully. 'How can you be so sure?'

She returned his stare. 'I knew him well and it was not in his nature to seduce a married woman. You will just have to take my word for it.'

He nodded slowly. 'I will do so unless I discover you are wrong.'

She hesitated. 'All right, I accept that because you didn't know him. Anyway this is not helping us discover who killed my father.'

'It could be that he had an inkling of who might have done away with Jonathan and he made the mistake of confronting the person he suspected.'

'I—I see.' She was silent a moment and then her eyes

widened suddenly. 'Do you think my father could have been killed by a religious fanatic?'

He marvelled at the way her mind so quickly grasped hold of possibilities. 'It has occurred to me that he might have been involved in printing some of the teachings of the heretic Martin Luther,' he said cautiously.

'Father was religious, but Jonathan was not. And I cannot believe that Father would be so foolish as to become involved in such a dangerous activity.'

'People can behave out of character when they strongly believe in something. Especially when they are grieving and deeply disturbed in their minds.'

She had a strange feeling that he was not only referring to her father, but someone else he knew, and wondered who it could be. 'That could easily apply to the murderer, too,' she said, moistening her lips that suddenly felt dry. 'If so, they could have a grudge against my family and I could be their next target.'

Gawain hesitated before saying, 'It is possible, but I gave my word to your father that I would take care of you if aught were to happen to him and I will do so.'

She gasped. 'Why should you make such a promise to my father when you were barely acquainted? What did he offer you?' she demanded suspiciously.

Gawain knew that the moment had come to tell her the truth. 'Shares in his business, but that is neither here nor there as I am not a poor man, Mistress Llewellyn. No doubt what I am about to say will vex you, but on your father's death I became your legal guardian.'

She was taken aback. 'Why should he ask you to do

that? There were other people he could have asked. His lawyer and man of business, for instance.'

The muscles of his handsome face tightened. 'I asked your father that same question. It might seem strange to you, but he trusted me. I refused at first, for I did not wish to be burdened with finding you a spouse but he persisted.'

'But I do not wish to marry,' blurted out Beth.

'So your father told me and frankly I do not believe it,' said Gawain with a shake of the head. 'Especially now your reason no longer exists.'

An angry sparkle lit her eyes. 'You are mistaken. I presume he will have left his business to me, so there is naught preventing me from taking control of it when I return to London. I will be able to support myself financially, so I have no need of a husband.'

'Impossible,' he stated, coming to halt outside his tent. 'It was your father's wish that you marry and you will do so. Nothing you say will persuade me otherwise. Now inside before you attract even more attention to yourself than you have already done.' He untied the flap and drew it back and ushered her inside.

'I—I will not s-stay here with you! I will not marry you!' She flung the words at him, making a bolt for the tent entrance, wondering whether Sir Gawain had designs on her himself and if he wished to have complete control over her, having killed her brother and her father?

Gawain seized hold of her and swung her against him. 'Where did you get that crazy notion from? I already have a wife, so do not be thinking me responsible for your father's death in order to get my hands on his business through you.'

Beth was stunned. 'A wife! You have a wife? Where is she? Is she here with you?'

A flush darkened his cheeks because he knew that he was going to have to lie to her. 'It really is none of your business, but, if you must know, she is tending an elderly sick aunt back home in England.'

'I—I see,' said Beth, wondering why she was having difficulty visualising him as another woman's husband. After all, he was handsome and strong, extremely attractive and possessed land and money. 'May I sit down?' she asked abruptly, her knees giving way.

He seized her arm and pulled forwards a stool. 'Naturally you are upset by the thought of having to obey a man who is almost a complete stranger to you, but it was your father's wish.'

She clenched her fists. 'It was wrong of Father to make arrangements for my future without discussing it with me. Why could he not treat me as he would have Jonathan?'

'I am sure you know the answer to that,' said Gawain, pouring wine from a barrel into a pitcher. 'You are not stupid.'

'Aye, because I am a daughter and not a son,' she said bitterly.

'Perhaps he also knew you well enough to know that you would argue with him if he told you the truth.'

She jerked up her head and glared at him. 'As I will argue with you. Do not think I will fall in with your desire to get me out of the way. I will not marry and become some man's possession, having no say in my own business.'

He said calmly, 'We do not need to discuss this now. Will you take a cup of wine, Mistress Llewellyn, and some bread and cheese? It is all I can offer you at the moment.'

The calmness of his manner frustrated her because she so wanted to vent her hurt and anger on someone. 'You said earlier that you came to the notice of the king. Why do you not eat at Henry's table?' she muttered.

'If you must know, I've had a surfeit of rich food since I've been here. Besides, those who fawn around the king these days are not to my liking. When I was at court it was because I had trained as one of the king's Gentlemen of the Spears, his élite mounted bodyguard.'

'Then what were you doing wrestling half-naked if you held such a position?' she asked.

'I used to wrestle with Henry but now I cannot.' He glowered at her.

'Why not? Because you would defeat him and the king is not a man to suffer defeat lightly?' she surprised him by saying.

Gawain shrugged. 'I wouldn't admit that, but the truth is that whilst fighting here in France a few years ago, my shoulder was dislocated. Now the joint has a habit of coming out of its socket when put unduly under stress and the pain can be debilitating. It does not happen often, but enough to embarrass me in front of my king and peers. Besides, I could no longer be relied on to defend the king if he were in danger, so I had to beg leave to resign from my position.'

'That must have been very upsetting for you,' said Beth, struggling with conflicting emotions. 'You must miss the life of a warrior.'

'Hardly that of a real warrior,' he said stiffly. 'Although life at court could be amusing, as well as exciting. As it is, Henry summons me to play board games or dice with him. He is an inveterate gambler and I have some skill.'

'That is why are you here now? He invited you to play with him?'

Gawain nodded. 'And there is no need for you to tell me that I should not be performing at the lists or wrestling with my disability. I have a wife to tell me that,' he added harshly.

'Is that the real reason why she is not here?' asked Beth. 'Because of your male pride being hurt? That is foolish.'

He handed a cup of wine to her. 'How well you understand me, Mistress Llewellyn,' he said sardonically.

'By St George, you took a risk,' she said, taking a sip of wine.

Their eyes met. 'You would say that pride comes before a fall, but I say a man needs his pride,' said Gawain.

'He could have flattened you,' said Beth. 'But I admit I found it admirable that you were able to throw that Breton wrestler.'

He shrugged and winced, determined not to show the pleasure her remark gave him. 'Shall we change the subject?'

She nodded, curious to know more about him. 'Tell me about your wife. Have you children?'

Gawain gazed into her attractive little face that was alight with interest. He imagined how her expression would change if he told the truth—that Mary had deserted him, taking their daughters with her. It would perhaps give Beth more reason to be against marriage. Of course, he could have told her how he had spent weeks searching for them, believing that his wife's wits were deranged after the loss of their son, fearing for the girls' safety and that of their mother. This had been after Mary's father's death when Gawain had taken on new responsibilities. Then he had struck lucky or so he had thought, only to discover that Mary had made a cuckold of him and when he had rode to the place where she had been observed, it was too late. She had vanished again. Then the king had summoned him to court and he'd had no choice but to abandon his search.

'I have two daughters: Lydia, who has seen seven summers, and Tabitha, who is three years old.' He found it too painful still to mention the loss of his son to her, but added swiftly, 'More recently I've been sorting out my father-in-law's affairs. He died a year ago and left it to me to rescue his ailing boat-building yard. I have hopes that in a few years it will be prosperous again.'

Beth frowned. 'You have enough matters of your own to sort out as it is without being bothered with mine. Why do you not allow me to handle my own affairs?'

Gawain was tempted to agree, but found himself

saying, 'I made a promise to your father that I would find you a husband. His dearest wish was that you provided him with a grandson.'

'A grandson!' This was news, indeed, to Beth and it angered and hurt her further. 'A daughter was not good enough for him,' she added in a trembling voice. 'Only a male offspring will do.'

Gawain paused in the act of setting the table. 'You must forgive him. It is natural for a man to want a son to carry on his name. No doubt your father had it in mind for you to marry someone who understood the printing- and book-selling business, but perhaps it would be wiser to sell it, so as to provide you with a substantial dowry to attract a gentleman so you would not be forever thinking of printing and books.'

'No! It cannot be sold,' she cried, starting to her feet and spilling a little wine on her gown. 'If I have a son, then he will inherit and carry on with my work.'

'What do you mean by that?' asked Gawain, frowning. 'What work is this? Tell me?'

Encouraged and filled with an overwhelming need to share her secret, Beth said, 'I know how to set type and to work the presses, and I have continued with the work Jonathan began. I write and print a newsletter and it is distributed in London and I am determined to carry on doing so.'

His eyes flared. 'By St George, I believe you are serious!'

'Indeed, I am!' Her face was alight with enthusiasm. 'I write about matters that I know will interest those who have learnt to read since their parents' generation grasped the first books that came off Master Caxton's presses here in England. They are eager for the written word and they desire more than just the gospels and stories of the saints. They enjoy the old tales from classical history such as *Aesop's Fables*, but they also want to be kept informed about what is happening today.'

'Are you saying that the printing and distribution of Holy Writ in our own tongue does not interest you?' he asked, his dark brows knitting.

'No, of course not,' she said, flushing. 'I am saying that the printed word has the power to do more than bring religious enlightenment to those who wish to read the gospels for themselves. It can educate, entertain and amuse on several topics.'

'I agree that there is much enjoyment to be found in such as Homer's *Illiad*, but the printed word can also be dangerous, as you well know. It can preach sedition and moral laxity,' he said drily.

'That is not my intention,' she said hastily. 'I sincerely believe there are many people who are eager to know what is happening in other countries. They are interested in the great occasions such as this one taking place here. They would also enjoy reading of the wonders of the Indies and the New World by those who have visited these lands.'

'I would not deny the truth of what you say, but those accounts will be written by explorers and no doubt printed by men. I would be doing you a disfavour if I allowed you to hold out any hope of continuing with this newsletter of yours, Mistress Llewellyn,' said Gawain, marvelling at the enthusiasm that gleamed in her lovely eyes. *If only she would look at him in such a manner!* He quashed the thought. 'Obviously your father would have disapproved and that is why you kept it a secret.'

Deeply disappointed in him, she said, 'Aye, because he thought, like you, that men can do most things better than a woman. We must be kept in our place under a man's heel, to keep house, to be faithful and do what a man says and to bear him sons. Daughters do not matter. I pity your wife, because no doubt you do not appreciate your girls but long for her to give you a son!'

The anger he had suppressed for so long exploded and he seized hold of her. 'I deem you have said enough, Mistress Llewellyn,' he said in a dangerously low voice. 'You have no idea of what is between my wife and myself. I, like many men, believe it is our God-given role to cherish and protect our women and children, whatever their sex. You would spread falsehoods and discontent if what you say is an example of your writing. I would be doing your readers a favour by taking your newsletter out of circulation.'

'I will not be silenced,' she said, glaring at him.

'Will you not?' he said harshly and pressed a fierce kiss on her lips.

A stunned Beth could do no more than remain still in his embrace, but her heart raced and her knees had turned to water.

He released her abruptly, furious with himself and her.

'You should not have done that,' she gasped, putting a hand to her tingling lips.

'No, I should not,' admitted Gawain hoarsely, turning his back on her and breathing deeply. 'But you would cause a priest to forget his vows. Your father held you in high esteem as a housekeeper and spoke fondly of you. He wanted you safely married and that will be my aim. I must ask you to forgive me for losing my temper and I assure you that it will not happen again.'

'I—I should think not! What would your wife say?' cried Beth.

'Shall we keep my wife out of this?' he said, clenching his fist.

Her eyes fixed on his whitened knuckles and she knew that she had touched him on the raw. 'I will not mention her again,' she said stiffly. 'Although if we were to meet in England—'

'You would tell her?' His expression was grim. 'It is possible she would not believe you.'

There was a long silence as they stared at each other. Then he reached for a knife. She shrank back and he swore beneath his breath and began to slice a loaf. 'Eat, Mistress Llewellyn, you need to keep up your strength if you are to survive the difficulties that lie ahead,' he rasped.

'I am no weakling nor did I say I would speak of that kiss to your wife. Rather I wonder how I could look her in the face, knowing that you had kissed me.'

'It is the swiftest way I know to silence a woman,' he said.

If he thought he had silenced her, then he was mistaken. *Yet it had been such a kiss that she could still feel his lips' impression on hers.* How dare he accuse her of spreading falsehood and discontent when he had not read a word she had written! She would show him—but in the meantime, he was right about her keeping up her strength. She reached for the bread and cheese, determined to have her way, but uncertain yet exactly how to go about it. She supposed it all depended on what happened when they reached England. He could not force her to marry and no doubt he would need to leave her in London if he were to visit his wife and children. The sooner they parted the better—they obviously struck sparks off each other, rousing feelings that had to be suppressed.

Gawain wondered what she was thinking. What would she say if he told her that Mary had borne him a son, but the boy had died? How in the weeks that followed he'd had to contend with Mary's coolness and impenetrable silences. He had tried to reason with her and get her to talk about their loss, but that had been a waste of time. Once he had discovered there was another man involved, it had caused him to wonder how long she had been making a cuckold of him and whether the boy had truly been his son or this other man's child. He had tried to be a good husband to her—never had he beaten her or forced her to bend to his will as she had told him her father had done. Gawain had treated her with respect and warmth as he remembered his father treating his mother. There had been great love between his parents, but still it had been a terrible shock when his father had died on the hunting field not long after his mother had passed away. Although he had left no message, Gawain was convinced his father had not wanted to live after his mother's death and had recklessly taken one risk too many. As if it had not been painful enough to lose his mother, he had felt utterly abandoned when his father died.

'I must speak to my servants, Jane and Sam,' said Beth, rousing Gawain from his reverie.

'My man, Tom Cobtree, and the lad, Michael, should be here soon,' he said, lifting his head. 'I will instruct them on how to find your tent. Hopefully, your servants will have returned and Tom will have your maid pack your possessions and bring them here. It is best you sleep in this tent tonight. You and she can have my sleeping quarters. I want the men to make a thorough search of your tent and its vicinity in the hope of finding the dagger and any other clues that might point to the identity of the murderer.'

Beth accepted Gawain's plan. She had no desire to return to the other tent where her father had met his death.

Within the hour, Tom and Michael had arrived; after a low-voiced discussion with Gawain, they left. Thankfully, Beth did not have to wait long before Jane came with some of her mistress's baggage. Gawain excused himself and left the two women to rearrange the sleeping quarters.

Jane was old enough to be Beth's mother and they were fond of each other. She was a widow and had lost two children in infancy. 'What a terrible thing to happen, Mistress Beth,' she said, dabbing her wet eyes with her sleeve. 'What is the world coming to? How will we manage?'

Beth placed an arm around her. 'I'm sure we will cope, Jane. It isn't as if I was unaccustomed to running the household and, despite what Sir Gawain says, I am determined that my father's business will not be sold.'

Jane's face brightened. 'That's the spirit, Mistress Beth, although, I will say that I deem it a good thing that the master thought to enlist him to keep an eye on you.'

'More than just an eye, Jane,' said Beth, scowling. 'Father asked him to find a husband for me. You can imagine how I feel about that.'

'Your father only wanted what was best for you, Mistress Beth,' said Jane, picking up the bundle of bedding she had brought with her.

'What he thought was best for me,' corrected Beth. 'But he didn't really know me. Even so, I'd like to go to the Church of the Nativity of Our Lady in the village and speak with the priest and have masses said for his soul. You can accompany me after we've finished here. I know some French and am sure I will be able to make my wishes known.' She sighed. 'Let's hope that Sir Gawain and the other men will find some clue to the murderer's identity.'

Gawain took the dagger from Tom and fingered the amethysts embedded in the hilt. 'Where did you find it?'

'In the corner over there,' said Tom. 'The grass hasn't been flattened by the groundsheet and the cloth

it was in was the same colour. Definitely worth a bit,'
he added with fine understatement.

'I've a feeling I've seen that dagger before,' said
Sam.

Gawain shot a glance at the burly figure of Beth's
servant. 'Are you sure? Think, man.'

Sam screwed up his lined face. 'Perhaps it was in
some nobleman's house when I was out delivering
books on the master's orders. Couldn't see any of our
other customers owning such a blade.'

'I presume there'll be a list of Master Llewellyn's
customers back in London,' said Gawain.

Sam nodded. 'Mistress Beth will be able to put her
hand on the book straight away.'

Gawain looked thoughtful. 'But she didn't recognise
the dagger.'

'She don't go delivering, has too much else to do.'

Gawain placed the dagger in its cloth inside his doublet. 'I'd best return to Mistress Llewellyn and inform
her that we've found the weapon. Sam, if you would,
pack your master's possessions and bring them to my
tent. Tom, you can come with me and cook us something hot for supper. You, Sam and Michael will share
this tent tonight.'

The three of them nodded.

When Gawain arrived back at his tent it was to find
it deserted. Where could Beth and her maid have vanished to? He was filled with unease, hoping they had
not been followed earlier. Then he remembered what
Beth had said about visiting the church in the village

and decided to go and look for her there. He told Tom what he was about and then set off in the direction of Balinghem.

'It is a sobering thought, Jane,' said Beth in hushed tones as they left the church, 'that my father's bones will lie here in France. A country that he long regarded as the enemy.'

Jane glanced over her shoulder as they hurried past the churchyard. 'You can't trust the Frenchies. Their king might be all smiles now, but give him another month and he'll be making up to someone else. The Scotties, mebbe, or even the Holy Roman Emperor Charles, himself.'

'The Emperor is Queen Katherine's nephew, so it is more likely that he and Henry might yet come to some agreement against the French,' said Beth. 'But these matters are for statesmen and royalty to sort out. We have enough problems of our own to deal with when we return home.'

'Do you think Sir Gawain will move us from Pater Noster Row?'

'I imagine that he has that in mind,' said Beth. 'With a murderer on the loose, no doubt he would consider it a sensible move.' Even as she spoke, Beth caught sight of Gawain coming towards them. She frowned, her emotions in a tangle, and thought how strange it was that in such a short time she was able to recognise his form and his stride from a distance. She determined not to dwell on the kiss he had forced on her or how much she had liked it.

She waited until he drew closer before calling, 'Good even, Sir Gawain. Did you find anything?'

'Aye. Tom found the dagger. Somehow it must have been knocked from the table and landed in a patch of tall grass in a corner.' Gawain gazed down at her and wondered if she was still angry inside because he had kissed her. 'Your man, Sam, thinks he might have seen it in some nobleman's house whilst delivering books. He can't remember his name. He suggested that you look through the account book and read the names out to him, so that hopefully it will jog his memory.'

Beth felt a stir of excitement. 'And if it can be proved that person was also here at the time of my father's murder, then we have our killer.'

'That is certainly a strong possibility,' agreed Gawain. 'In the meantime I must speak with Monsieur Le Brun and intend visiting Calais early tomorrow morning. I will return in time for your father's burial.'

'May I come with you?' asked Beth. 'I would like to see him.'

Gawain hesitated, then agreed.

The rest of the evening passed without further incident and although Beth slept only fitfully, towards the dawn she finally fell into a deep sleep.

When at last she did wake, Jane told her that Sir Gawain had given orders that she was not to be disturbed and had set off for Calais with Tom Crabtree, leaving Sam to keep a watch out for any sign of trouble. She was annoyed at being left behind, but soon decided there was little point in feeling that way. After a breakfast of bread and ham, she took paper and quill and ink and began to write down all that happened in the last twenty-four hours.

By the time she had finished the sun was climbing high in the sky and Gawain had returned.

One look at his face told Beth that something momentous had occurred. 'What is wrong?' she asked, starting to her feet.

'Monsieur Le Brun has been murdered,' said Gawain grimly.

Beth felt the blood rush to her head and collapsed on the ground.

Gawain cursed himself for his thoughtlessness and went down on one knee, placing his arms beneath her and lifting her up. He sat down with her on his lap and glanced at Jane, who had put down her mending and stood up. 'Don't stand there like a stock,' he roared. 'Fetch some wine.'

Jane hurried to do his bidding while Gawain tried to rouse Beth by patting her cheek and calling her name. He needed her to be strong when he was feeling aroused by simply holding her on his lap. He was annoyed with himself; he should not be feeling like this about her.

Beth's eyelids fluttered open and she gazed up into his face. Realising that she was sitting in her guardian's lap, she sat bolt upright. 'Put me down at once!' she ordered.

'There is no need to panic,' he said roughly, wishing she would keep still and hoping she was unaware of his arousal.

'You—you did say that Monsieur Le Brun had been murdered?' She swallowed a lump in her throat and, despite her earlier demand that he release her, clung to his doublet.

'Aye, it was completely unexpected.' His expression was serious. It appeared that perhaps after all they had a religious maniac on the loose. He could think of no other reason why the French master printer should have been killed, but one of his sons had told him that he had been providing Master Llewellyn with information about the teachings of the heretic Martin Luther for more than a year now, so maybe that was reason enough for a lunatic.

Beth's eyes filled with tears. 'He was such a kind, harmless old man,' she whispered.

'I'm going to get you on a ship to England today,' said Gawain. 'Whilst in Calais, I spoke to the master mariner of a vessel that is sailing this evening.'

'Good,' said Beth, relieved. 'I will be glad to leave this place.'

Before she could say any more Jane brought the wine. Gawain took the cup from her and held it to Beth's lips. She drank, but, despite feeling light-headed, as soon as she had drained the cup she insisted on getting to her feet. Gawain wasted no time in helping her up and then ordered the men to make ready the horses and to pack the tents, bedding and baggage in a wagon.

Beth and Gawain conversed little on the journey to Calais. She could not deny that she would have been more anxious if it were not for his presence. Yet she knew she could not depend on him to keep her safe once she arrived home, despite his promise to her father. He had a wife and children and she would not have him risk his life for her. One thing was for certain—the death of Monsieur Le Brun proved that her father must have had something to do with the printing of religious information coming out of Europe. She still could not believe that Jonathan was involved. Yet if he had not been, then why had he been killed? Could it have been purely because he was his father's son? If so, that meant her life really could be in danger, too.

# Chapter Three

Gawain stood at the side of the ship, gazing towards the port of Smallhythe, positioned on the bank of the River Rother where his boatyard, amongst others, was situated. Raventon Hall lay further inland up a hilly road that led to the town of Tenderden and beyond to the Wealden forests, nestling between fields where sheep grazed. He felt a swell of emotion, glad to be back despite the difficult situation he found himself in. If it were not for his concern for his daughters and the hope of having news of them, he would have sailed for London first to visit Beth's father's lawyer before going home. He needed to get her off his hands before he succumbed to temptation again. She held an attraction for him that went beyond mere physical beauty that he found baffling. She was self-opinionated, stubborn and had no mind as to how a lady should behave. But she was also well-read and clever and he could see her attempting to best him at every turn, especially when it came to choosing her a husband or deciding what to do with her father's business.

Of course, he could send her to London by road with her servants and his own man, Tom, but would she be safe? It all depended on the murderer's motives and whether he was a dangerous fanatic or a person of intelligence and cunning. He came to the decision that for now Beth would be safer at Raventon than in London. He would place her in the care of his Aunt Catherine, who hopefully knew better than to discuss her nephew's most private affairs with anyone. He didn't want Beth knowing what had been happening between him and Mary.

'Do you have your own boat, Sir Gawain?' asked a voice at his shoulder.

He turned and stared down at his ward's sombre wind-flushed face. 'Aye. Why do you ask?'

'Because I am wondering if you will be taking me to London in it rather than continue there in this ship.' Beth had also been wondering what he had meant when he'd said that she did not know what was between him and his wife. Perhaps she was not the wife he had desired or maybe he loved her and she did not love him?

'Certainly not today,' he answered.

She hesitated. 'Of course, you will be hoping that your wife and children are home now. Surely that is all the more reason for me to leave you to enjoy their company. I and my servants could travel by road if you will lend us horses.'

Gawain shook his head. 'It is best you rest after the

journey. My wife has most likely not returned, but my aunt will make you welcome at Raventon Hall. There you will find peace and solitude and that is needful whilst you mourn your father. You need time to recover from the terrible shock you have suffered.'

Having hoped that she might gain some control over her own life once back in England, Beth was disappointed, thinking now of what she had been going to write for her news sheet, but she kept a grip on her emotions. 'How much time are you talking about? It is thoughtful of you to consider my feelings in such a way, but I would prefer to go home,' she said firmly.

'Of course, but I doubt you will find much in the way of peace and solitude in London's streets at this time of year, Mistress Llewellyn.'

'I would not gainsay you, but I will need more clothes and items for my *toilette* if I am to stay in your home for more than a few days and there is much in my house that will need my attention,' she said in a polite little voice.

'Shall we leave the decision about the length of time you will stay until the morrow?' suggested Gawain.

Beth decided she would have to be content with that suggestion for the moment. She did not want to appear to be difficult so that he would feel a need to have a watch kept on her. She nodded, adding, 'Should you not warn your aunt of my arrival? I know how having unexpected visitors sprung on one can put all planning of meals askew and I do not wish your aunt to take a dislike to me.'

Gawain agreed.

* * *

As soon as the ship had anchored and all their goods were unloaded, Tom was sent on ahead to Raventon Hall. Beth gazed about her at the bustling little port. 'Most of the buildings appear quite new,' she said, accepting Gawain's help up on to his horse; Sam was driving the cart with Jane sitting alongside him.

'There was a fire here a few years ago and most of the houses were destroyed,' Gawain said, swinging up into the saddle in front of her. 'The majority of the buildings are of half-timbered design, but the new church is of red brick.'

'I've never seen a redbrick church before,' said Beth, hesitating to slip her arms about his waist and link her hands together despite knowing she would feel so much safer if she did so once the horse broke into a canter. Instead she gripped the back of his doublet and hoped for the best. 'How far is your home?' she asked.

'Tenderden is less than a league's distance from here. Most of the timber for the boat-building yards is transported by river via the town.'

Beth gazed about her as they made their way out of the port of Smallhythe. 'Tell me more about the area, if you would?'

Gawain was pleased by her interest. 'Tenderden is a centre of the broadcloth industry and so there are many spinners and weavers plying their trade. Some are of Flemish descent. Edward III forbade the export of unwashed wool and so they brought their specialist skills here.'

'How interesting,' said Beth, her fingers tightening

their grip as the horse broke into a trot. She shifted closer to him and felt more secure moulded against his back and even a little excited. She blamed that on the speed at which they were travelling.

Conscious of Beth's comely form in a way that he knew was not sensible, Gawain attempted to block out such thoughts by pointing out the church of St Mildred on the hill as they came into Tenderden. He thought of Mary and how glad he was that they had not married at the parish church. The one in Smallhythe had burnt down and in one of her rants she had stated it was a sign from God that their marriage was not of his will. His eyes darkened. In the light of what had happened since, it seemed she was right.

As they approached the house, Beth's stomach began to tie itself into knots. What if the elderly sick relative had died and Sir Gawain's wife had returned? She might resent his having brought a strange young woman to her home. Whilst Beth did not doubt that Gawain was the master in his own home, she knew enough about her own sex to realise that if his wife took a dislike to her, then she could make her stay very uncomfortable, indeed.

As Gawain reined in his horse in front of Raventon Hall, Beth saw that whilst it had decent proportions, it was not large, as he had mentioned, so she would not have to worry about finding her way about. It was half-timbered, with mullioned windows that reflected the sunlight and had a welcoming aspect.

A metal-studded wooden door opened and out came a tall lanky woman. She wore a brown gown trimmed with lace and wisps of greying hair clung to a damp, smiling face framed by a starched white headdress. 'You have returned safely, nephew,' she cried. 'I cannot express too much how glad I am to see you.'

'It is good to be home,' said Gawain, a question in his eyes.

She glanced briefly at Beth, flashing her a slight smile, before saying to her nephew in a low voice, 'A missive arrived, addressed to you in Mary's hand. I have placed it in your bedchamber.'

He felt a sinking feeling in the pit of his stomach, but his voice showed no emotion when he spoke. 'May I introduce my ward, Mistress Elizabeth Llewellyn. Beth, this is my aunt, Mistress Catherine Ashbourne.'

'Mistress Llewellyn, you are very welcome. I extend my condolences on your very sad loss,' said Catherine, inclining her head.

'Thank you. It is good to meet you and I am pleased to be here,' said Beth politely with a smile, relieved that his wife must still be away if the mention of a missive was anything to go by.

Gawain dismounted and, with a brief word of apology to Beth, headed for the house. The smile on her lips died and she managed to get down from the horse, unaided. 'You must forgive my nephew,' said Catherine. 'It is some time since he has seen his wife and daughters and he is impatient to have news of them. I dearly miss the girls myself. The house is not the same without them. Do come inside.'

Beth followed her and paused just inside the doorway to gaze about the hall. It had a timbered ceiling that ran the full length of the house. Sunlight flooded in from a window at the other end of the hall, to the side of which was a raised area, partially concealed by an intricately carved wooden screen. Two settles with cushions stood close to the hearth where a fire burnt, a necessity even though it was summer because the stone floor struck chill through the soles of her shoes despite the rushes and herbs that covered it. Against one of the walls were a couple of benches, trestles and a table top. Set against another wall was an iron coffer and a large wooden chest with metal bands and a large keyhole. Perched on top of it was a travelling writing desk and several books. On two of the walls there were tapestries.

'It is a fine hall,' said Beth, curious to inspect the books as she remembered Sir Gawain mentioning his own reading.

'Do sit down and I will have refreshments brought to you as it is still a few hours until supper,' invited Catherine. 'Whilst you take your ease, I will ensure that your baggage is taken up to your bedchamber, so your maid can unpack for you. There is a small ante-chamber adjoining yours with a truckle bed where she can sleep.'

Beth thanked her and relaxed against a cushion, wondering what Gawain had learnt of his wife and daughters and whether he would be joining her for refreshments.

Gawain entered his bedchamber and wasted no time breaking the seal of his wife's missive. Not once had she written to him since that first note she had left on his pillow after she had disappeared. That had been brief and to the point, simply stating that she could no longer live with him and that he must not try to find her and the girls. He unfolded the sheet of paper and spread it on the small table over by the window and began to read.

Gawain,
It has come to my ears that you have been searching for us. I should have expected this, but I hoped that you would heed my wishes, but no, you have grown obstinate and uncaring since I first met you. In the past I respected and admired your strength of character and appreciated your generosity and warmth of manner, but I have to tell you that I only went through a form of marriage with you because Father insisted on it. I loved another. We met whilst I was staying with distant kinsfolk of my mother's. We were scarcely more than children when we plighted our troth without benefit of clergy, but simply in the eyes of God. Then our parents parted us and we were both forced into marriages not of our making.

Gawain gave a mirthless laugh. He could remember no force being exerted. Rather he recalled how willingly Mary had come into his arms. He found it hard to believe that it had all been a pretence on her behalf. He was tempted to screw up the letter and throw it away, but he needed to know how his daughters fared and the identity of the man she was now claiming was her husband. He read on with growing incredulity and anger.

Despite our conviction that we were really tied to each other and our other marriages false, I dared not cause a scandal and bring my father's wrath down on my head. We did not see each other for a year or more after I went through a form of marriage with you and then fate intervened and we met again and became lovers. Then my dear love's so-called wife died in childbirth and shortly after my father passed away. We decided that we could no longer live apart and so I went to him. Of course, I could not leave my sweet girls behind; besides, it is possible that Tabitha could be my dear love's daughter. Accept, Gawain, that we will not be coming back to you. I was never, in truth, your wife, Mary.

Gawain's emotions threatened to choke him. Who did Mary think she was, deciding what was lawful and what was not? He knew that in some cases such ceremonies were accepted as binding, but as far as he was aware they were only considered legal if the parties lived together afterwards. He needed to know where Mary and this man were living and sort this matter out even if he did not want her back. Separating the girls from him was cruel. Gawain had always been the girls' provider and protector. He knew they looked up to him. What had Mary told them about him and this other so-called husband? They must be utterly confused. He ran a hand through his hair, wishing he had Mary and this man in front of him now. He would show them who was in the right here. Instead, he had to control his anger and frustration, needing time to think about what he must do to get the girls back. Tabitha could still be his daughter, but even if she were not, he still loved her and wanted her home. As for Mary—he could be right in believing her wits had gone begging after the loss of their son.

He placed the missive at the bottom of the chest at the foot of his bed and locked the chest. Then he left his bedchamber and went downstairs, but there was no one in the hall, yet he could hear voices and recognised that of Beth Llewellyn. He guessed that his aunt had taken her into the smaller, more comfortable parlour for refreshments. He decided he could not face them right now. As he crossed the hall and went outside, he remembered lifting Beth off her feet after the wrestling match and that moment when she had trapped her hand and he had caught a glimpse of her cleavage. It had been as revealing a moment as when her cap had slipped and her braids had tumbled free. She must have been mortified, yet she had kept her wits about her, called a warning to him and, making the most of her opportunity whilst he faced the Breton, made good her escape. He needed to keep his wits about him right now. He might desire her, but he needed to keep his hands off her.

A wry smile twisted his lips and then he scowled. Beth's shocking behaviour in dressing as a youth was far less damaging than Mary's actions. How on earth was he going to bring matters to a satisfactory conclusion where the girls were concerned without creating a scandal? As if he didn't have enough to do in the next few months: securing a safe future for Beth, finding a murderer and managing the Raventon estate, his forests on the Weald and the boat-building yard at Smallhythe. He swore beneath his breath and then squared his shoulders and went in search of his steward.

Beth was feeling pleasantly sleepy when she was shown into a bedchamber that was furnished with all that was necessary for her comfort. She was happy to see that Jane was there unpacking her clothes; on a table over by the window her writing implements had been laid out.

'It is a pleasant room,' said Catherine, drawing back one of the bed hangings and fastening it securely to a hook on the wall.

Beth smiled. 'I certainly cannot find fault with it. Do you have many guests staying here?'

'Not since the Christmas revels when my nephew had a couple of friends to stay with their wives and children. The mummers from the village came and entertained the guests. We sometimes took part and it was immensely exciting and amusing dressing up and wearing masks. Have you ever done so, Mistress Llewellyn?' asked Catherine.

'Indeed, I have done so in London. I deem that such moments are also spiced with danger because one cannot always guess the identity of the person behind the mask.'

Catherine agreed. 'You are so right. I have felt fearful more than once on such occasions. There are some people who exude an air of madness or menace so that you wonder if they are Old Nick himself.' Her hand quivered as she smoothed down the blue-and-green woven counterpoint on the bed.

'You are thinking of a specific person?'

Catherine shook herself. 'I will say no more. I do not want you to have bad dreams.'

Beth's curiosity was roused. 'I deem you have a story to tell.'

'Aye, but I'll not be telling it,' said Catherine firmly. 'I will leave you now to do whatever you see fit. Do feel free to walk the grounds. At this time of year the rose garden in particular is lovely. When it is time for supper, I will send a servant to find you.' She made for the door.

'Please do not go yet,' said Beth, stretching out a hand to her. 'I would that you would tell me something more about Sir Gawain. I know so little about him. His parents—who were they?'

Catherine hesitated. 'I cannot linger long as I must go to the kitchen and see that the preparations for supper are advanced. His father, Sir Jerome, fought on the old king's side during the wars and was rewarded for it, although he already owned Raventon and forest on the Weald, supplying oak for the shipyards.'

'And what about his mother? How did she and his father meet?'

Catherine's homely features took on a grave expression. 'Ah, my sister, Margaret, she was one of the old queen's ladies-in-waiting. She had a lovely nature and was perhaps too good for this world. She died after she miscarried twins.'

'That is sad,' murmured Beth, wondering how old Gawain had been at the time. 'Sir Gawain's wife—'

'Enough, child, I must go,' said Catherine and hurried out before Beth could delay her further.

Jane glanced at her mistress. 'She sent shivers down my spine with her talk of Old Nick. Despite her welcome, Mistress Beth, I did wonder if she wants to be rid of us. It would be strange indeed if Sir Gawain had brought you here, thinking you'd be safe, when the place could be haunted by nasty demons.'

'We have no reason to believe this house is haunted. You are putting words into her mouth,' said Beth, sitting on a stool and removing her shoes. 'You can leave me now, Jane. I would like to be alone for a while.'

Jane smiled. 'That's right, Mistress Beth, you have a lie down. I'll go to the kitchen and ask one of the maids where I can wash some of the garments you wore in France.'

'You don't have to worry about that now, Jane,' said Beth, stretching out on the bed and closing her eyes. 'We'll be returning to London in a few days.'

'I'd rather have some work to occupy my hands, Mistress Beth,' said Jane.

'Then do what you wish,' murmured Beth, yawning.

Jane tiptoed out of the bedchamber and the room fell silent.

Beth tried to sleep, but the talk of Old Nick, demons, madness and menace had unsettled her. Briefly she had been able to put out of her mind what had happened in France, but now she wept for her father. Part of her regretted leaving France so swiftly and she could only pray that some kind Frenchwoman would tend his grave until she could return there one day. She gave up trying to sleep and rose and went over to the window. The glass was thick with a whirly pattern embedded in its surface in some of the tiny panes, but others were clear, enabling her to see through them. There was no way of opening the window, so she decided to go outside shortly and get a better view of the gardens. Right now she would use the time to write down her first impressions of this house and the gist of the conversations that had taken place since her arrival.

She took a sheet of paper and picked up her writing implement, sharpening it before removing the top from her ink container. She wasted no time gazing into space, but began to write. When she had finished and read through what she had written, she felt a stir of excitement. Here she felt there could be a thrilling tale in the making; all she needed was a little more information and then she would allow her imagination to take flight. She thought of Sir Gawain. There were questions she needed to ask him, but whether he would provide her with the answers she wanted was a different matter entirely.

Gawain had spoken to his steward before saddling up his horse and visiting the forest that could be seen in the near distance. After having a word with his forester and woodcutters, he returned to the stables and was making his way back to the house when he saw Beth strolling in the direction of the rose garden. He was tempted to call out to her. The garden would be a pleasant place to linger and would delay the moment when he would have to make certain decisions. Yet although drawn to her, he doubted he would ever trust a woman again. Had Beth wanted her father dead? As she had said herself, she had much to gain.

Then she turned her head and looked at him. 'Sir Gawain, I was hoping I would see you,' she said, giving him an unexpected dazzling smile.

'Mistress Llewellyn, what can I do for you?' he asked with chilling politeness.

The smile died on her lips. 'Have you discovered something that displeases you?' she asked.

'I don't know what you mean,' he rasped.

Beth was reluctant to bring up the subject of the missive he had received from his wife, so instead she said, 'You have obviously been out and about your lands and I wondered if some calamity had struck your trees or your sheep in your absence.'

'Nothing like that.' He hesitated before saying, 'Perhaps you would like to see the rose garden?'

'Your aunt told me it was a lovely place to stroll at this time of year,' said Beth, glad of his change of manner.

'My mother had the garden laid out with roses brought from many different places in Europe and their perfume is such that I remember her saying that she could never have enough of it.'

Beth was pleased that she had not needed to initiate a conversation about his mother, but that it had come naturally from him. 'You miss your mother? I know I miss mine.'

A shadow darkened his handsome face with its fine straight nose and sculptured cheekbones. 'I was only twelve when she died and my father died shortly afterwards.'

'Their deaths must have been a great loss to you,' she murmured.

Gawain had never spoken about his double bereavement and had no intention of doing so now. Instead, he simply said, 'One has to accept life as it is.'

Beth wondered if he was giving her a subtle hint about her need to accept her fate. She allowed several moments to pass before saying, 'My father might have told you that my mother was his third wife. I don't think his feelings for any woman surpassed the passion he felt for printing. Jonathan did not feel the same about the business. It is true he enjoyed finding out snippets of information that would amuse and interest people, but his real passion was for play-acting. I only wish he could have told Father. Our lives would have been so different and perhaps he would have been happier.'

'You cannot know that for certain.' Gawain opened a wicket gate and she went on ahead of him. The scent of roses instantly assailed her senses and she walked slowly along the path, stopping every now and again to sniff the fragrant heart of a blowsy deep-red or purple-pink bloom. She knew little about flowers but here and there was a name, such as Belle de Crecy. In her eagerness to read the label, she pricked her finger.

'Ouch!' she exclaimed. 'That was careless of me.'

Gawain resisted taking hold of her hand as he gazed at the torn flesh from which blood oozed. 'You'll need some salve for that.' He peered closer. 'Two of your fingers are discoloured.'

'It's ink,' said Beth.

'Ink.' He raised his eyebrows. 'You have been writing?'

She hesitated. 'Aye. My mother encouraged me to note down my thoughts and the events of each day and this I have tried to do.'

'And where do you keep all these pages of writing?' he asked abruptly.

She slanted him a glance from beneath her eyelashes. 'I really shouldn't tell you. You might want to destroy them.'

He frowned. 'You really believe I would do that?'

'You've already made your feelings clear about how you feel about my writing,' retorted Beth.

'That is because I do not want you wasting your time when you can be more gainfully occupied. You will marry shortly, so what is the point of writing if no one is to read it?' Even as he spoke, Gawain wondered if Mary had any scribblings secreted away in her bedchamber that might provide a clue to her and the girls' whereabouts.

Beth's brown eyes glinted. 'Another woman might read them one day and it would give her an insight into how a woman of my day lived. Unfortunately, most histories are written by men. Have you given any thought to your daughters' education? I doubt it. Most men don't.'

He drew his breath in with a hiss. 'You go too far, Mistress Llewellyn. Of course I have considered my daughters' education. And if you had a pennyworth of sense you would accept that you could be mistaken at times. If you only thought like a man, then you would consider charming me into finding you an indulgent husband who will allow you to have your way in all things.'

'I don't believe it. Rather you would marry me off to a man like yourself, determined to force his will on me. A man who has no experience of printing or how to recognise a market for a news sheet and a different kind of book. A man who won't heed aught I say to him,' replied Beth fiercely.

'Enough,' warned Gawain. 'You will go to your bed-chamber and stay there until I give you permission to come downstairs again. It is possible that you will never enter a print room again!'

Beth stared at him and her mouth quivered, then, without another word, she turned and ran towards the house.

# *Chapter Four*

Beth spent the next hour angrily filling one side of a sheet of her precious supply of paper with suggestions of what she would like to do to Sir Gawain. Eventually she put down her quill and stretched before going over to the bed and dropping onto it. She was hungry, but she was not going to go begging for food from him. She pillowed her head on her arms and thought of her father and Jonathan and tears oozed from beneath her eyelids. It seemed so much longer than three days since she had discovered her father's body. If only she had not been drawn to the wrestling match, then she might have returned to the tent in time to prevent his murder, but her curiosity and love of writing had led her into trouble and turned her life upside down. Why did her father have to choose Sir Gawain, a man whom he scarcely knew, to be her guardian? Why had he had to bribe him by offering shares in his company?

It was enough to tempt some men to commit murder; although Sir Gawain had said he didn't need money, he was having to spend his own in the shipyard that had belonged to his father-in-law. What if he had bribed someone to kill her father, not knowing that the dagger would be recognised by her servant? No, he would not do that. Somehow she sensed he was not a man to get someone else to do dangerous acts. Nor did she really believe he had killed her father. No, she believed Jonathan and her father's deaths were connected and she could not think why Sir Gawain would wish her half-brother dead.

She yawned, realising how tired she was; maybe it was that which was causing her to allow her thoughts to run away with her. Her father had trusted Sir Gawain. Maybe she could trust him, as well? A vision of the knight half-naked swam into her consciousness and she was filled with an inexplicable longing. She hated herself for finding him so physically attractive when he had set his mind so firmly against that which she so wanted out of life.

A sudden knock at the door caused her to start and she called, 'Who is it?'

'Gawain.'

Her heart seemed to kick against her ribs and she rolled off the bed and smoothed down her gown. 'May I ask what is it you want?'

'I thought you might be hungry so I have brought you some food,' came the reply.

She was taken aback and wondered why he had not asked Jane or his aunt to bring it up. Should she refuse it? She decided that would be churlish; besides, she was hungry. She went over to the door and opened it, intending to thank him politely, accept the food and wish him a good-night and close the door.

But he was too swift for her and barged right in before she could speak or prevent him from entering the bedchamber. She watched with annoyance as he strode over to the window and placed the tray on the table there. Instantly she remembered the sheet of paper with her scribblings on it and almost ran after him. Obviously he had come to spy on her! She was too late, for already he had picked up the sheet of paper.

'I see you have been writing despite hurting your finger,' said Gawain, glancing down the page.

'Please, give that to me! You have no right to read it.'

She tried to take it from him, but he brushed her hand away and carried on deciphering her untidy script. When he came to the end, he lifted his dark head and stared at her.

'Boiling in oil? Stung to death by bees? Do my words and one kiss really merit such a fate?' There was a quiver of amusement in his voice.

'I was angry,' she muttered, lowering her gaze and toying with the binding on her finger.

'So was I, but I would not have considered meting out such punishment to you for your rudeness,' he said idly, his eyes running over the page again.

'No, you simply silenced and threatened me in a manner you thought fit,' she said indignantly.

'But I did not silence you, did I? You still ran on

and judged my relationship with my wife and children without knowing the facts.' His voice was flat. 'I should put you on bread and water and take away your writing implements and paper. Then when you feel ready to beg my pardon for your ill manners, I should refuse to accept your apology and send you home with Sam and Jane and leave you to your fate.'

Beth's head shot up and there was a sparkle in her eyes. 'Then send me home. It is what I want, after all. But you won't, will you? Because if I was left to fend for myself, then I could prove how well I could manage without you. My thoughts were for my eyes only and you should have respected my privacy. Although, you can't really believe I want you boiled in oil or stung to death by bees.' She could not resist adding in an undertone, 'I pity the poor bees who would attempt such an act.'

'If your words are meant to be some sort of apology then you really do need to curb your tongue and learn a few lessons in good manners,' said Gawain, a glint in his eyes. 'Explain why you pity the bees?'

She bit her lower lip. 'I spoke without thinking. Couldn't I just beg your pardon?'

'No, you are not getting off so easily!' Gawain folded his arms across his chest. 'The thought must have come from somewhere. Explain what you meant, Mistress.'

'It was just a jest.'

'Then why am I not laughing?' He raised his eyebrows. 'Perhaps you were insinuating that their stings would have difficulty penetrating my hide because I am tough and unfeeling. If so, I would like to know on what hypothesis you have come to that conclusion? You scarcely know me.'

'And that is why my father should not have made you my guardian,' said Beth promptly, a flush on her cheeks. 'Now I would rather not continue with this conversation, if you please.'

'In that case, all I have to say is that your time would be better spent considering the kind of husband who would suit you so our relationship can be terminated as soon as possible, rather than you waste it writing nonsense.' He gathered together her writing implements and the sheet of paper containing her scribblings before she could make a move to prevent him.

'No!' she cried. 'Please, I beg your pardon! Forgive me and return them to me!'

He ignored her protests, telling himself that he should never have given in to the impulse to show compassion towards her. What she had written down proved that she had a temper and who was to say that if she wanted something badly enough she might not commit murder to get her way? He made for the door and could not resist calling over his shoulder, 'I'm surprised you never thought of *having me hung, drawn and quartered*, Mistress Llewellyn.'

'Maybe I should have,' she said through gritted teeth, 'only it was far too horrible to contemplate.'

'Should I be grateful for that?' he asked, pausing by the door. 'Or perhaps you really would like to murder me?'

'I do not find that the least bit amusing,' snapped Beth, considering picking up one of the items on the tray and flinging it at him, only the door was already closing. Oh, why did she have to write such nonsense? Sir Gawain would now rate all her thought processes as emotional, foolish and inferior to his own. If only she could prove to him that she could reason as sensibly as many a man. A thought struck her. Perhaps she could begin by trying to recall at least some of the names of the customers in her father's account book!

Her stomach rumbled and she remembered the food he had brought and was glad to see that he had thought to include a cup of wine, as well. Perhaps she should be grateful to him for thinking of it and she felt ashamed of her behaviour. Had he meant the food as a peace offering? A sigh escaped her. Should she beg for his pardon again on the morrow?

The mutton broth had cooled, but it was still tasty and she ate the lot and downed the wine. She decided not to wait for Jane to come and help her undress, but did so unaided and performed her *toilette* before saying her prayers and climbing into bed. The mattress felt as if stuffed with sheep's wool and the boards beneath were hard. Even so, the wine had made her drowsy, so she turned on her side and fell asleep, only to dream that she was trapped in a tent. There seemed to be no opening and she was trying to crawl beneath the walls but there were too many pegs holding them down. Suddenly she sensed that there was someone in the tent with her. Then she saw a figure dressed in red and the head was hooded and a mask covered the face. She opened her mouth to scream, but no sound came out.

She tore herself out of the dream, her heart thudding. What had the dream meant?

She slid out of bed and, still drowsy, made her way over to the table, meaning to write down the dream whilst it was fresh in her mind, only to remember that Sir Gawain had removed her writing implements. Exasperated, she returned to bed and tried to hold the dream in her mind. Perhaps in the morning she could go into Tenderden and find a stationer's. That was, of course, if Sir Gawain did not prevent her from doing so.

It was the following morning and Gawain had slept little due to spending too much time thinking of Beth and whether she was capable of murder and arguing with himself that was nonsense. She was obviously not herself at the moment after the terrible shock she had received and had behaved stupidly and out of character. His thoughts had veered between giving her a good spanking and taking her into his bed and making love to her, which proved that he was capable of thinking and behaving just as foolishly as she, as well. Due to the shock he had received on reading Mary's missive, no doubt. But he did not want to dwell on that right now when there was a murderer on the loose. Beth must stay here when he eventually travelled to London. In the meantime he would entrust Sam to take a message to the Llewellyns' man of business. He only hoped that when he did leave Beth alone, her curiosity about people did not mean she would go prying into his business or that of his neighbours.

He dressed practically in brown hose, plain grey

shirt and a brown, unadorned, broadcloth doublet, clothes that were very different from those he wore when he attended court. Later that morning he would visit the boatyard. He left his bedchamber and went downstairs and found not only Catherine sitting at table, but also Beth. He noticed that she was wearing the same blue gown that she had worn yesterday, but she had dispensed with the headdress and was wearing a simple black kerchief over her hair. She looked demure and far removed from the angry shrew she could be likened to yesterday. *Boiled in oil, stung by bees!* he thought, and his lips twitched. He found himself remembering how she had not struggled when he had kissed her in France. Had she perhaps enjoyed it? No, he must not consider for a moment that she might have done so, despite her knowing it was wrong with him being a married man. Better to believe that she had not struggled because he had taken her by surprise.

A serving man was hovering and Gawain asked him to bring collops of bacon and bread, as well as a tankard of ale. He was aware of Beth's eyes on him and wondered if she was bubbling with resentment beneath that demure exterior. As soon as the serving man departed, Gawain turned his full attention on her. 'You slept well, Mistress Llewellyn?' he asked.

'Surprisingly well in the circumstances,' she responded.

'I am relieved to hear it. No bad dreams?'

She smiled sweetly. 'Normally if my dreams are so vivid and frightening that they wake me, then I write them down. As I did not write anything last night, then I mustn't have dreamed, must I?'

Gawain guessed that she had dreamt and she was still annoyed with him. But before he could comment, Catherine leaned forwards and said, 'I do believe dreams have meaning and it is God's way of trying to tell us something. Do you remember in the Old Testament how Joseph was able to interpret dreams?'

'Indeed, I do, his story is one of my favourites,' said Beth. 'That is why it is so important to make a note of dreams.'

'If you do not have the means to do so, there are writing implements here in the hall,' said Catherine. 'Although I deem we will soon run short of paper.'

'Will they have supplies in Tenderden?' asked Beth.

'Certainly.' Catherine gazed at Gawain. 'Will you be going to the boatyard today? If so, then perhaps you can take Mistress Llewellyn with you.'

'Please, call me Beth. Mistress Llewellyn is such a mouthful,' said Beth.

Catherine smiled. 'If that is what you wish, then I will be pleased to do so.'

Gawain had not expected the two women to become friendly so soon and thought it possible that they could be sharing secrets in no time at all. He must have a few words with his aunt. The last thing he wanted was Catherine falling victim to Beth's charm and inquisitive nature. He would need to separate the two and so would begin by doing as his aunt suggested.

'I am willing to take Mistress Llewellyn with me this morning as I am sure she will find it interesting taking a look at the boatyard, as well as having a stroll around the village.'

'You must have a look at the churches, Beth,' said Catherine. 'They are both fine in their different ways.'

'If there is aught you wish for me to fetch for you, Aunt Catherine, then let me have a list,' said Gawain.

'I will waste no time doing so,' said Catherine, rising from the table and excusing herself.

Beth was about to follow her when Gawain indicated that she should sit down. After the barest hesitation she did so and gazed at him warily. But before he could speak the serving man returned with his breakfast and set it before him. 'Perhaps what you have to say to me can wait until after you've eaten,' she said hastily, rising again.

But Gawain waved her down. 'I won't keep you long because I have every intention of setting out shortly. I give you credit for being cleverer than I deemed you to be, but don't attempt to win my aunt to your side so you can conspire with her to get your own way.'

Her eyes flared, but she did not pretend to not know to what he alluded. 'I need to write, even if no one else is to read what I have written,' she said in a low voice.

'For your eyes only,' he said drily.

'Indeed.' She hesitated before adding in a stiff little voice, 'I must beg pardon for my rudeness to you yesterday. You were right. I know little about you.'

She had surprised him and he found himself saying, 'I accept your apology. I would like to ask where you would hide your scribblings if you did not want anyone to find them?'

A tiny laugh escaped her. 'Do you take me for a fool?'

'No. I give you my word that I will not read anything you write without your permission. I cannot say fairer than that,' he said, taking up his knife.

How could she believe him when he had already done exactly that? 'Allow me time to consider your question.'

'Certainly.'

She hesitated. 'Does this conversation mean that you will return my writing implements to me?'

'There is little point. You need new writing implements, more ink and, of course, paper,' replied Gawain, thinking that perhaps it would be a mistake to try to prevent her from writing altogether. 'You will need to visit the stationer's in Tenderden. You have coin?'

'Enough,' she said, wondering if his manner was genuine.

'Then I will meet you in front of the house within the hour,' he said. 'And bring a cloak with you. It can be chilly down by the river and it's possible we're in for a change of weather.'

'I appreciate the warning,' said Beth, flashing him a smile as she hurried out.

Gawain thought that when she smiled at him so delightfully, he really did want to kiss her again. He could almost feel her soft lips beneath his and scowled; he must not allow himself to be tempted to ravage them again or he just might find himself featuring in that news sheet of hers in the guise of a rogue in a dramatic tale.

\* \* \*

Beth stood outside the front of the house, gazing up at the white clouds that moved like sailing ships blown by the wind against an expanse of deep blue sky. Despite the mixed emotions she felt every time she thought of her father and Jonathan, she looked forward to the outing. At the moment it did not look the least bit like rain, but she was no weather seer and could only hope Sir Gawain was mistaken.

She did not have long to wait before he appeared, riding a horse and leading another. He dismounted, helped her into the saddle and then led the way along the path towards the main highway. Living in London, Beth scarcely ever rode a horse and would have much preferred to ride pillion behind him, but pride prevented her from admitting her lack of horsemanship and she could only pray that he would not urge his horse into a gallop and expect her to keep up with him.

Fortunately there was no need for her to worry; he kept to a steady trot because as they approached Tenderden, the traffic on the road increased. He told her that they would not stop there now, but would do so on the return journey, weather permitting. As they drew nearer to Smallhythe, Beth thought she could smell the sea, although they were some distance from it. She followed him closely as they made their way through the narrow streets until he called a halt.

Gawain was in the act of helping her to dismount when a voice hailed him. He turned to face a stocky young man with a shock of reddish-brown hair and a broad flat face with a snub nose. 'James, it is good to see you,' said Gawain, taking the young man's hand and shaking it. 'Fare you well?'

'Very well, thank you, Sir Gawain,' said James, grinning. 'Mildred and I are to be married and we would be honoured if you and Mary would come to the wedding.'

After the barest hesitation, Gawain asked, 'When is the ceremony to be?'

'Not until the beginning of August when my elder brother, Hugh, hopes to be able to preside at the ceremony,' replied James.

'I saw Father Hugh briefly a few days ago,' said Gawain. 'I remembered when he was in charge of your family shipyard that he was a regular visitor to Raventon Hall, but after my father died, everything changed.'

'Aye, I remember it well,' said James, stroking his chin. 'Hugh was deeply upset by his death. I was only apprenticed at the time, but he decided then to train me to take over his position so he could join the priesthood. We see him rarely these days. He has become so grand now he is in Cardinal Wolsey's employ and spends most of his time at York Place in London, although, as you know, he is in France at the moment.'

James glanced at Beth admiringly. She had wandered off whilst the two men were talking. 'May I ask who is that young woman?'

'She is my ward,' said Gawain, frowning. 'I am burdened with the task of finding a husband for her.'

''Tis a pity I am already spoken for,' said James, his eyes twinkling. 'But your task should not be too arduous. She has lovely features and a comely figure. What is her fortune and is she biddable?'

'Her fortune is adequate and she took her mother's place in organising her father's household several years ago,' replied Gawain. 'As for her being biddable, I have no complaints on that score so far,' he lied smoothly.

James nodded thoughtfully. 'If you are of a mind to, then you must bring her to the wedding. There is likely to be a choice of possible suitors amongst the guests.'

'I will consider it,' said Gawain. 'I must go now, James. I have much to do.'

They shook hands again.

'I will let you know the exact date of the wedding. I trust Mary will have returned by then,' said James. 'Your aunt, of course, is also welcome. My mother always enjoys her company.'

Gawain thanked him, even as he was thinking how best to avoid attending a wedding where he would have to make excuses for Mary's absence again. He was gripped by frustrated rage at being trapped in a situation not of his making and from which there seemed no easy escape. Fortunately most of his neighbours had no real notion of how long Mary and the children had been away, but if he were to attend this happy occasion and she were not there, questions were bound to be asked.

He turned to Beth as she approached. Her cheeks were flushed prettily with the sharp breeze but she was shivering slightly and had her light summer cloak wrapped closely around her. He frowned. 'You are cold?'

'A little chilly.'

'Then let us go inside the yard. You can take shelter in one of the workshops or, better still, the smithy,' he said, pushing open a gate and leading both the horses inside.

'So you and your wife are invited to a wedding,' murmured Beth.

'You overheard,' said Gawain sharply.

'He had a loud voice,' she said hastily. 'I was not eavesdropping.'

'Really?' His voice was dry.

Beth's lips tightened and she glanced about her, deciding to ignore his question. Instead, she thought that this yard was where Jonathan's small boat had been built. What had brought him here when there were boat-yards nearer to where they lived? She breathed in the scent of wood and the strong pungent odour of pitch, noticing the hull of a boat on wooden stocks and several men at work on it. There were others in the yard, obviously absorbed in a variety of tasks. Could one of them be responsible for what had happened to Jonathan's boat? But if so, why?

She was roused from her reverie by Gawain's voice. 'Did you hear James extend an invitation to you and Aunt Catherine?'

'Aye,' replied Beth, 'but I cannot see how I can accept.'

He met her eyes. 'I see no reason why the two of you should not attend.'

'But I will be in London surely by then. Besides, I am in mourning.'

'I am sure your father would be in favour of your attending such an event as there could be one or two there who might make you a suitable husband,' he said.

'You really do want to get rid of me as soon as possible, don't you?' she blurted out. 'Well, the day can't come quickly enough for me, either. But you could save yourself time and trouble if only you would accept that I am capable of running my own business.'

He wondered if he was imagining the hurt in her lovely eyes. 'It makes sense that we make the most of every opportunity to find the right husband for you and to give you both time to get to know each other,' he said. 'The man you saw is James Tyler, who owns the shipyard just a little farther along the river to this one. Few shipwrights are wealthy, but he is and has many rich friends who will be invited to the wedding and in the market for a wife.'

'You mean those connected with shipbuilding, suppliers, prospective buyers, merchants, mariners,' said Beth hotly. 'What use will they be to me and my business?'

Gawain shrugged. 'If we were to sell the business—'

'I will not agree to sell it. I would like to return home before the wedding, so it is unlikely I will be able to attend,' she said firmly. 'Father, Jonathan and I always attended Bartholomew Fair in August and I intend to do so this year,' she said.

'You will not be returning to London until I am convinced it is safe for you to do so,' said Gawain heatedly. 'And now I am being signalled, so must leave you for a while. The smithy is only a temporary building, but it is the one to your right. You might find it interesting to visit. We will talk of the fair later.'

She fought to hold on to her temper and show interest. 'All right, I agree. Now tell me—what is a smith doing here?'

'He is making nails and an anchor. Now I must go.' He left her alone.

Beth walked over to the smithy and went inside, convinced Gawain would prevent her from going to the fair just to assert his will over her. She felt cold and was glad of the warmth inside the smithy, holding her hands out to the fire glowing in a brazier. She stood to one side away from the giant of a man with a gleaming bald head and arms like hams. Except for one brief glance her way, he ignored her as he hammered metal into shape. She did not linger long and next visited a workshop filled with clay pots and a variety of tools where she noticed a considerable number of items she couldn't name. One of the men told her they were augers, used for drilling holes for the clench nails to go through when nailing planks together. She was struck by how easy it would be to take one and sabotage a vessel. She wondered if Gawain had already thought of it and questioned the men. Most likely he had done so. She decided to explore the port to see if this, too, had a stationer's, but she could not find one and to her disappointment had to return to the yard, empty-handed. Still, there was always the town up the hill.

On the return journey beneath a louring sky, Beth asked Gawain whether he believed it was an auger from his yard that had drilled the holes in Jonathan's boat. 'Possibly, but there is no way of knowing for certain,' he answered. 'As you will have noticed, they are in plentiful supply because a ship requires many nails to hold it together and the auger is soon damaged.'

'You do not suspect any of the men at the yard?'

He shook his head. 'None of those that are there today, but labourers come and go and not all who have worked here in the past dwell in this area and not all their names are written down.'

She was taken aback. 'So someone could have worked in the yard, damaged Jonathan's boat and then just left?'

'Aye, it is possible Jonathan's murderer is a common labourer who was paid to hole your half-brother's boat after he sailed it back to London,' said Gawain.

Filled with dismay, she burst out, 'This is hopeless! We'll never find him.'

'We still have the dagger that killed your father and Sam's conviction that he has seen it before, so you must not lose hope,' said Gawain, deciding it would be best to change the subject. 'You mentioned Bartholomew Fair. I agree with you that it is not to be missed. It is a great event for the cloth trade, as well as being a pleasure fair that draws the crowds from all layers of society, including those spinners and weavers in Tenderden.'

'I have seen the Guild of Merchant Taylors process to the cloth fair to test the measures for cloth,' said Beth excitedly.

'People come from far and wide to buy Kentish broadcloth.'

'So you will not prevent me going to the Fair?' she said eagerly.

'No, but whether we will stay for the full two weeks depends on several factors,' said Gawain.

'I know,' said Beth, sighing. 'The date of your friend's wedding and whether your wife will have returned by then.'

'That would not prevent me from attending the fair,' said Gawain, thinking how easy it was to deceive people, although such deceit could not go on for ever. 'Anyway, as the wedding is likely to be at the beginning of August and the fair does not open until the twenty-fourth, you can attend both events.'

Beth's spirits, which had lifted at the thought of attending the fair, plummeted, but she told herself most likely that was due to the thought that this would be the first time she would be there without her father or Jonathan. She felt a tightness in her throat and tears pricked her eyes. 'Are you still intent on selling my father's business?' she asked in a husky voice. 'If so, then I have a suggestion to make. Could it not simply be moved elsewhere? To Aldersgate or Cripplegate to the north of London, for instance. There are several other such businesses in those areas.'

'Are you still dreaming of continuing with writing and printing your news sheet?' groaned Gawain.

'And what if I were and had a son one day? I do not need to be married to do so,' she said daringly.

A muscle tightened in Gawain's cheek. 'Now that is foolish, although I deem you would enjoy causing a scandal.'

'I speak the truth, but I admit I was teasing you.' There was a blush on her cheeks. 'I suggest that you listen to what my father's associates and employees have to say when you visit London. They might surprise you by telling you that I am not as foolish as you think in some matters.'

'I will consider what they have to say, of course.'

'So have you decided when you will go?'

'Not until you have had the opportunity to scrutinise the account book and see if your servant recognises any name he could associate the dagger with,' said Gawain.

'That could be within just a few days,' said Beth.

'Aye, so you will have to be patient until then,' said Gawain firmly. 'And in the meantime you could do as I suggested and give thought to the kind of man you could accept as a husband, not just a lover.'

She put her tongue in her cheek. 'I could certainly make a list of possible traits in a man I approve of.'

'As long as you do not expect perfection,' he said drily.

She was about to say that was the last trait in a man she would expect, but at that moment there came a flash of lightning and a crack of thunder. Their exchange came to an abrupt end as the heavens opened and they made a dash for cover.

## Chapter Five

Beth blew on the strand of hair that dripped water into her eyes and fell into Gawain's arms as she slid from her horse. She could hear the rain hammering on the stable roof as he set her down on the ground. She remained leaning against him, her breath coming fast due to that final gallop that had filled her with terror. Gawain had dismounted and opened the stable doors for her to enter on horseback. Despite his sodden clothing, Beth could feel the heat of his body penetrating her saturated cloak and the clothing beneath and she was reluctant to abandon that warmth. The memory of how he had kissed her in France popped into her head and her heart began to thud in her chest. She wanted to lift her face to his and have him kiss her again. It did not make sense that she should feel this way. He obviously did not approve of her and, besides, he was not at all the kind of man she wished to marry, even if he were free. He was high-handed and intent on crushing that creative spirit in her because it was not acceptable that a woman should write and influence people. And yet she could not deny that he roused feelings within her that she had never experienced before.

Gawain knew that he should move away from Beth, but he blamed some primeval instinct for keeping him rooted to the spot, holding her so close that he could feel every contour of her shivering form. She needed his warmth. What good would it do if he protected her from a murderer, only for her to die of a fever brought on by being chilled to the bone? He rested his wet cheek against her drenched hair and closed his eyes. He would like to strip her naked and roll her in the sweet-smelling hay and make love to her.

Beth stirred in his arms and Gawain released her instantly. What did he think he was doing? He was behaving foolishly and he imagined her writing about this in her journal and embellishing it with God only knew what else. 'These summer storms are generally of short duration—do you want to make a run for the house?' he asked roughly.

'I am of a mind that the sooner we get out of these wet clothes the better,' croaked Beth, stepping away from him.

'Make haste, then,' urged Gawain, closing his mind to the picture her words conjured up. 'I will need to see to the horses. I don't know where the blasted stable lads are,' he added vehemently, removing his sodden hat and slinging it on to a hook.

Beth hesitated. 'I could help you.'

'No, I will manage without you.' He opened the door
and pushed her out into the rain and slammed the door
behind her before he could weaken.

For a moment Beth felt like banging on the door and
demanding to be let back in, but it was obvious he could
not wait to be rid of her. No doubt she had embarrassed
him by leaning into him the way she had done. What a
fool she was for wanting to feel his lips pressed to hers
and to yield to him! To experience what it was like to
be possessed by a man. Perhaps any man would do to
rid her of this overwhelming urge for physical affection
and fulfilment she felt when in his company? Maybe
she really should give serious thought to taking a husband after all and she would no longer need Gawain as
her protector! In the meantime she must get out of her
wet garments. She took off through the rain towards
the house and entered the hall in a rush.

Catherine and Jane were sitting together on the
settle by the fire. Catherine had a book on her lap and
was pointing at a page and obviously trying to explain
something to the maid. Not wanting to disturb them,
Beth headed for the stairs, but they must have heard her
because both women turned and looked in her direction.

'Holy Mary, Mother of God!' cried Jane. 'Mistress
Beth, you're soaked!'

'Aye, I must get changed,' said Beth, not pausing.

'I will come and help you,' said Jane. 'If you'll
excuse me, Mistress Ashbourne, it's been very interesting what you've read to me and I did so enjoy seeing
the drawings.'

'Where is Gawain?' asked Catherine.

'Seeing to the horses,' called Beth from the stairs. 'I offered my help, but he refused it. No doubt he will be with you shortly with your wares.' Only now did she remember that she had left her own purchases in the saddle bag. Would Gawain remember to bring them to the house or should she go and fetch them?

Before she could make a decision Jane took her arm and hurried her up the stairs. 'Come on, Mistress Beth, before you catch your death,' said the maid.

Jane opened the door of the bedchamber and ushered her mistress inside. She wasted no time helping her undress. As Beth rubbed herself dry and wrapped a cloth around her head Jane fetched her a clean chemise. 'Now you get into bed, Mistress Beth, and I'll go down and make you a hot drink and bring it up to you.'

Beth thanked Jane and donned the chemise and climbed into bed. She drew the covers up to her chin and soon felt much warmer as she thought back over the day. No doubt Gawain was regretting having brought her here. It was not only the even tenor of her life that had been interrupted, but her father's death had turned his life upside down, too. She grimaced, remembering how he had shoved her out of the stables. Definitely he'd had enough of her company and no doubt could not wait to head for London. Maybe whilst he was away he would take the opportunity to see his wife and daughters. She felt an odd ache inside her. Surely it could not be jealousy? Of course not! she thought firmly. Even so, she wondered where they were staying and concluded that, if it were some distance from London, then she should seize the opportunity to visit the capital and print an updated version of her news sheet. After all, it was she who had stepped into her father's shoes and surely her employees would be loyal to her and not Sir Gawain?

As she snuggled beneath the bedcovers she considered the description of the wrestling match she had noted and wondered if she dared to include it in her news sheet. A tremor ran through her as she imagined Gawain's reaction if he were to see it. She frowned, thinking that she should never have been so foolish as to blurt out her secret passion and asked herself what Jonathan would have done in her position. It needed some thought.

A short while later Jane entered her bedchamber, bringing not only a steaming fragrant cup of mulled wine but also a plate of small simnels and wafers flavoured with nutmeg and currants. In between mouthfuls of food washed down with wine, Beth asked, 'Has Sir Gawain returned from the stables?'

'Aye, he has, Mistress Beth, just as the rain stopped and the sun came out. He left something downstairs for you, but I couldn't bring it up because I had my hands full.'

'I will get dressed and fetch it,' she said, pleased that he had not forgotten her purchases.

'I can do that if you want it brought up here,' said Jane. 'I have to take the tray down.'

'Thank you, Jane.'

\* \* \*

By the time Beth was dressed and drying her hair in the sunshine that now poured in through the window, her maid had returned. Beth unpacked the parcel and had the pleasurable task of laying out her new quills, sharpening knife, ink bottles and writing paper on the desk. She remembered how Mistress Ashbourne had been showing Jane a book and asked if it were a printed book.

'No, it was handwritten by Sir Gawain's great-grandmother. It's full of recipes and spells for all kinds of ailments,' replied Jane. 'She read some of them out to me. They sent a shiver through me from head to toe with their mention of hairs of donkeys and drinking water from a boiled mouse. I can't see how they could do you any good at all. It fair made me baulk, the one that told you to take six dead spiders in a muslin bag and hold it in the mouth of a child that had the whooping cough.'

Beth smiled faintly, 'Mother used to say that when people sickened and feared they were close to death, they'd try anything to be cured.'

'I remember her saying so, too,' said Jane with a sigh. 'But I'd need to be really desperate to put spiders in my mouth.'

Beth's smile deepened as she picked up one of the quills and sharpened it. 'So does Sir Gawain know about this book that his great-grandmother wrote?'

Jane shrugged. 'I don't know. Mistress Catherine, who is his mother's older sister, told me that their mother passed it down to her.'

'I wonder why she has never married.'

'Perhaps she had no mind to, but preferred keeping her mother company after she was widowed,' said Jane.

'Or maybe there was a man she loved, but she lost him and so refused to accept any other suitor,' mused Beth.

'What an imagination you have, Mistress Beth,' marvelled Jane, watching her. 'Are you going to write one of your tales now?'

Beth shook her head. 'Not now, but I have been thinking that if I am to fulfil Father's wishes by marrying, I might as well start writing a list of the attributes I would like in a husband.'

'You want a fine set-up figure of a man to begin with,' said Jane firmly. 'Although, having said that, it's no guarantee that he won't succumb to the sweating fever or the plague and leave you a widow. My Arthur did and he always seemed so strong.'

'How cheerful you are,' said Beth drily. 'Even so, Jane, I think you are right in suggesting a fine-looking man who is strong in the body. I want a husband who is able to protect me if our home was ever broken into by robbers or we were attacked on the highway.' She removed the top of one of the containers of ink and dipped in the point of her quill. She began to write down the description and then paused, nibbling on the end of her quill. 'Dark or fair-haired? What do you think, Jane?'

'I like them flaxen-haired, myself,' mused Jane, 'but you might like them dark.'

'I'm not so sure. Sir Gawain is dark and—' She

sighed. 'I don't know. Do you not think that dark men have a stern aspect when they lour? Their eyebrows seem to bristle.'

'But Sir Gawain has blue eyes, Mistress Beth, so perhaps not so grim an aspect when he is not vexed,' said Jane.

'You have noticed his eyes,' commented Beth, writing down *blue eyes and dark hair*.

'Aye, real piercing they can be. He has a fine nose, but he doesn't stare down it at me in a disdainful manner like some men do when they're speaking to a servant.'

Beth stared at her. 'You are saying that he is not proud and haughty?'

'I wouldn't say that he hasn't got some pride in him—why shouldn't he? He's a knight of the realm, has a fine house and land and also is often invited to the king's court. But he's also considerate,' added Jane.

'Considerate?'

'Aye, Mistress Beth. Look at the way he brought us here, knowing that you needed peace and quiet to mourn your father.'

'I suppose a husband who is considerate of a wife's feelings is definitely to be desired,' murmured Beth, realising that her maid was more observant than she had thought.

'I'd certainly write it down,' said Jane.

'What else?' mused Beth, chewing on her quill again.

'You don't want one that's tight-fisted. I like an open-handed man, myself, but my second husband could be a bit too open-handed with the wrong people. He also liked a wager and tossed good money away at cock fights.'

'So a husband who is not miserly, but generous with his wife and children and the poor, whilst not foolish enough to gamble his money away,' said Beth, a smile tugging her mouth as she wrote it down.

'You also don't want a man who never takes you anywhere, but leaves you at home whilst he's enjoying himself elsewhere. You just never know, Mistress Beth, what men get up to when they're out of your sight for too long. There's other women, as well as gambling you have to be aware of,' warned Jane.

'So I need a husband who is faithful and wishes to spend as much time as he can in my company,' said Beth, writing it down and thinking of that kiss Sir Gawain had impressed on her lips. Odd, how she could still feel it if she dwelt on that moment.

'That's as long as you want it, as well,' said Jane.

'You mean I have to care enough about my husband to want to spend time with him,' said Beth, trying not to think of Gawain's wife again. Yet she could not help but wonder if she cared for him, why she could not have allotted someone else to tend her old aunt for a few days in order to spend time at home with her husband as any caring wife should and then return to her? She recalled what Gawain had said about not expecting perfection in a spouse. In reality, most marriages were simply ones of convenience.

'Temper!' Jane's voice roused her from her thoughts.

'Pardon?' Beth looked up at her maid.

'You don't want a husband who's quick-tempered or downright bad-tempered,' said Jane.

'Certainly not,' said Beth firmly. 'Although, how one is to know without spending some time beforehand in his company—?'

'That's why a maid should be courted and so you mustn't rush into marriage, Mistress Beth, but spend time getting to know your suitor.'

'True,' murmured Beth. 'And there is another aspect of marriage that would be important to me, Jane. Conversation. I do not want a man who is strong but also silent. I enjoy conversation and discussing what is going on about me, as well, as in the wider world if possible. Then there are plays and stories and matters pertaining to religion and books that I enjoy. I also want a husband who can see the amusing side to life.'

'In my experience, most men don't like a woman that rattles on too much,' said Jane.

Beth raised her eyebrows. 'We are not considering a man's desires at the moment, Jane, but mine.'

'Fair enough, Mistress Beth, but the day will come when you'll have to do what the man wants and there's a side of marriage that could come as a terrible shock to you.'

Beth stared at her. 'I deem you are referring to the marriage bed, Jane. I am not completely ignorant, you know. I admit that the whole process of begetting a child sounds a messy, unpleasant business. But I remember what Father used to say. "We are not put on this earth to enjoy ourselves."' She pulled a face. 'But my brother thought differently.'

'Aye, Master Jonathan knew how to enjoy himself. He liked folk dancing and singing on May morning and during the twelve days of Christmas.'

Beth considered Jane's words and thought that perhaps sharing the marriage bed with Gawain might be rather pleasant than otherwise. She remembered the warmth of his body and the strength in his arms and the sight of him half-naked. But he was forbidden fruit. She sighed. 'If only Jonathan had met a lass I could have called sister, how glad that would have made me. If they'd had children, then I would not have to be making this list now in order to fulfil Father's wish.' She put down her quill and leaned back in the chair and yawned. 'I deem I have written enough for the moment.'

'Why don't you have another rest?' Jane scooped up the wet clothes that her mistress had discarded. 'I'll deal with these and, if you fall asleep, I'll wake you in time for supper.'

'I will rest, but I have no intention of sleeping,' said Beth. 'I will read the Book of Hours that was my mother's and try to meditate. How I wish she was still alive,' she said sadly.

'You do that, Mistress Beth,' said Jane, bustling from the bedchamber.

Beth settled on the bed and opened the Book of Hours, but she had read only two of the meditations when she felt her eyelids drooping. She had no wish to doze off if it meant she would lie awake at night, worrying, so she rose and went over to the table again.

She picked up the sheet of paper on which she had

written her list, thinking to put it away. It was then she remembered Gawain's enquiry concerning places of concealment. Her eyes searched the room and she thought of the obvious ones, such as the bottom of a chest beneath clothes or bed linen, or under the mattress. Less obvious would be to prise up a floorboard and hide the papers in a box in the space beneath. One did not want a mouse to get at it or insects and a box would also be necessary if one took a brick or a stone from the wall over by the fireplace. If the lintel was wide enough above the door, it could be concealed there, too, although one would need to be tall or have a stool to stand on to reach that position. Then one could also sew it into a garment or the hem of a curtain or a hanging. She could not believe he planned on searching her bedchamber, so whose was it and what was he searching for? she wondered.

She glanced down at her list of desirable masculine attributes and thought how she would enjoy watching Gawain's face when he read it. She wondered where he was now and what he was doing.

Gawain rubbed his hair dry as he stood in the middle of Mary's bedchamber that was adjacent to his own, wondering if he was crazed to even consider that she might have kept a journal. He could not imagine her showing the same enthusiasm as Beth Llewellyn for the written word, yet Mary had plenty to say in the missive she had sent him and he thought of Lydia and Tabitha. One dark like himself and the other fair like Mary. He did not want to believe another man had

fathered Tabitha. He had to get them back! Perhaps
Mary might not have kept a journal, but she and this
other so-called husband of hers could have written to
each other. What would she have done with any billets-
doux she might have received from him? Destroyed
them or hidden them away so she could take them out
and re-read them when the mood took her? Who would
have delivered such messages without rousing suspicion? Money would have to be paid over to a messenger. Of course, if she had kept them, they could still be
here if she had left in a hurry, fearing he might return
from court before she could escape.

He tossed the drying cloth on a chair and went
over to the bed and slid his hands beneath the mattress. No doubt this would be one of the places that
Beth Llewellyn might suggest he search. He frowned,
remembering the feel of her in his arms. Damn! He
had to get the chit out of his head and keep his mind on
what he was doing. He tried the other side, but without
any luck. He looked in the chest at the foot of the bed,
but again without any success. It occurred to him that
even if he found any missives from Mary's lover, they
might be of no help to him in finding her and the girls,
as it was unlikely he would write down his address
when Mary already knew where to find him. Deciding he was wasting his time searching any further, he
returned to his bedchamber. He knew that he could not
let matters remain as they were for much longer. He was
in need of a male heir. Beth might feel strongly about a
daughter being able to inherit all that was her father's,
but he knew his own sex better than her. Most would

not give women the same respect as they would a man and would attempt to trick and cheat a female. He considered how if he did not beget another son and Lydia were to marry, then it would be her husband who would eventually take control of Gawain's land and other possessions. He felt a spurt of anger and decided that, if he were to find his daughters and Mary refused to return home with them, he must seriously consider what action he could take to free himself of her. But first he must deal with the dilemma that Beth Llewellyn presented him with. Right now he found himself sympathising with her in her position. Really, he could not blame her for wanting to have possession of her father's business and not handing it over to a man who was a complete stranger to her.

He did not see Beth again until supper and, as he had mentioned his meeting with James Tyler to his aunt earlier, it was not surprising that the main topic of conversation was James's approaching nuptials.

'He has made a good choice in his wife,' said Catherine. 'Mildred is warm-hearted and patient and her mother has trained her well. She will run his household and entertain those with whom he does business in an exemplary manner.'

Beth paused with her spoon held halfway to her mouth. 'And will he make her an excellent husband?'

'They have known each other since childhood, as have their families, so I am sure they will rub along perfectly amiably,' said Catherine.

'Amiably—so they are not in love?' asked Beth thoughtfully.

Catherine smiled. 'Surely that depends on what you mean by love? From what I have seen, as an onlooker, love can grow between husband and wife after a while. Besides, I deem it far better for a couple to like each other and then they are more likely to be tolerant of the other's shortcomings. No one is perfect.'

'As I have already said to Sir Gawain, perfection in a man is not a trait I desire,' said Beth promptly. 'I consider it would be exceedingly uncomfortable living with such a person. As I am far from perfect myself I would prove a disappointment to him.' She glanced at Gawain. 'Still, I would hope that those suitors you will eventually consider as a husband for me would appreciate my finer qualities.'

'Do you know that part in the scriptures where it lists the attributes of the most excellent wife?' asked Catherine.

Beth frowned in thought. 'Does it not say something about her excellence when it comes to spinning and making fine clothes and her being worth her weight in rubies?'

'It says a lot more than that,' said Gawain, frowning, 'including that a virtuous woman's price is far above rubies.'

Beth shot him a glance, recalling the way she had made no attempt to remove herself from his embrace in the stables. Perhaps he thought she was not as virtuous as she should be. He had entered her bedchamber the evening before and a gentleman should not have done so but most likely he did not consider her a lady. After all, her father had been involved in trade. Even so, she found herself saying, 'But should a woman not expect the same behaviour in a man as he does from her?'

A muscle clenched in Gawain's cheek. 'Of course. I'm sure you'll be able to discuss with my aunt the different merits of any suitors I present to you when the time comes,' he said.

'I have compiled a list as you suggested, Sir Gawain,' she said, holding his gaze steadily. 'You might wish to see it before you choose someone amongst your acquaintances that might suit me.'

'No doubt it will prove interesting,' said Gawain. 'I have wondered if perhaps a much older man might be best for you. A kindly gentleman who will indulge and dote on you.'

Beth was startled by his suggestion. 'You would marry me off to a man who would soon make a widow of me?'

'Why not? For a woman who has stated that she'd prefer to remain a spinster, but knows that she must marry, I would have thought that an ideal choice.'

'It is worth considering,' said Beth coolly. 'Only we are both forgetting that I need a man who is capable of fulfilling my father's wish for a grandson. A lusty man, who is also physically strong and so able to protect us both from those who might seek to harm us.'

'Are those qualities on your list?' asked Gawain wryly.

'Some of them,' replied Beth with a sudden smile.

'And for the rest I would that you will bear them in mind.'

'Of course! I am not an ogre,' replied Gawain, warmed by her smile. 'Just as long as you remember that the odds against my finding you the kind of husband who would meet all your requirements are likely to be high.'

Beth shrugged and said in a droll fashion, 'That is what bothers me.' She gave her attention now to her food.

Catherine's eyes darted from Beth to her nephew. 'The Hurst brothers might be at James and Mildred's wedding. You remember them, Gawain?'

'Of course,' he said in a toneless voice.

'You do not like them?' asked Beth, lifting her head and staring at him.

Gawain hesitated. 'One of them will definitely not fit your criteria as Christopher is already married with four offspring.'

'What about his brothers—are they older or younger than him?' asked Beth.

'Younger,' replied Gawain. 'The Hurst family home is near Greenwich. They have a large shipyard and have built ships for the king and his father before him. Just like James Tyler, they also hire out their ships and are involved in trade.'

'So they live closer to London than you do,' mused Beth.

'Obviously,' said Gawain, cutting up a slice of meat on his plate.

'And their names?'

'Nick and Pip.'

'Pip?'

'Phillip. He's the youngest.' He raised his eyebrows and felt a spurt of irritation. 'I see I have roused your curiosity.'

'Was that not your intention? It is you who is set on my marrying,' she challenged.

He frowned. 'Aye, because it was your father's wish. But perhaps it is best I say no more about the Hurst brothers now, so you can make your own judgement when and if you meet them.'

'Surely you can describe their appearance?' said Beth.

'No.'

'Are they ugly?' she persisted.

He sighed and shrugged.

Catherine glanced at her nephew. 'You should not tease Beth.'

'All right, they are not ugly,' said Gawain, putting down his knife. 'But I am not convinced either would make you a suitable husband.'

'Why?' asked Beth. 'Is it that they are not brave and daring?'

'Ha! You want brave and daring, too, in a man?' said Gawain, his blue eyes glinting.

'I might not have written those down but, aye, I would like a brave and daring suitor,' she replied seriously.

'They don't always make the best husbands if they are off on adventures all the time,' grunted Gawain.

Beth frowned. 'I had not thought of that. Tell me—'

'No more questions,' said Gawain firmly. 'The wedding is still weeks off and there is much to be done to set your affairs in order before then! As soon as Sam returns I will have to go to London, remember? Perhaps I'll find a husband for you there. Let us pray that Sam has had no difficulty finding the account book or delivering my message to your father's lawyer or I shall have to set aside all thought of seeking a husband for you.'

'You're saying that finding the murderer must come first,' said Beth slowly.

He hesitated, then nodded.

Sam returned three days later, bringing with him not only the accounts book, but an offer of a bed for the night from Master Llewellyn's lawyer.

'I will bear that in mind,' said Gawain. 'So how did you find everyone in Pater Noster Row, Sam?'

'The printers and the bookbinders seem to have plenty of work, sir,' replied Sam. 'But all came to a standstill when I told them what had happened. Naturally they were shocked and Edward Stanton, the master printer, was especially angry. Apparently there had been talk of an important pamphlet to be printed to be distributed at Bartholomew Fair, when, as you know, thousands come from all parts of the country.'

Gawain frowned. 'Did he tell you what this pamphlet was?'

Sam shook his head. 'But I can tell you that the news of the master's death has spread like wildfire because there were visitors aplenty coming into the bookshop and expressing their sympathy for Mistress Beth.'

Gawain said, 'I hope you did not tell anyone, Sam, where your mistress is staying?'

Sam shook his head. 'I just told them that she was spending time in the country mourning her father, but plenty showed concern about what will happen with the business. I told them that you were her guardian now and would be visiting London within a week or so.'

Gawain wished that Sam had kept his name out of this a bit longer, but as it was likely to become public knowledge once he arrived in London, he made no comment. 'I'll have food and ale brought to you here in the hall, Sam, whilst you and Mistress Beth see what you can discover from the accounts book.'

'I've thought of a name, sir, but I'm saying nothing until I see the dagger again and Mistress Beth reads out the names.'

Gawain went and fetched the dagger and gave it to Sam. 'Whilst you're inspecting it again, I'll fetch your mistress,' he said, having noticed her heading for the garden.

Beth had been gathering herbs and was cutting stems of fennel to serve as a vegetable to accompany the fish for supper when she saw Gawain approaching. Her heart performed an odd little leap. 'You look to be in a hurry, sir,' she called. 'Is something amiss?'

'Sam has returned and I thought you would wish to set aside what you're doing and take a look at the accounts book with him,' said Gawain, stopping a foot or so from her. He noticed that the sun had brought out a sprinkling of freckles across the bridge of her nose and that there was perspiration on her brow. 'Where is your hat?' he asked, frowning. 'Your skin will burn if you do not protect it.'

'You deem that a suitor will not accept me with a sun-kissed face?' she said lightly.

'No, only that you could end up with a megrim.'

She flushed. 'I beg pardon. The truth is that I forgot it and did not wish to waste time going back to the house.'

She placed the scissors and fennel in the wicker basket on the ground, but it was he who picked it up and carried it. 'Come, let us get you indoors,' he said, taking her arm.

She felt a tingle of pleasure go through her and tensed, knowing she really must keep her distance from him, but before she could do so, he slackened his hold and she went ahead of him, calling over her shoulder, 'What news has Sam of those in Pater Noster Row?'

Gawain told her and caught up with her, watching her expression change. 'Have you any idea what this pamphlet might have been? Could it have been a religious tract?' he asked.

'I suppose it's possible Father intended spreading news of Martin Luther's latest teachings that Monsieur Le Brun might have informed him about. If so, it is too late now for anything to be done about it so we might as well forget it,' she said swiftly. 'So, when will you go to London?'

'If you are able to name the person Sam believes to

own the dagger, then possibly I will go in the morning. He is in the hall waiting for you. I will take the basket to the kitchen and then join you both there.'

She thanked him and hurried to the house, taking off her gloves as she approached the table in the hall. 'Sam, it is good to see you safely returned. Did you remember to bring the other books and pamphlets I asked for?'

'Aye, Mistress Beth. I gave them to Jane to take up to your bedchamber.'

She thanked him and sat down and drew the accounts book towards her. She unfastened the metal clasps that kept the book closed, opened it and gazed down at her laboured neat hand that declared this to be the accounts book of Master David Llewellyn and Son, of Pater Noster Row. For a moment the words blurred as tears filled her eyes. Her poor father, he had not deserved to die the way he did and neither had Jonathan. She mopped her eyes, wondering whose name would replace that of her father. She hated the thought of it being some stranger that he never knew.

'Are you all right, Mistress Beth?' asked Sam gruffly.

She nodded, took a deep breath and turned a couple of pages until she came to a list of names, purchases and figures. Most of the names she knew well and found it difficult to believe that any of them would want her father dead. She began to read them out, as well as the purchases they had made, thinking that perhaps that, too, might help to jog Sam's memory. She was on the second page of names when Gawain entered the hall and sat at the table. Immediately she was self-conscious about the sound of her own voice, aware of his dark blue eyes fixed on her face as she read out the name of Sir Ralph Pennington.

Instantly Sam reacted by saying, 'I deem I saw the dagger at his house!'

Beth stared at him and then turned her gaze on Gawain. 'I can't believe it! Surely Sir Ralph has no cause to kill my father and I am certain if he were to kill anyone he certainly would not stab them in the back in such a cowardly fashion.'

'I was just about to say that myself,' said Gawain instantly.

'You are acquainted with Sir Ralph?' said Beth.

'Aye, he was a friend of my father's and took me under his wing when I was doing my training to be one of the king's Gentlemen of the Spears,' replied Gawain.

'I'm not saying it was Sir Ralph who killed your father, Mistress Beth,' interrupted Sam, his expression earnest. 'It was his nephew I saw toying with the dagger. A real popinjay he was, obviously thought himself a cut above ordinary folk. That was until Sir Ralph spoke to him real sharp and he addressed him as Cedric.'

Gawain rapped his fingers on the table. 'I have met him! He is one of those new young men around the king and likes to gamble.'

Beth stared at him, bright-eyed. 'I think I also have seen him! Is his hair as fair as barley and does he have the face of an angel?'

Gawain looked at her in surprise. 'That sounds like him. Where did you meet him?'

'We didn't meet exactly. He was buying a book and was with Jonathan and I overheard them talking and—' She stopped abruptly.

Gawain's eyes met hers and a blush rose in her cheeks. 'I—I don't think I was meant to hear what they were discussing,' said Beth. 'And there is no need for you to look at me like that,' she added indignantly. 'I was not eavesdropping! They knew I was there, but must have forgotten.'

'Calm yourself,' murmured Gawain. 'I am not accusing you of anything. What we need to know is whether Cedric was in France at the time of your father's death. Sir Ralph certainly was, I know that for a fact.'

'Do you consider it possible Cedric owed my brother money?' asked Beth. 'Jonathan did like to gamble on occasions, although he kept that secret from my father.'

'It is worth looking into,' said Gawain, 'and if you were aware of your brother's...' he hesitated before adding, 'friendship with Cedric, then your father could have been aware of it, too. He could have suspected Cedric of trying to get money out of Jonathan and your brother refusing to lend him any more.'

'Cedric could have lost his temper, but hadn't the courage to face Jonathan in a straight fight,' said Beth rapidly. 'The way my brother met his end and the fact that Father was stabbed in the back points to a person who is a coward.' Her eyes sparkled with sorrow and fury. 'Cedric must be brought to justice!'

'If he is guilty I would agree, but we do not have proof yet,' said Gawain grimly.

'Then we must get proof,' retorted Beth. 'It can't be that difficult now we have linked him to Jonathan and the dagger.'

Gawain reached out and placed his hand over hers. 'A word of caution, Beth. Leave this matter to me. He might have remembered your presence in the print room and that you could have overheard their conversation, so you must not do anything foolish that could put your life at risk.'

'It is my father and half-brother who have been murdered, not yours,' she said angrily. 'I will not sit back whilst you give him time to make his escape.' She would have withdrawn her hand from beneath his if he had not gripped it tightly.

'If Cedric is found guilty, he will not escape. Trust me! I will find him and see what he has to say for himself,' said Gawain. 'I will go in search of him in the morning.'

With that Beth had to be content and she nodded. 'In the morning.'

'You will stay here,' said Gawain firmly. 'And do not be so foolish as to attempt to follow me,' he added in softer tones. 'Your promise on it, Beth. I would not like to leave orders to have you locked in your bedchamber for your own protection.'

She hesitated, but the expression in his eyes told her that he meant every word he uttered. 'I promise.'

He responded with a smile of such charm that she

felt a peculiar melting sensation inside her. Then he raised her hand to his lips and kissed it before releasing it. 'I will not fail you,' he said.

# *Chapter Six*

Beth's book lay open on the bench beside her as she watched a pair of butterflies fluttering in the air before landing on a clump of marigolds. The heat of the sun was making her feel drowsy and she stifled a yawn, wondering when Gawain would return. It was a month since he had left for London and there had been no word from him. Considering the short time she had known him, it was surprising how much she missed his presence. Several times she had considered breaking her promise to him, but it was as if there was an invisible barrier preventing her from doing so. A promise was a promise and he had asked her to trust him. She felt she had no choice but to do so because he was obviously trusting her to stick to her promise.

What could be keeping him? She gnawed on her lip, trying not to dwell on the conversation she had overheard between Jonathan and Cedric. It had not been about money and she had feared that her brother was involved in an unnatural relationship with the fair-haired angelic-looking young man, but she had managed to convince herself afterwards that she had read into their words more than there was intended. She had remembered since that there had been a large woman present and she had slanted them a sharp look and the two younger men had smiled at each other. Then Cedric had asked her brother whether he had a copy of Chaucer's *Canterbury Tales* and they had moved away from her. She'd had another thought about the two since. What if they had fallen out and the result could have been Cedric trying to blackmail her brother and Jonathan refusing to hand money over and that was why he had been murdered?

Not for the first time she prayed that Gawain had not met with an untimely end and told herself that surely if something terrible had befallen him, then they would have heard. Perhaps Gawain had discovered that Cedric had accompanied his uncle to France; maybe they had not returned when Gawain arrived in London and he had decided to visit his wife and children in the interval before seeking out Sir Ralph and Cedric again. She did not want Mary to return home, if she were honest. During the last few weeks Beth had started to feel very much at home at Raventon Hall, despite longing to step foot into the print room and smell the familiar odours of ink, fresh paper and vellum. It would be foolish to put herself into danger. She was also finding the tranquillity here in the garden away from the hustle and bustle of London another factor in the healing of her grief, although she had suffered from recurring dreams about that time in France. Instead of Sir Gawain entering the tent after her, she was confronted by a young man with the face of an angel who then somehow turned into a terrifying figure clad in red and black.

'So there you are!'

Beth jumped at the sound of the voice and her heart fluttered in her breast as she gazed up into Gawain's attractive features and she felt warmth and excitement flood through her. For a moment their eyes held and she was convinced that he was as glad to see her as she was to see him, but perhaps she was imagining it. She must not forget he was married and of a mind to find a husband for her once the murderer was captured. Yet she could not help saying, 'Where have you been all this time? I worried in case you had met some ill fate.'

He was touched by the thought that she had worried about him. 'Is that is why you started and looked at me as if you'd seen a ghost?' he teased, cocking a dark eyebrow.

'You've been gone a month and there's been no word from you,' she protested.

Gawain grimaced. 'You have every right to rebuke me.' He picked up her book and sat beside her, wincing as he did so.

'You are in pain,' said Beth, unable to conceal the concern in her voice. 'Is it your old injury?'

'Aye, we were attacked on the road and had to fight our way out.'

She gasped. 'How terrible! Perhaps you should be in bed resting?'

'I admit that the thought of sleeping in my own bed is extremely appealing after so many nights spend on floors or the ground. Fortunately Tom was able to deal with it and I suffer more right now from too much time on horseback. I intend staying put for the next few days.'

He stretched out his legs and his shoulder brushed against Beth's as he stifled a yawn. She once again felt that pleasurable sensation his slightest touch caused her and she experienced an urge to draw closer to him, but fought it. 'You are weary. Perhaps you should, indeed, have gone straight to bed,' she said in a low voice.

He glanced at her. 'I'll last out the day. I have much to tell you. I would have sent Tom with a message, explaining why I was away longer than I intended, only I had need of him and I had no intention of entrusting my message to anyone I did not completely trust.'

'So did you find Cedric?' she asked eagerly.

'Patience. First I had to find Sir Ralph Pennington.'

'And did you?'

'Aye, he was newly returned from France and had gone to stay at his country residence in Berkshire, preparing for a visit from the king some time in August. Unfortunately Cedric was not there, but Sir Ralph assured me that he had not accompanied him to France. Apparently he sent a message saying he had been called home at the beginning of June to his father's deathbed.'

Beth was taken aback. 'Did you believe him?'

'I believed Sir Ralph, but I wasn't so certain about Cedric, so I travelled to his father's castle in Yorkshire to speak with him.'

'Yorkshire!' she exclaimed in astonishment.

'Aye.' He frowned. 'When we arrived there the old man had indeed died. Cedric sent a message out to me, saying that he was too distraught to see anyone. I asked one of the servants when his master's son had arrived and the date he gave me definitely meant that Cedric could not have murdered your father in France.'

'So Sam made a mistake!' said Beth, her emotions in turmoil.

'No.' Gawain smiled grimly. 'I had not gone all the way up there to be fobbed off so easily. I was determined to confront Cedric about the dagger. Besides, Sir Ralph had told me that his nephew was desperate to come into his inheritance because he had gambling debts and had been waiting for months for the old man to die.'

'So we were right about his need for money,' said Beth, her eyes brightening. 'Did he agree to see you?'

Gawain nodded. 'I sent a message in to him that he could not resist. We had a short conversation about the dagger during which he told me that he had picked it up somewhere, but could not remember where, but had mislaid it long before he left London for Yorkshire.'

Beth frowned. 'It sounds suspicious to me.'

'I deem he has light fingers and panicked when someone saw the dagger and commented on it, so he decided to return it to its rightful owner,' said Gawain.

Beth felt a stir of excitement. 'Who is the rightful owner?'

Gawain stretched his arm along the back of the bench. 'He refused to tell me. It could be that he is truly frightened of naming the person because it could be someone in a position of power. The other possibility is that Cedric intends to blackmail whomever it is. From the castle's appearance there is not as much money to inherit as he might have hoped.'

'He would be a fool to blackmail a murderer!'

'I would not argue,' said Gawain. 'Anyway, Tom is keeping a watch on him and he also has one of the lads to act as messenger or relieve him.'

A thought occurred to Beth. 'What if he tells the murderer that you have the dagger? Are you not putting your own life at risk if he attempts to get it back?'

'Your lack of faith in my ability to defend myself and those in my protection surprises me, Beth,' drawled Gawain.

She flushed. 'I did not say that I doubted your strength or your wits,' she said swiftly, stretching out a hand to him.

He took it and kissed it. 'I am glad to hear it.'

The palm of her hand where his lips had touched thrummed; she longed for him to kiss her mouth again. This, indeed, was a foolishness. No doubt he was only comforting her because they still did not have their murderer. Her throat felt suddenly tight and she had to clear her throat before managing to say, 'I—I did w-wonder whether you had visited your wife and daughters whilst you were away.' She withdrew her hand.

Gawain wished vehemently that Beth had not reminded him of Mary right now. But perhaps she had done so deliberately to prevent him from overstepping the mark. For a moment he considered telling Beth the truth, but that would only make her think the worse of him for deceiving her in the first place; he wanted her to not only trust him but, God forgive him, to grow fond of him enough to not want to leave his home. 'I stayed only a short time. Mary knows that I have much to do that keeps me here or in London.'

'I see,' said Beth. 'I presume that you have told your wife that you have to find me a husband and that she knows that I am staying here and about James and Mildred's wedding on the sixth of August.'

'Is that when it is?' he said, frowning.

'Aye, we had a visit from Mildred.'

'Then it is unlikely Mary will be home in time for the wedding,' he replied after a brief hesitation. 'Her aunt is very ill and will not be able to spare her. Besides, Mary was never a particular friend of Mildred's.'

No wonder his wife does not mind missing the wedding then, thought Beth. But to stay away from Gawain for so long surely meant there was no real love lost between them. That thought lifted Beth's spirits, but they plummeted just as quickly because he knew he was still married to her. 'Of your courtesy, may I ask one more question and then I will bother you no more?'

'What is it now?' he drawled, a hint of humour in his eyes.

'The wedding. You will attend? I cannot possibly choose a husband from amongst James Tyler's guests without you there to help me,' she said.

Gawain, who had been looking forward to spending a few days at home relaxing, really was in no mood to vet suitors for Beth and yet he knew it made sense to do so. Part of him had hoped the tug of attraction he felt towards her might had waned during his absence, but it hadn't. His feelings were definitely all mixed up where she was concerned. 'So you are prepared to start looking for a husband despite our still not having captured the murderer?'

Beth sighed. 'It was your original idea that we view prospective spouses at the wedding.'

Why had he had to tell her that? groaned Gawain inwardly. He cleared his throat. 'No doubt you are eager to meet the Hurst brothers?'

'It should prove interesting to meet the gentlemen you don't consider suitable for me.' She gazed at him archly.

'Did I say that?' asked Gawain.

'You know you did!'

'I have forgotten. Anyway, there is no guarantee they will be there,' he warned.

'Indeed,' said Beth, thinking it most likely that he sounded so irritable because he was tired and in pain. She reminded herself that was because he had been working on her behalf as her guardian and added softly, 'I know you wish to rest, but could you spare me a few more moments of your time and tell me of your visit to the lawyer and my father's business?'

Gawain relaxed. 'I have signed all the necessary documents and your father's business now belongs to you. When I arrived back from Yorkshire I discovered that several people had already shown an interest in buying it.'

Her expression swiftly altered and she frowned. 'But I have already told you that I do not wish to sell it. Rather I would find other premises in Aldersgate.'

'I have visited Aldersgate and did not see any premises that I deemed suitable,' said Gawain. 'What I have considered—'

'But you know naught about printing, bookbinding and selling,' she interrupted, springing to her feet and dislodging the book she had been reading.

He caught it before it hit the ground. 'You have said that before, but I know enough about business to realise that your moving there would not be welcome,' he said firmly, handing the book back to her.

'Why not? Because I am a woman?' she said in a seething voice.

'That has naught to do with it,' he snapped, 'because I and your lawyer would deal with the move and you would have the same employees working for you. Rather it is because you would have to build up a completely different clientele in Aldersgate. The area is not so conveniently situated for your present customers and the income from the business would plummet. It is best either to sell it or to keep to the present premises and sell shares and become a company. Also, by selling shares you will have a dowry to attract the right husband and still have an interest in the business, as well as an income.'

She stared at him, then sat down again. 'You seem to have it all worked out. No doubt you are trying to do what is best for me, but I would like some time to consider your suggestion.'

Gawain's eyes narrowed. 'Are you thinking still of continuing with your news sheet?'

'In truth, I was wondering if the murderer might decide to put in a bid for the business if it were to go up for sale. I will not have him gaining control of that which was my father's life and the same goes for selling shares,' she said, her brown eyes hard.

'We would sell only to a person we trusted,' said Gawain.

'Who can we really trust?' asked Beth, exasperated.

'Each other,' suggested Gawain, raising an eyebrow. 'I already have some shares in the business that your father left me, if you remember.'

She stared at him and wondered if she was too trusting of him because she was attracted to him. 'So you would buy more. Why? So you can gain control?'

He flashed her a startled look. 'Of course not! You would retain more shares than you sell to me and that way you will always have control.'

'Again I need to think,' said Beth, feeling she had been wrong-footed.

'Whether or not you can trust me?'

She flushed. 'I have not known you long.'

'Long enough, I would have thought, to realise I have your well-being at heart,' he said, leaning back and closing his eyes. 'Forget my suggestion. Let us instead discuss the list you gave me,' he murmured.

'List?' she said evasively.

'Do not pretend, Beth, that you do not know what I am talking about,' said Gawain, stifling a yawn. It had not slipped his attention that she had mentioned a liking for blue eyes and dark hair such as his own. 'Your ideal husband, remember? I spent some time whilst I was away, considering those amongst my acquaintances who might make you a suitable match.'

'You mean rather than the Hurst brothers?' teased Beth. 'I, too, have been giving thought to those men I know who might possibly suit me.'

'And what conclusion did you reach?' asked Gawain, stifling another yawn.

'That the only way to be sure is by living with them,' she said loudly, wondering if he was now about to fall asleep before her very eyes when they were in the middle of such an important discussion about her future.

Gawain's eyelids slowly opened and he gazed sleepily at her. 'I presume you are jesting?'

She smiled. 'What do you think? Perhaps I simply wanted to shock you awake. No doubt you thoroughly disapprove of the thought of my living with a man without being married to him?'

'You might stay under his roof,' murmured Gawain, 'as long as you are chaperoned. If he has a mother or sisters or an aunt living with him, you might find out more about him than you would like.' His eyes closed again.

The silence seemed to stretch between them and the hum of the bees in the flowers was hypnotic. The mention of an aunt had not slipped past her.

'I am glad you raised the subject of liking,' said Beth loudly. 'Do you not agree that it is essential to like one's spouse? I should imagine that even if a man had all the attributes I mention on my list and there was something about him that I could not like, then one could be very unhappy.'

Silence.

Beth allowed several moments to pass before asking, 'Are you listening, Sir Gawain?'

No answer.

She gave up trying to rouse him. 'I wonder what it is that makes one grow fond of a certain person and dislike another? What is it that makes one love someone?' she murmured, watching the steady rise and fall of his chest. 'What magic is it that draws one irresistibly to another?' She sighed, knowing he needed his rest. Should she leave him to sleep, undisturbed? Unless by getting up she disturbed him? It was peaceful here in the herb garden and she could gaze openly at him without worrying about what he might make of her staring at him. There was stubble on his jaw and she was tempted to touch it and see how bristly it felt. She noticed how long his eyelashes were and how in slumber the lines of his face were relaxed and he appeared less careworn and, hence, younger.

He shifted slightly on the bench and his head slipped down on to her shoulder. Her heart quickened its beat and she gave in to the impulse to rest her cheek against his hair. She closed her eyes and imagined what it would feel like to sleep with him. It would be much more comfortable sharing a bed than a bench. Her thoughts began to drift and then suddenly she caught herself up. What was she thinking of? She could never live with him as a wife. Hadn't he told her in France about his wife and that he had no intention of taking another? That would be bigamy. But what if his wife were to die and he were to ask her to marry him? Would she accept such a proposal? She felt certain he was still of a mind to silence that creative voice of hers and keep her away from the printing presses. Suddenly she heard voices and lifted her head. Digging her elbow in her companion's side, she said loudly, 'Sir Gawain, wake up! Your aunt and Jane are coming.'

Gawain winced and rubbed his side and forced his eyes open. He blinked up at Beth and then slowly moved away from her. 'I beg your pardon.'

'You are obviously more weary than you realised,' said Beth, her cheeks rosy. 'I'll leave you now and keep your aunt in conversation, so you have time to gather your wits.' She hurried away.

Gawain stretched, knowing he had not behaved chivalrously by pretending to be asleep instead of in that state betwixt waking and sleeping where one can hear, but the body is so relaxed that it refuses to respond to stimulus. He thought about Beth's words and asked himself what magic was it, indeed, that drew a person to someone? She obviously had someone in mind. Perhaps it was him? She had not pulled away from him when he had rested against her. What could he read into that? Perhaps she was as attracted to him as he was to her despite their mutual suspicion of each other.

What else had she said earlier? The only way to be sure of knowing someone was to live with them. He could have told her that you could live with someone for years and think you knew them, but you didn't. He rose and followed the voices and hailed his aunt. Catherine's face lit up at the sight of him, for she had been out visiting when he had arrived home. Beth excused herself and taking Jane with her, left aunt and nephew to catch up on each other's news.

Later that day over supper Catherine brought up the subject of what she was thinking of wearing for the occasion and mentioned what gift they should take for the bridal pair, as well as the small cakes that it was customary for guests to give for the wedding feast.

'I have never been to a wedding,' said Beth, smiling at them both. 'I will wear my dark blue gown,' she announced. 'Tell me about these cakes, Mistress Catherine.'

'They will be piled high and the bridal couple must try to kiss over them without their toppling them if they are to have luck and prosperity.'

'That sounds as if it could be fun,' said Beth.

'It is because all couples setting out together along the marital path need all the luck they can get,' said Catherine, glancing at her nephew. 'Is that not true, Gawain?'

Beth saw him frown and, without a word, he left the table.

'You must excuse him,' said Catherine hastily. 'He is weary after being away so long.'

Beth wondered if that was really the reason for his sudden departure, or his aunt's pointed question. Perhaps Gawain's marriage really was not a happy one. 'Were you at his wedding?' she asked of Catherine.

'Of course, and Mary was a lovely bride. Eighteen he was and the match arranged by her father, Master Marston, and Sir Ralph, his guardian.'

'And did they manage to kiss over the cakes?' asked Beth.

'One would have thought it an easy matter to do so with my nephew being so tall, but as he reached across and lifted her up, her elbow caught a cake that was jutting out and several toppled on to the tablecloth. He claimed that he would make his own luck and prosperity and not leave it to superstition.' Catherine glanced guiltily in the direction of the door. 'Do not mention this to my nephew. He will say that I have allowed my tongue to chatter on far too much.'

Beth promised that not a word would escape her lips and finished her supper. At least when James and Matilda's wedding was over, she could look forward to attending Bartholomew Fair and returning to her own home for a while.

'Here, Beth, shower the bride and groom with these,' said Catherine, thrusting a handful of seeds at her, 'and let us pray that their marriage really will be fruitful.'

'Have you enough?' asked Beth, taking the seeds from her.

'Aye, come before they leave the churchyard and lead the procession to the house.'

Beth hurried over to the smiling couple. The bride wore a blue gown, a popular colour for weddings as it symbolised purity. Her flaxen hair hung down her back and on her head she wore a floral wreath consisting of gilly flowers, marigolds, lavender, thyme and rosemary. In her hand, she clutched a posy of the same flowers and herbs. Beth soon realised that she and Catherine were not the only ones showering the bride and groom with seeds, which no doubt the birds would swoop on if they did not lodge in the clothing or hair of the bridal couple.

Beth stepped back to allow James and Mildred to make their way out of the church grounds and, as she did so, became aware that she was being watched by a small group of men, consisting of Gawain, another man of a similar age, an elderly man and the priest who had presided over the service. She could hear the latter's melodious voice wafting towards her on the breeze, asking whether the young woman wearing the dark blue gown was Mistress Elizabeth Llewellyn and remembered how she had thought in the church that he looked vaguely familiar. She did not hear Gawain's reply because Catherine took her arm and they joined the bridal procession.

It was not until later, after Beth had eaten her fill and wandered out into the garden overlooking the river to escape the heat in the hall, that she was introduced to the man who had stood at her guardian's side earlier. 'Beth, this is Christopher Hurst, whom I have mentioned to you,' said Gawain, surprising her by adding, 'He wished to make your acquaintance as soon as I told him that you were the owner of a printing-and-book-selling business in London.'

'It is a pleasure to make your acquaintance, Master

Hurst,' said Beth, gazing up into a pair of twinkling pale blue eyes.

'The pleasure is all mine, Mistress Llewellyn,' he replied, 'because I would ask a favour of you.'

'A favour?' Beth shot a questioning glance at Gawain.

'Remember my telling you that Master Hurst has two younger brothers?' he said.

'Of course,' said Beth, wondering what was coming next.

'Well, Nick is fond of travelling and managed to buy his way on to a Portuguese ship sailing to the New World,' said Gawain. 'He kept a journal of his travels and when I told Chris of your interest in printing such experiences and selling it in book form, it struck a chord with him.'

Chris said, 'It is the twenty-fifth anniversary of Nick's birth in November and I thought it would be the ideal gift for him to see his tale in print.'

Beth's eyes gleamed. 'You have captured my interest, Master Hurst. No doubt it is too much for me to expect that you have the journal with you?'

'Alas, no, but I do have it at home. At the moment Nick has gone off to Venice, so I am not expecting him to return any time soon before his birthday. I could have my youngest brother, Phillip, deliver it to you at Raventon Hall. If Gawain and yourself could read it, I am certain you will find it interesting.'

'I am sure I will,' said Beth eagerly. 'I assume this is to be a surprise for your brother Nick?'

'Indeed,' said Chris, beaming at her. 'And you will

let me know the cost of the printing, binding and what not. A vellum backing, I think.'

Beth said, 'Do you want just the one copy for him or do you wish for more copies for yourself and members of your family? Naturally the cost will depend on the number of copies.'

'Of course,' said Chris. 'I am sure you will find it such an interesting tale that you might find a market for hundreds of copies.'

'That is possible,' said Beth cautiously. 'How would your brother feel about strangers reading his journal?'

'How could he not be delighted if it makes him money?' asked Chris.

Beth thought she could see his point, yet what if he was mistaken?

Gawain had been watching Beth's expression and now said, 'We will consult you, Chris, after we have both read Nick's journal.'

'Good,' said Chris, beaming at them both. 'And now I had better go and find my good wife.' He hurried off.

Beth said hesitantly, 'You have surprised me and I really appreciate your encouragement in allowing me to be involved in this reading and printing.'

'I knew it would give you pleasure and I do not doubt your ability to judge what makes a good book,' said Gawain.

'Thank you.' She paused, flattered by his remark and wondering whether speaking to her employees had caused him to change his mind about her abilities. But she would not pry into his reasons right now. Instead she said, 'Master Hurst is almost more handsome than you are, Sir Gawain. Are his brothers just as hand-some?'

Gawain gazed down at her with an arrested expression in his eyes. 'You flatter me. It is a pity Chris is not a widower—you and he might have suited as he has a most amiable nature and might have allowed you the freedom to do whatever you wished.'

'Thoughtful and generous towards his brother, too,' said Beth slowly.

'Aye, I just hope Nick's journal proves not to be a disappointment,' said Gawain.

Beth stared at him, surprised. 'Why should it do so? He must be a man of courage and daring if he has sailed to the New World.'

'I would not dispute that, but it is disappointing that he is not here for you to discover that by meeting him face-to-face.'

She agreed, adding, 'And the youngest brother?'

'Another disappointment for you,' said Gawain smoothly. 'He could not come today as he had some task to complete. Mind you, thinking about it, Pip is far too young for you. But I have a widower who is interested in meeting you.'

'Is he very old and likely to die soon and leave me a rich widow?' asked Beth, a mischievous note in her voice.

Gawain smiled faintly, but before he could answer there came the strains of music from inside the house and instantly she asked, 'May we go inside and watch the dancing?'

'You like dancing?'

'Who does not? Although, the last time I danced was at Bartholomew Fair when my mother was alive. Then we danced in the streets to the music of the hurdy-gurdy.'

'Then let us go inside,' said Gawain, taking her hand and leading her towards the house. 'Today is a celebration and I deem your father would rejoice in your enjoying yourself.'

Beth's face lit up and, impulsively, she reached up and kissed his cheek. 'If I dance gracefully enough,' she said with a saucy gleam in her eye, 'then perhaps your widower will ask me to marry him.'

'You are teasing me,' said Gawain, amusement in his dark blue orbs. 'Master Bigbury does not meet with all your requirements, so no doubt you will turn him down. He grows hops and brews beer, as well as having several fruit orchards. I deem he has passed the anniversary of his fiftieth year, but from what I know of him, he has a kindly disposition and is not parsimonious at all.'

She paused in the doorway to a passageway that led to the hall. 'Was he, by any chance, the aged gentleman whom I saw with you and Master Hurst and the priest outside the church?'

'Aye, that is Master Bigbury,' said Gawain. 'Unfortunately, years spent outdoors has aged his skin, but he still has a lust for life and there is no doubt he can beget children.'

'You mean he already has children?' asked Beth, frowning.

'He did indeed father several children, but unfortunately none of them survived childhood.'

'Hmm! Perhaps I shouldn't write him off too soon then,' said Beth, thinking that Gawain was less likely to present her with another suitor if she spent some time deliberating over this one.

'Good,' said Gawain. 'I will make you known to him.'

As they approached the hall, their ears were assaulted by the sound of viols, recorders and bagpipe. The rhythmic sound of feet clumping on the floor shook the building. There was a hum of voices, as well as those raised in song. It struck Beth that everyone appeared to be enjoying themselves. Even James's priestly brother had a smile on his face. He was standing next to Catherine, who was chattering away to him. She was about to point them out to Gawain when he surprised her by leading her on to the floor and they joined one of the sets for a country dance.

Beth had never thought she would enjoy herself so much, but she found such pleasure in dancing with Gawain, that she was unaware how many pairs of eyes were turned on the pair of them. Not that she danced solely with him as there were several traditional country dances and the movement of the dance involved processing in such a way that changed one's partner several times.

It was during one such dance that Beth came face-to-face with Master Bigbury. He looked delighted to see her.

'Mistress Llewellyn, I did not think I'd get to meet you like this. Let me introduce myself,' he said eagerly.

'I know who you are,' said Beth in a friendly manner. 'Sir Gawain spoke well of you, Master Bigbury. I am pleased to make your acquaintance, although I do believe the dance is hardly the right place for us to converse.'

'Aye, you're perfectly correct,' he said hastily. 'I will speak to Sir Gawain about dropping by at Raventon if that is acceptable to you?'

'Of course, I look forward to seeing you,' said Beth, knowing she lied.

She breathed a sigh of relief when the movement of the dance took him away from her and she found herself confronting Gawain once more.

'I saw you talking to Master Bigbury,' he said.

'He is going to ask your permission to call on me,' said Beth with a wry smile.

'You agreed then,' said Gawain, surprised.

'Aye, as it will be good practice for me. I will converse with him as long as I am chaperoned by your aunt,' she said with aplomb.

'I would not allow him to speak with you, otherwise,' said Gawain, amused.

When the dance came to an end and Gawain went to speak to Master Bigbury, Beth hurried over to where Catherine sat alone, pale-faced and gazing into the distance. 'Are you feeling ill?' asked Beth.

'A little faint. It is so hot in here,' said Catherine, fanning herself with her hand.

Beth felt worried about her because she was a person who never complained. 'Would you like to go outside?'

Catherine nodded and Beth helped her to her feet and, arm in arm, they left the hall. They went into the garden and sat on a bench overlooking the river. Both were silent for a while and then Catherine sighed. 'My heart is heavy. I used to be extremely fond of Father Hugh, well before he became a priest. Earlier when I was speaking with him, I forgot that he was no longer the young man I used to know. I spoke of matters that were burdening me, but I should have kept them to myself.'

'Is there anything I can do to help?' asked Beth.

Catherine shook her head and stood up. 'If you will excuse me, Beth, I must speak with my nephew.'

Beth could see she was really worried. 'Of course. Would you like me to come with you?'

Catherine shook her head and walked away.

Beth wondered what it could be that was bothering Catherine so and hoped that Gawain could ease his aunt's mind. As for herself, she remained where she was, gazing out over the river and thinking of Gawain and how it felt when his arm had slipped about her waist and he had held her close during the dance. She closed her eyes and could almost feel his lips on hers before trailing a path down the side of her face and her throat. Then she heard footsteps behind her; thinking it might be Gawain, she turned her head. Her smile faded as she saw that it was the priest.

He was staring at her in a way that made her feel ill at ease, then suddenly he gave a wolfish grin and fear trickled down her spine.

## Chapter Seven

But when Father Hugh spoke, his words were commonplace and not frightening at all. 'Good evening, Mistress Llewellyn. I see you are making the most of this charming location.'

'Aye, it is hot and noisy inside, but I must not linger as my guardian will be wondering what has happened to me,' said Beth, a hint of breathlessness in her voice as she stood up. She felt less scared, but was convinced she had seen him before this day and intuitively knew the memory was not a good one.

'I will not keep you long.' His elongated eyes appeared to be silver slits in this light. 'I was greatly saddened to hear of the deaths of your menfolk.'

'You knew them?'

'I visited the shop in Pater Noster Row once or twice to purchase books.'

'So that is where I have seen you before,' said Beth slowly.

He looked startled. 'You have a good memory as you must have only been a young girl at the time. Jonathan's passing must have been a great loss to your father. Such a clever and witty young man, if wrong in his thinking on occasion.' He pursed his lips and, for a moment, Beth thought he was going to say something more about her half-brother, but when he spoke, it was only to say, 'And your father gone, too, now. A double tragedy for you, Mistress Llewellyn. No doubt you will be seriously considering selling his business now you are in the market for a husband.'

'Did my guardian tell you that?'

'Who else?'

'Then perhaps you should have asked him that question.' Beth was unconvinced that Gawain had discussed the matter with the priest. It was more likely to have been Catherine after what she had said earlier to her. 'Now if you will excuse me, Father Hugh, I really must return to the house.'

He put out a hand and clutched her sleeve. 'Dally a little longer, daughter, and tell me if Sir Gawain has got any further in his search for their murderer?'

'Why did you not ask him yourself?' said Beth, noticing that the priest's fingernails were long, like a falcon's talons, and she wanted to shake off his hand.

'Alas, Gawain is not prepared to discuss the matter, not even with his father's old friend.'

Beth's throat was suddenly tight with emotion. Where was this priest's compassion that he should persist in his questioning? 'You deem he would talk to me, a grieving daughter, about it?' she asked.

She could see that her reply surprised him. 'You were dancing earlier so it appears to me that you have decided to leave mourning behind. Surely you want your father's murderer caught?' he said.

Beth felt the colour rise in her cheeks. 'That goes without saying, but I am only a woman and leave such matters to Sir Gawain. Just as I accept what he says about my father approving of my behaviour here this evening. It was his will that I should take a husband, not mine.'

Father Hugh said sharply, 'I watched you dance with your guardian. I do not know what he has been telling you about his wife, but he can never be free of her whilst she is alive.'

Beth was taken aback. 'Why do you say this to me? It has never crossed my mind that he and I...' Her voice trailed off because she knew that was a lie and it appeared to her that the priest saw more than she wanted him to. She had no idea what would have happened next if they had not been interrupted.

'Father Hugh, by St George, what do you think you are doing?' said Gawain angrily. 'Unhand my ward immediately! You forget yourself.'

The priest released Beth instantly and faced Gawain, a slight smile playing about his thin lips. 'Such fury, Gawain. I hope that you are not forgetting your position.'

'I know exactly where I stand,' said Gawain, his expression uncompromising.

'Good.' The priest fiddled with his sleeve. 'I hope you have also remembered that the Cardinal is expecting you to bring him up to date on what you might have discovered. I can tell you that his investigations in France came to a dead end. Is there aught you can tell me and I will pass a message on to him?'

'I will seek an audience with the Cardinal when I am ready,' said Gawain.

Father Hugh clicked his tongue against his teeth. 'I am only trying to help you, my son, but I can see that you have inherited your father's unwillingness to accept the truth, so I will leave you.' His robes brushed the ground as he swept past Gawain.

Once he was out of earshot Gawain turned to Beth and took her by the shoulders and gazed down at her with concern. 'If it were not that he was a priest I would have punched him for his behaviour towards you. Did he force you into telling him anything? I know he used to scare me when I was a lad, but I always tried to conceal it.'

'He did scare me, but I responded to his questioning by referring him to you,' said Beth, feeling safer now and wanting to rest her head against his chest and have his arms around her but knew she must not give in to her longings. Whilst dancing with him, she had forgotten about his wife, but Father Hugh had forced her to remember her existence.

'Clever girl,' said Gawain, his hands moving gently over her shoulders in a soothing manner. He knew he should be keeping his distance, but the need to touch her and give her reassurance was overwhelming.

'He said I should not have danced with you.'

'Apparently he said something similar to my aunt,'

said Gawain. 'Do not mind what he says as he is priest to neither of us and should look to his own faults and the grand style in which he and his Cardinal live before he criticises others.'

Beth sighed. 'I wanted to escape his company the moment he approached me. Close up to him, I knew that I had definitely seen him before. Then he told me that he had visited the shop to purchase books and had met Jonathan. My brother had little time for those in holy orders except Franciscans, whom he admired for their vows of poverty and obedience to Christ.'

'Unlike Father Hugh,' said Gawain grimly. 'He is a member of that rich-and-proud hierarchy of the church and belongs to Cardinal Wolsey's household, as you might have guessed.'

'So what do we do now?' asked Beth.

He held her gaze for several moments and then smiled. 'You must stop fretting about all this and leave it in my hands. Master Bigbury has asked permission to call on you in a few days. We can also expect a visit from Pip Hurst with his brother's journal.'

Beth's face brightened. 'It should make interesting reading.'

'Let us hope so. And now my aunt would like to go home and I think we should go with her.'

'Gladly will I leave,' said Beth. 'Father Hugh has quite spoilt my enjoyment of the evening.'

'I must go to London and speak to the Cardinal, but I should be back in a few days,' said Gawain, as they went to fetch his aunt.

Beth knew that she would miss him.

\* \* \*

The following days had passed slowly and on the fourth day she woke late to be told that a message had arrived saying that Gawain was at the shipyard and would be home later that morning. Beth was glad to hear it because she was expecting a visit from Master Bigbury that evening. She wished now that she had not shown willingness to see him and said as much to Jane.

'Describe him to me, Mistress Beth,' said the maid, pouring hot water into the basin on the washstand.

'He is a wealthy widower, landowner and brewer of beer. He is much older than me.'

'And how do you feel about marrying a much older man?'

'I am of a mind that would depend on whether we were able to come to some agreement about his letting me have my way,' said Beth, picking up the jar of home-made liquid soap, perfumed with rose petals. 'Which will mean my being able to spend time in Pater Noster Row in the running of my business.'

Jane looked startled. 'But is that likely, Mistress Beth? Will he rather not expect you to organise his household and for you to be there for him when he comes home after a long day seeing to his brewery and his fields?'

'Exactly, so I consider a match between us unlikely,' said Beth, trying to work up a lather with the soap. 'But I suppose I will have to go through the motions of being willing to give his offer fair consideration to please Sir Gawain.'

Jane agreed and asked what her mistress planned to wear today.

'The russet gown and the cream-coloured chemise,' replied Beth.

Once her *toilette* was finished and Beth had dressed and put on her slippers, she went downstairs, thinking that no doubt Catherine would have already broken her fast. It was as she thought and Beth was eating a solitary breakfast when there was a banging at the door.

Before she could get up and see who was there, it opened and a flaxen-haired young man stood in the doorway with a parcel under his arm. He smiled at Beth.

'You are Mistress Llewellyn?' he asked.

'I am,' she replied, returning his smile. 'And you? Could you be Master Phillip Hurst?'

'I am and I have brought you my brother Nick's journal.'

She signalled to him to come forwards and saw that he had the same blue eyes as his oldest brother and was just as good-looking except his face was a little leaner. 'Would you like a drink of ale?' she asked.

'Thank you,' said Phillip. 'May I sit down?'

'Please do. Would you like some bread, butter and ham?'

'Aye, indeed I would,' he said, those blue eyes gleaming. 'It seems an age since I left home and have had little to eat since.'

Beth noticed a servant hovering in the doorway and presumed that he had heard Phillip Hurst banging on the door. She told him to bring some refreshments for their guest and then she gave her attention to Phillip once more.

'I will not open the parcel just yet because I do not wish to get butter on the pages,' she said, smiling, 'but tell me, do you read?'

'Aye, Father reckoned it was a necessity. I've read parts of Nick's journal, but I've been kept busy in the shipyard whilst we've the long daylight hours, so I haven't finished it.'

'But that which you have read, did you find it interesting?'

He hesitated and then said cautiously, 'There's plenty of information about the Portuguese galleon he sailed on and he had adventures, but he writes about them in a way that lacks excitement. Perhaps he did not want to make too much of the danger so as not to worry our mother or Chris. He writes about the most fantastic happenings as if he were at home and just crossing the street in a storm, instead of which he is in the middle of a mighty ocean and almost loses his life.'

Her eyes twinkled. 'You think you could write it better?'

Phillip hesitated, then nodded. 'I tell stories.'

'You mean you are a real storyteller?'

'Since I was a boy I have created tales in my head.'

'That is a real gift,' said Beth admiringly. 'Who doesn't like a good story told by a gifted storyteller or a play-acted out by travelling players?'

His face lit up. 'That is how I feel. I would like to

join one of the troupes such as those I have seen perform at the king's palace of Greenwich.'

Beth could not conceal her surprise. 'You have visited Greenwich Palace?'

'Aye, the king is open-handed and extremely hospitable, appreciative of the ships that my family have built for him,' said Phillip. 'Although it is true to say that Henry likes to slip away with a few friends to his smaller palace of Eltham to hunt.'

'And what does your brother think of your talent for storytelling?'

Phillip looked alarmed. 'God's blood, he doesn't know! He is only interested in designing and building ships, as well as his home and family. He believes that's all I should care about, too. He has it in mind to find me a wife this year. I have told him I am too young to settle down. Besides, I could not support a wife.'

'How old are you?'

'Seventeen. I suppose he'll have his way if I don't do something to prevent it,' he said gloomily. 'If I were not the youngest brother with scarcely any money of my own, unlike Nick, whose godmother left him her fortune, I would join a troupe of travelling players and roam the country having adventures of my own.'

An idea struck Beth and impulsively she said, 'My guardian, Sir Gawain, is set on finding me a husband. I accept that I must marry if I am to bear a son as my father wished, but I would much rather be in control of the printing business he willed to me.'

''Struth! I wish someone had left me a business, but no such luck,' said Phillip.

'Sir Gawain is of the opinion, and so is my maid, that most husbands will not allow me to do what I want,' said Beth, gazing at him pensively. 'But I deem someone, such as yourself, would do so if we came to an agreement that meant you could join a travelling troupe of players and have the adventures you so long for.'

Phillip chuckled. 'If only that were possible, but I cannot believe you are serious.'

'Why should I not be serious?' asked Beth, her eyes dancing. 'Would not a rich wife suit you?'

'Aye, but I cannot see Sir Gawain allowing it.'

'Why not?' asked Beth, although she thought he was most likely in the right of it.

'Because he will say that I am too young for you and it is a crazy notion.'

'You are but three years my junior and he would have me off his hands sooner rather than later. He is of a mind to marry me to a rich old man, but I am not interested in money. What I need is a healthy virile young man who will give me a son.'

Phillip grinned. 'Well, I suppose I could help you out there. I've never had a day's sickness in my life. We could marry and I could go travelling whilst you busied yourself with the printing of books.'

'What is this you are talking about?' asked a voice behind Beth.

She started and turned to face Catherine. 'I was proposing that Phillip marry me,' she said boldly. 'Do you not consider that a good idea, much better than marrying an old man?'

Catherine gazed at Phillip and breathed out a sigh.

'If I stood in your shoes, I could certainly see why that idea would be so appealing, but I cannot see my nephew agreeing with it.'

'I told you,' said Phillip ruefully.

'I know you did, but it's possible that you both could be wrong. I must marry and Sir Gawain needs me off his hands,' said Beth, clapping her hands.

'I don't suppose there is any harm in your speaking to him about it,' said Catherine. 'But don't say I didn't warn you, as he will most likely reject the idea.'

Before the matter could be further discussed, the door opened and Gawain appeared. He smiled when he saw Phillip. 'So you have brought Nick's journal, lad,' he said.

Phillip stood up. 'Aye, Sir Gawain. But Mistress Llewellyn has not yet had the opportunity to look at it.'

Gawain glanced at Beth and raised an eyebrow. 'You surprise me. I thought you'd have torn the wrappings off in your eagerness to get your hands on it.'

'Butter,' said Beth, licking a finger. 'I was late rising and have only just broken my fast. Perhaps you would like to look at it first?'

'If that is your wish,' said Gawain, picking up the parcel as the serving man entered the hall, carrying a tray.

He set the tray on the table and asked Gawain if he wished him to fetch some food and drink. Gawain asked for more ale to be brought. As Phillip began to eat, Beth watched her guardian take out his eating knife and saw at the twine on the parcel. As if aware of her eyes upon him, Gawain looked across at her. 'What is it?' he asked. 'You look as if you want to say something.'

Beth glanced at Phillip. Instantly, he seized his cup of ale and took a deep draught and swallowed before saying, 'Sir Gawain, I am of a mind to marry Mistress Llewellyn.'

Gawain narrowly missed slicing the top off his thumb and swore as he dropped his eating knife. 'Are you hurt, nephew?' asked Catherine, hurrying to his side.

'It is nothing,' he said, sucking his finger. 'I am just wondering whether I've gone deaf. I thought Phillip here said that he is of a mind to marry Beth. Now who could have put that idea into his head?'

Catherine looked at the two younger people. 'It is very sudden, but one can see the attraction.'

Gawain stared at the young shipbuilder and his heart sank; he could certainly see why marrying young Phillip Hurst was a far more attractive proposition than Master Bigbury to Beth if physique and health were what mattered in the marriage stakes. Young, vital, handsome, glowing with health and strength—what woman wouldn't want to be made love to by such a Grecian, godlike figure? He wanted to throw him out of the house and prove to Beth that he, himself, could satisfy her in the marriage bed if only he were free to do so.

'There's nothing wrong with your hearing, Sir Gawain,' said Beth, amused. 'As soon as Master Phillip and I met we realised we had much in common and were able to speak our minds. He has confessed to me that which he would most like to do with his life and I have told him my dream. Instantly, we saw a way that we could both have what we desired.'

Gawain scowled. 'I'm damned if I know how marrying you would help Phillip when his life is already mapped out for him.'

'Phillip doesn't want his life mapped out for him, do you?' she asked the younger man.

Phillip swiftly washed down a mouthful of food with more ale. 'No, I don't,' he said firmly. 'Mistress Llewellyn is in the right of it. I've had enough of being told that shipbuilding is what my father did and it's what he wanted for me, as well as Chris and Nick. Nick wouldn't buckle down and went and did what he wanted, so why shouldn't I?'

'But according to Chris, you're already a skilled craftsman for your age,' said Gawain exasperatedly. 'He depends on you and when you finish your apprenticeship, most likely he'll make you a partner in the business.'

'He's never said that to me,' said Phillip, his blue eyes mutinous. 'Besides, if I become a partner, I'll be stuck at the yard for ever and never go off and have adventures.'

'It is most young men's dream to go travelling, to seek their fortune and have adventures, but that is all it is for most—a dream.' Gawain glanced at Beth. 'You should not be encouraging him by making him dissatisfied with his lot, which is a good one.'

'He was already dissatisfied,' said Beth, tilting her chin, annoyed that Gawain should blame her. 'I simply asked him what he would like to do if he could do whatever he wished and he told me.'

'That's true,' said Phillip, nodding his flaxen head. 'I want to join a troupe of travelling players and put on plays all around the country and at the king's court.'

Gawain blinked at him in astonishment. 'And what kind of adventures do you deem you will find as an actor, lad? Make-believe ones? It is true that some actors can make a decent living by entertaining the nobility, but not all. Consider also the travelling and that you could be living from hand to mouth in winter.'

'Then I will come home to Mistress Llewellyn and we will beget children and I will be of help to her in her business,' said Phillip. 'She's fair and comely and there is but two or three years between us. Many a young man has married a much older woman. Even the queen is several years older than the king.'

Gawain could not argue with that, but he certainly did not want Beth marrying Phillip. In truth, he didn't want any other man having her. 'Am I to believe that the pair of you did not fall in love at first sight? That this is simply a convenient match you speak of?'

'Aye, love has naught to do with it,' said Beth. 'Although any woman would find Master Phillip extremely attractive.'

'That may be so, but a wife needs a husband at her side, not one that spends most of his time travelling around the country,' said Gawain impatiently.

'I disagree,' said Beth firmly. 'I need a young lusty husband to get me with child and then I can happily get on with the life I dreamed about. My father did not stipulate the kind of man I should marry.'

'That might be true, but only because he trusted me to choose the right husband for you. No offence meant, Pip,' said Gawain, getting to his feet.

He drew Beth to one side. 'You need a husband who is there to protect you. Have you forgotten your situation so soon?'

'I had for a while,' said Beth, sighing. 'Why did you have to remind me when I was having such an amusing time?'

'So you find this episode amusing!' Gawain swore. 'Phillip Hurst is immature and you could put his life in danger if you persisted with this foolishness. Have you forgotten so soon the danger you could be in? I cannot allow you to marry him, Beth.'

Beth was guilt-stricken. 'Aye, I had, but frankly neither of us believed for a moment you would agree.'

Gawain groaned. 'Then why did you bother continuing with this farce?'

She sighed. 'I understood his frustration for not having had the opportunity to do what he so longs to do.'

'We all have our frustrations, Beth,' said Gawain, his dark blue eyes fastened on her mouth, 'and must deal with them as best we can. Still, I wonder if Chris Hurst knows of Pip's ambition to be an actor.'

'No, he does not,' said Beth, frowning. 'Which I deem is a pity. If he did know, then perhaps he might allow his brother to live his dream for a short while? Even if it is simply in the hope that Phillip will see the perils and pitfalls that such a life would entail so that, when he returns home, he will be content to settle down again.'

'Perhaps you have a good idea there,' said Gawain, struck by her perception. 'I will speak to him, but in the meantime you can read Nick's journal.'

Beth nodded. 'Pip seems to think it can be improved on.'

Gawain raised his eyebrows. 'An expert, is he?'

'He told me that he is a storyteller,' said Beth. 'If he is good, then he could earn himself a fair purse in the halls of noblemen.'

'Perhaps, but that is not my concern,' said Gawain. 'Hopefully I will also be able to read the journal before we attend Bartholomew Fair.'

Beth felt a stir of pleasurable excitement. 'I will need to arrange with Master Stanton and the bookbinder when the journal can be printed and bound. Hopefully it will be done in time for Nick Hurst's birthday.'

Gawain nodded. 'I can see no cause for delay. Now you may go whilst I speak to Pip. Don't forget the journal. I am hoping it will guarantee that you will stay out of mischief,' he added drily.

Beth smiled. 'May I ask of you a boon?'

'If it is in my power to grant and is within reason,' he said cautiously.

'I am in no mood to entertain Master Bigbury. Could you not send a message saying I am indisposed? You can cross him and Phillip off the list of suitors,' she said, her eyes twinkling. 'We shall have to conjure up some others.'

He shook his head at her, a smile hovering about his lips. 'All right! But go now before I lose all patience with you.'

Without thinking, she blew him a kiss and went to collect Nick Hurst's journal and took her farewell of Phillip before hurrying from the hall.

Gawain stared after her hungrily and wished they could have kissed in reality. She had such soft lips and he longed to explore the sweetness of her mouth. He groaned inwardly and knew he must soon remove her from his sphere before he gave in to temptation. If only he had thought to discuss his marriage with the Cardinal whilst he was there, he might have known where he stood in regard to his relationship with Mary, but it had been somewhat of a hasty meeting. Perhaps next time.

Beth had forgotten completely about Gawain's plan to speak to Cardinal Wolsey. Instead her mind was occupied with deciphering Nick Hurst's handwriting, but she had no real difficulty as it was clear and precise. She soon realised that his younger brother had hit the nail on the head in his opinion of his brother's writing. *Restrained* was the word, thought Beth. There was much to interest and fascinate and it just needed some alteration here and there.

When Beth had finished reading the journal she handed it over to Gawain on his return from the Weald two days later.

'So, what is your opinion of Nick Hurst from what you have read?' he asked, gazing down at her.

'He's probably the right kind of man to have with you if you find yourself with your back against the wall,' she replied.

'Definitely one of your brave and daring heroes, then,' said Gawain, his fingers brushing hers as he took the journal from her.

Their eyes caught and Beth found herself waiting expectantly as her heart raced at that brief contact with his skin, which had sent a tingle right through her.

Gawain cleared his throat. 'You have nothing more to say about him?'

Beth recollected herself. 'Disappointingly he also seems to be a man lacking in wit.'

'Perhaps he thought it would be wasted if he was only writing for himself,' said Gawain, knowing that he must keep his thoughts firmly focused on the subject in hand instead of ravishing her. 'He does have a dry sense of humour.'

'I'll take your word for it,' said Beth. 'There are also some drawings that would make excellent woodcuts. Especially for those readers interested in shipbuilding.'

Gawain turned over the well-thumbed pages. 'I see what you mean. The Portuguese ocean-going vessels are different in construction from the English ships that are used to sail along the coast and cross to Europe.'

'Perhaps he is of a mind that one day Englishmen will decide that they, too, would like to see the New World for themselves,' said Beth in a careful voice.

Gawain glanced at her swiftly. 'Are you hinting that there is work for our shipyards if this were to happen?'

'Aye, but perhaps Master Nick Hurst would rather not have those drawings included in any book of his travels that we might decide to print for the general reader,' said Beth. 'He might wish to keep them to himself.'

'Clever, thoughtful Beth,' said Gawain, respect in his eyes. 'I will read this and we will discuss it when I have done so.'

Beth almost burst with pleasure due to the compliment he had paid her. As she went upstairs to her bedchamber to change for supper she thought how good it was to converse with him on matters that interested them both. She was glad that he had made no more mention of selling the business or buying shares in it, but had found work for the presses instead.

It was several days before Gawain was ready to talk to Beth about the journal.

'So, what is your opinion of it?' asked Beth eagerly. 'Do we print a hundred copies?'

'Not so fast, Beth,' said Gawain, grinning. 'Certainly print a single copy of the actual journal as it is for Nick, but then I would split it into two separate slim volumes, one to be a tale of his adventures. You might wish to involve young Pip in any improvements to make it more exciting than it is at the moment.'

She was disappointed, although she knew what he said made sense. 'And the other volume?'

'A shipwright's handbook with drawings, but it

might require more information. We would need to speak to Chris Hurst about that in Nick's absence.'

'Having read it, are you not tempted to build one of these ocean-going vessels in your shipyard?' she asked.

'Perhaps, but I am no shipwright and have no love of the sea or travel,' he said. 'My heart is in the land.'

Beth could understand how he felt. She had grown fond of this corner of England despite her eagerness to visit the print room again. 'Can a messenger be sent to the Hurst household to inform the brothers of our plans?'

Gawain nodded. 'I am glad that you are able to accept that it is best that we work together, you and I, so that your business continues to be a success.'

Had she accepted that they work together? thought Beth. 'Are you still of a mind that I should sell shares in the business?' she asked in a careful voice.

He gave her a quizzical look. 'Shall we make a decision about that after our visit to London to attend Bartholomew Fair?' he suggested. 'What I do suggest is that, if Chris Hurst agrees, we start by printing the hundred copies of Nick's adventures I put to you earlier.'

She agreed, believing that they would sell and knowing she was looking forward to spending time in the city with Gawain, hoping to enjoy all the fun of the fair despite that which still gave her cause for concern on occasions: finding her father and Jonathan's murderer.

## Chapter Eight

Beth unfastened her cloak and hung the garment on the back of the door of her bedchamber at her London home. She had experienced a deep sadness entering the building, knowing that she was the last of the family who had once spent happy hours here. As she had passed through various rooms, she could almost hear her mother's warm voice welcoming her. In a way it was good to be home because there were so many memories tied up with this house. Yet at the same time she questioned whether she'd ever be able to become accustomed again to the noise and the bustle, as well as the stench of the narrow city streets in high summer.

Already she was missing the fresh Kentish air of Gawain's manor, but at least he was here with her. An overwhelming happiness shot through her at the thought of spending the next few days in his company. Up until recently, Catherine was supposed to be accompanying them to London, but then suddenly she had changed her mind, saying that she could not cope with the hustle and bustle of the city. Beth did attempt to try to persuade her to come, but Gawain's aunt would not budge.

Beth hummed a country tune as she unpacked and thought how it would be good to lose themselves in the crowds. For a moment she thought of Gawain's wife and then she tilted her chin and told herself that she was not going to feel guilty. If Mary bore him any love at all, then she should be spending time with him herself. Beth was beginning to have her doubts about Mary's reasons for staying away so long. Even if the old aunt was ill unto death, surely she had servants enough to take care of her so as to allow her niece to go home every now and again with her children to visit her husband?

The song died on Beth's lips and she sighed, wishing Gawain could be honest with her. If he had made an unhappy marriage himself, she wished he could swallow his pride and tell her. If it were so did that bode well or ill for any advice he might give about her entering the matrimonial state?

She changed out of her travelling garments and washed her hands and face and tidied her hair before taking Nick Hurst's journal and two handwritten revised copies of it from the top of the chest where she had placed them. As she left her bedchamber and went downstairs there was no sound or sight of Gawain. Neither could she see Jane anywhere, so she must be doing

what she would said she would do and was hiring a
cook and a couple of maids for their sojourn in London.

Beth went into the yard to the rear of the house and
passed through a door in a dividing wall, so entering
her other premises. She walked up the yard and into the
printing workshop to discover that Gawain had arrived
ahead of her and was talking to Master Stanton, the
master printer. She stood watching them, feeling slightly put out that her guardian had not waited for her so
they could enter the building together. She breathed in
the familiar, comforting odours of ink and glue and
leather and watched the compositor locking lines of
lead type together in preparation of inking them with
a leather pad ready for the printing press that was not
in use.

The bookbinder and his apprentice sat at another
bench, sewing pages together and appeared completely
absorbed in their task. She noticed printed pages hanging on a line for the ink to dry and thought of her father
and the pride he had taken in producing tidy copy. She
swallowed the sudden lump in her throat.

Suddenly Gawain turned his head. 'So there you
are,' he said, smiling.

'Aye, I'm here,' she said lightly. 'And little seems to
have changed, except for—' She did not finish because
there was no need.

A pause and then her master printer said, 'It's good
to see you back, Mistress Llewellyn. I don't think I
need to say what is in my heart about the master as you
know how fond we all were of him.'

'Of course I do,' said Beth, walking slowly over to

Master Stanton. She shook his hand and then asked what work it was that was on the press that was in operation.

'It's a reprint of Chaucer's *The Canterbury Tales*,' he replied. 'It was Sir Gawain who suggested it when he was last here. With all the folk in town for the fair, he thought that we could sell quite a number of copies if we had them in the shop in time.'

Beth considered it an excellent idea, but why had Gawain not mentioned it to her? Surely they should have discussed it before his giving the order to go ahead with the print run. She tried to conceal how she felt as she did not wish to spoil this time together, so said, 'What an excellent notion of yours, Sir Gawain! The very best of books for those who have travelled in any kind of company to get here.'

Gawain's eyes rested on her face. 'I am glad you feel like that. I should perhaps have consulted you, but there was not much time. And talking of travellers—do we not have a different kind of traveller's tale for the presses, Beth?'

'Oh!' said Beth, taking the journal and manuscripts from beneath her arm. 'You have mentioned it already?'

'Only briefly. Your part in preparing it for the presses has been much greater than mine and you know much more about the whole process of printing, so I thought you'd enjoy explaining exactly what you want done to Master Stanton yourself.'

She thought his words went some way to lessen her concern that he might ease her out from too much involvement in the business. 'That is generous of you, but if you were to stay here long enough, then I'm certain you will soon know as much as I do about the whole process.'

'Another time,' he said, touching her cheek lightly. 'There are people I must see before tomorrow.'

She felt a mixture of relief and disappointment. 'Will you be back in time for supper?'

'Hopefully. In the meantime, see what you think of the suggestion I have made to your master printer.' He took her hand raised it to his lips and kissed it before taking his farewell.

Beth brushed her lips with her hand where he had touched it and sighed. Then she became aware that the men were watching her and she flushed before turning to Master Stanton. 'I would like some woodcuts made of the drawings that you will find within the board-bound pages here, but they are also to be included in the pages I have tied with a blue ribbon. I want just two copies of the original journal and a hundred of the thicker of the other two manuscripts. Hopefully we will need to print more of that one if the first hundred sells well. See the original journal is taken to the woodcutter today. You will store it until then in the metal box. Also make certain the other two manuscripts are placed with your other copies waiting to be printed in the iron chest here and locked away.'

'Certainly, Mistress Llewellyn. When do you want us to make a start?' he asked.

'As soon as you have finished the work you have on the presses at the moment.' She smiled. 'So what did Sir Gawain suggest to you?'

'That the wood from his forest on the Weald be used for the woodcuts,' said the master printer. 'He will supply it free of charge.'

'That is thoughtful of him.' Beth hesitated before asking her next question. 'Have there been any unsavoury characters snooping around here after the news of my father's murder was made known?'

'None that I noticed, Mistress Llewellyn.'

'And our regular customers—they have not fallen away because of what happened?'

He shrugged. 'One or two, but most appeared as shocked as we were by your father's murder and want to continue to give you their support. Don't you worry, Mistress Llewellyn, I'm sure the filth who perpetrated this terrible crime will be caught before he can do any more harm.'

Beth could only hope that was true and left him to get on with his work, whilst she checked the accounts. She thought again of her father and wished he could see her now and be pleased. She spoke to the other men and the apprentice, helping to carry in some of the books that were ready to be sold; one she took home with her, loving the feel and smell of the small volume, straight off the press.

Several neighbours had got wind of her return and had come not only to express their condolences in person, but were also curious about Sir Gawain, wanting to know if her return was permanent or whether she would be returning to his country house. She decided it was best to provide them with no definite answer. It was a relief when Jane arrived with the women she had hired and her neighbours left her alone. She approved Jane's choice of temporary servants and then, after deciding what to have for supper, she retired to her parlour to read about Chaucer's pilgrims until her guardian returned.

Beth glanced up with a welcome in her eyes as the door opened. Gawain entered the parlour, but he looked none too happy and the light in her face died.

'Dare I ask what is wrong?' she asked.

He did not immediately answer, but slumped on the settle across from her and gazed into the fire. She waited several moments before saying, 'You're late, so I thought if you had not eaten you could have supper in here.'

He nodded. 'That's fine.'

'Good.' Beth closed her book and, getting up, placed it on her seat. 'Have I done something to vex you?' she asked.

Gawain lifted his head and looked across at her. 'Not you, Beth.'

'Then who?'

He washed his face with his hands and rubbed his eyes. 'God's blood, I'm tired.'

'It's been a long day,' she said softly.

'Aye, but it is not that which is the problem. I went to see Wolsey, but he is away on the king's business. Tom was outside York Place. He'd been keeping an eye on Cedric and had followed him to his uncle's house in Berkshire, but on the departure of the king and his entourage, he left with them. Tom decided he wouldn't have any difficulty following their progress, so he decided to have a rest as he hadn't had much sleep. When he eventually traced the king and his train to the next noble house on his itinerary, he had no sighting of Cedric. When the king moved on again, Cedric was not amongst his followers, so Tom decided to head back to London, knowing I was coming here for the fair.'

'So he has lost him.' Beth counted silently to ten before saying, 'I will make no further comment at this point, but fetch your supper and a jug of ale.'

'Thanks, Beth. You can imagine what I said to him.'

'Aye, but you do not have to repeat it,' she said with a wry smile, placing a hand on his shoulder. 'At least you are not to blame.'

Gawain covered her hand with his a moment before withdrawing it and changed the subject. 'Have you had any visitors?'

'Aye, but none for you to worry about.' She hesitated. 'I did wonder, when you were away so long, whether you had been to see your wife and children.'

He shook his head.

After a few moments, she left the parlour, wondering why she had felt she must remind him that he was married. Perhaps because there was a certain intimacy in them staying in this much smaller house without his aunt to chaperon her and her tending to his needs.

Gawain gazed into the flames, thinking about his feelings for Beth, and decided he had to tell her the truth. It was possible that by doing so he would give her reason to believe he was untrustworthy, but he felt he could not continue living a lie.

The door opened and Beth entered, carrying a tray. She set his supper down on a small table close to the settle. 'I brought you wine as the ale seems to have already run out. Most likely Jane did not order enough. I will see that she does not make the same mistake on the morrow.'

'You have not brought a cup for yourself?' asked Gawain.

'No, I had a cup earlier and too much red wine can bring on a megrim.'

'But you will sit down,' said Gawain firmly. 'There is something I have to tell you about Mary and the children.'

Beth gazed across at him and her heart gave a peculiar leap. She did not know whether after all she was ready to hear what he had to say about his wife. Knowing so little about her and not having seen her, she was a shadowy figure and, if she were honest, Beth preferred her that way. 'Do you not think it best if you eat your supper first before it gets cold?' she said rapidly.

'No, I have to get this off my chest now,' said Gawain and took a gulp of wine. 'I have not been honest with you, Beth.' He hesitated.

Her heart began to thud. 'Go on,' she said breathlessly, holding his gaze steady.

'She and the children are not staying with her aunt. I lied about that so people would not suspect the truth. She has left me for another man,' he growled.

'I—I see,' said Beth carefully, shocked beyond

belief. How could Mary possibly prefer another man to him? 'Who—who is this man?' she added, twisting her fingers together.

'I do not know his name. On the day I returned to Raventon Hall with you, I found a message from her.' He took another gulp of wine. 'She says he is her true husband because she went through a form of marriage with him before she married me.'

'What!' Beth's brown eyes mirrored her incredulity. 'Are you saying that she married you bigamously?'

He lifted his head and smiled wryly. 'Now that was not a word she used. Maybe she should have done. If I could find the pair of them and get them to agree to attend a court of law, then my marriage could hopefully be annulled.'

Beth's spirits began to soar. 'Was their marriage in front of a priest?'

'No, and there is the difficulty. Apparently she and her lover were very young when they plighted their troth simply before God.'

Beth's heart sank. 'I have heard of such matches being made in the past being accepted as binding, but are they still legal?'

'That I do not know. I have spoken of this only to my aunt. She realised that something was very wrong when Mary left with the children without saying where she was going. I searched for them, of course, but then I had to go to France without having found them. I told my aunt of the contents of the missive Mary had sent me. I wish now that I had kept my own counsel because she spoke of it to Father Hugh.'

'Father Hugh!' exclaimed Beth. 'So that is what she meant at the wedding and what he was hinting at when he spoke of you to me!'

'What did he say?' demanded Gawain.

Beth flushed. 'It does not matter right now. Carry on with your story.'

'Of course it matters!' he said harshly. 'Did he hint that I was less of a man because I couldn't hold on to my wife and that I was not fit to find a husband for you?'

'No!' cried Beth. 'I deem he believed you had told me about your wife's missive and that you had hinted that you could marry me yourself!'

Gawain stared at her and there was an expression his eyes that caused the colour in her cheeks to deepen. 'Why do you think he thought that?' he asked softly.

'He mentioned watching us dance together,' she replied huskily.

Gawain nodded. 'That would do it,' he murmured.

Beth did not catch what he said and burst out. 'It is beyond my comprehension that your wife should behave so badly towards you. She must be crazed to leave someone so considerate and responsible towards others as yourself!'

'She says she loves him,' said Gawain soberly.

'Even so, what she has done is cruel! What reason has she given to your daughters for leaving you? Has she told lies about you? It is wicked of her to take them from you,' said Beth vehemently.

Gawain's eyes darkened. 'I admit I am furious with her for removing them from my protection. I fear she might have told them that I no longer want them or even that I am not their true father.'

'What of her father?' Beth asked. 'Am I to presume he knew naught of these other vows she took?'

'According to Mary her father did know, but he disregarded them as did the parents of her lover. I can only believe that was because Mary's father was in desperate financial straits and he knew if he accepted my offer then he'd not have to worry about money.'

'But obviously he must have also considered you a better choice of husband for his daughter than this other man,' said Beth firmly.

Gawain's expression lightened. 'Carry on like this, Beth, and you'll have me believing that I am the better man and Mary has committed a great error.'

Beth said scornfully, 'Of course you are the better man, otherwise this other husband would not have given her up so easily to you in the first place. I have no doubt you treated her well, so what was the catalyst that caused her to leave you when she did and go to him?'

'His wife died shortly before Mary's father, so no doubt you can imagine the effect that had on both of them as apparently they had been seeing each other for a while. She even hinted that Tabitha and even my son who died might not be mine.'

Beth was taken aback by his mention of a son and she was conscious of the pain in his eyes and voice. She reached for his cup of wine. 'May I?' she asked.

'Please do.'

'I had no idea you'd lost a son.' Beth swallowed a

mouthful of wine and then said fiercely, 'I hate her for causing you such suffering.'

'I would not have her back if she came crawling. The children are another matter,' he said, reaching for his knife and cutting up his meat. 'I intend on finding them and bringing them home. Of course, it will cause a scandal if the truth were to get out.'

'You want Tabitha even though she might not be yours?'

'Aye! In my heart she is still my daughter.'

Beth thought it was noble and generous of him to feel like that. She felt certain there were many men who would not. 'But you still have to find them.'

He nodded, his expression was suddenly bleak. 'So much else has happened to prevent it.'

'You mean that your time has been taken up due to your involvement in my affairs,' said Beth quietly. 'A fact that I have not appreciated enough in the circumstances. So what are you going to do now?'

He put down his knife and reached out a hand to her. 'I have strong feelings for you, Beth, and I sense you feel the same towards me, too. I admire your courage and intelligence and want to go on protecting you. I certainly don't want you marrying anyone else other than me. As it is you can see the tangle my life is in. I do not know if the church will accept Mary's first marriage as binding. They might not do so. I did intend to speak to Cardinal Wolsey about it today, but now it will have to wait.'

Beth understood what he was saying perfectly and had noticed that he did not mention the word love when he spoke of his feeling towards her, but then she did not know if what she felt towards him was love or simply lust and a great deal of liking for the man he appeared to be. She placed her hand in his and said, 'Thank you for being honest with me. Father Hugh obviously saw more than either of us were aware of that day of the wedding.'

She moved closer to him and placed an arm about his neck and drew his head down to meet hers. She kissed him, thinking royalty and the nobility found no shame in begetting bastards. She would like to bear Gawain a son for both of them even if they could not marry. For a moment Beth thought seducing him was going to be easy because he returned her kiss with passion and his hands roamed her body. When she had to break off the kiss to draw breath, he enveloped her in a bear hug and covered her face with kisses before claiming her mouth once more.

Then suddenly he pushed her away. 'This will not do, Beth,' he said, breathing heavily. 'You must do as I say and go up to your bedchamber and lock yourself in,' he ordered.

'Lock myself in! Surely you jest?' said Beth, startled.

He shook his head. 'I might yet be tempted to come to you in the dark watches of the night and lie with you.'

'Then do!' she cried, clutching his sleeve. 'Can you not see how much I long for you to claim me for your own? Ever since I saw you half-naked wrestling in France, I have lusted after you.'

The silence that followed felt so charged with emotional tension that she wondered if she had been too honest with him.

'I am shocked, Beth,' said Gawain, trying to keep the smile out of his voice.

'I thought you might be,' she said, sighing.

'I am also flattered. I wish I had known then that is how you felt. It would have done my self-esteem no end of good, but really I am glad I didn't know because...' He paused.

'You deem we might have become lovers,' she said daringly.

He did not answer, only saying, 'I spoke to you of how you tempted me even in those first few days. If I had known for certain you wanted me, as well, it would have weakened my resolve to keep my promise to your father,' said Gawain, rifling his dark hair with a trembling hand. 'As it is, I must think seriously if he would consider me the right husband for you if my marriage was to be annulled.'

'Forget your promise to him!' said Beth. 'Would you like to know how you have haunted my dreams? You have such a manly chest that, in my imaginings, I would run my hands over it and press my lips to your skin and feel your lips on mine and—' She swallowed. 'I could go no further because that is beyond my—my—'

'Experience,' finished Gawain hoarsely as a vision of Beth's bare breasts rose before him. 'You must not say such things to me, love.'

*Love! He had called her love! Did that mean he not only desired her, but loved her?* 'I know,' she said meekly, her spirits soaring. 'But a writer needs to hone their skill with words, as well as their imagination. Yet, I would put into action those desires I long to have fulfilled,' she added, running a hand over his shirt front. 'I would have us make love.'

'Beth, stop it!' He could not help smiling.

Her lips twitched. 'Why must I stop it if dreams are all I am to have where you are concerned right now?'

'Hush!' He placed a hand over her mouth and drew her close to him. 'You will wake Jane and—'

'Once before you silenced me by kissing me,' she said in a muffled voice between his fingers. 'Do so now?'

'If I kiss you, will you then go to bed?' asked Gawain.

'If it is a kiss that is worthy of carrying into my dreams,' said Beth.

He removed his hand and gazed down at her. There was that in her eyes that caused the breath to catch in his throat, whilst he was roused to such a painful intensity that he knew that only by either letting her go or making love to her would it be eased. Why should he not possess her when she was offering herself to him? He swung her up into his arms and, with his mouth on hers, carried her out of the parlour. She breathed directions to her bedchamber into his ear. They reached the door, only to stop at the sound of snoring within. It was like a dash of cold water in his face and brought him to his senses.

'I don't believe it,' whispered Beth. 'Jane must have been waiting for me to come to bed and has fallen asleep. We will have to go to your bedchamber.'

'No, Beth,' said Gawain quietly, placing her feet on the floor.

She looked up at him with disappointment in her eyes. 'Why not?'

'You know why.' He held her hand against his chest. 'Dream well, Beth, and I will see you in the morning.'

'You are leaving me to dream alone?' There was a tremor in her voice.

'I must! Your father trusted me to do what was right by you.' He released her with difficulty and walked away.

# Chapter Nine

Beth had slept fitfully that night after spending hours awake, thinking of what had taken place between her and Gawain. If only it were possible for his marriage to be annulled. As it was, for now she must adopt a cheerful attitude as she did not wish him to see her downhearted. After all, they had come to London to enjoy themselves at Bartholomew Fair.

Gawain looked up from the small single sheet of paper he was reading as Beth entered the parlour and she thought he looked tired. Did that mean that he had not slept well, either? She sat down opposite him as one of the new maids entered. Beth asked her to bring her some bread, butter and ham. With a whisk of skirts the girl left the room.

'Would you like some ale?' asked Gawain.

Beth nodded and watched him pour the liquid into a pewter cup. 'We'll have to leave soon if we wish to get a good view of the Drapers and Merchant Taylors' Company leading the procession,' he said.

'Of course, you'll know all about that exalted company due to your interest in the cloth trade,' she murmured, sipping her ale.

'I won't be purchasing any cloth, but I want to see what price that from the Cotswolds, as well as our own fetches. I also wish to look at some sheep in Smithfield.' He paused and passed the slip of paper he had been reading over to her. 'We'll be distributing that. It contains information about our reprinting of Chaucer's *Canterbury Tales*, the cost and where it can be bought.'

Beth was impressed. 'You thought of this?'

'Aye,' said Gawain. 'What do you think?'

She hesitated. 'Did you consider how it would cut into our profit on the books sold?'

'Your master printer pointed that out to me, but I decided I would bear the cost myself and hopefully this will bring customers to the shop.'

Beth frowned. 'That is good of you. If we had thought about it, we could have set up a stall at the fair.'

'That would have entailed more labour,' said Gawain. 'No, Beth, I wish you to enjoy yourself at the fair, not work.'

It was true that she did want to enjoy herself with him and not be thinking of sales of books and profit margins, but even so part of her would have enjoyed making sales. 'You must have been up very early to have had this set up and printed,' she said.

He nodded. 'It's a pity that Nick's journal is not yet in print. The more those who are literate know about it, then the more we will have them clamouring to buy yours and Phillip's version of it.'

'I'm glad you're putting your heart into this venture,' said Beth, smiling, as the maid entered with her breakfast.

'I want the business to prosper for your sake and...' he lowered his voice '...hopefully by not printing religious tracts there will be no attempts on your life.'

Beth felt that familiar trickle of fear as she spread butter on a slice of bread. 'I know you are right, but have you thought that by simply accepting the role of my guardian you could have put your own life in danger?'

'That is a risk I am willing to take and you know why,' he said quietly. 'Tom and Sam are sharing the task of keeping a watch on York Place. When the Cardinal or Father Hugh returns, one of them will come and inform me of it.' A muscle clenched in his jaw. 'I plan to take the dagger with me this time and I have the missive that Mary sent me also with me. It's possible the Cardinal might recognise it and also know where Cedric is—if he does, he can question him further. Now make haste and finish your breakfast, so we can be on our way.' He stood up and left her alone to finish her meal.

Beth sighed, thinking even last night might never have been if it were not for his mention of Mary's missive. But she would not allow herself to be low spirited, but look forward to the fair.

She and Gawain stood, watching the guilds and dignitaries of the city enter the churchyard of the priory of St Bartholomew. She forced herself to concentrate on what was taking place. After a silver measure of an exact yard was produced and all other measures laid against it to ensure customers would not be cheated with a false measure, the fair was declared open. She and Gawain joined the crowd gathered in the large green space that was part of the priory grounds and where the clothiers and drapers had set up their stalls. There was not only cloth to be had, but also gloves, ribbons, lots of different colours and textures of thread, as well as needles and pins.

Gawain tucked Beth's hand in his arm and smiled down at her. 'I don't want to lose you,' he said, 'so best you hold on to me.'

'I have no objection to that,' she said, returning his smile, remembering when she had first set eyes on him. Never had she thought she would be contemplating marriage with him. 'May we just wander around first and see what else there is on show?'

He agreed.

The west gate of the churchyard led on to the field known as Smithfield and there not only were animals being sold at market, but there stood other stalls, selling all kinds of goods, as well as booths where various sports took place, including wrestling, rope dancing and cockfighting, as well as miming, plays and dancing to the music of fiddles, pipes and the hurdy-gurdy. She thought of Phillip Hurst, wondering if, one day, she might see him here performing in one of the plays.

Whilst Gawain went to inspect some sheep, Beth decided to spend her pennies on fairings. Unexpectedly, she caught sight of Father Hugh watching her and she wondered if he had seen her with Gawain. For a moment she was filled with trepidation in case the priest should come over and question her, but then he turned and hurried away. On impulse she decided to follow him, only to lose him in the crowd. She wondered if Tom and Sam were concealed amongst the throng, keeping their eye on him. She hoped so and returned to her enjoyment of the fair. She purchased a pair of gloves, several new ribbons, a posy of wild flowers and a corn dolly. There was food to be had, too, and she bought wafers, cakes, as well as mince pies from a pie man shouting out his wares. She also noticed one of the apprentices talking to folk and handing out strips of printed paper.

Gawain rejoined Beth as she was eating a pie and watching a juggler perform. She handed over the pie she had bought for him and gave him a smile, but he did not return it.

'What is wrong?' she asked.

'Nothing for you to worry about,' he said, biting into the pie.

She hesitated, wondering if he had noticed Father Hugh and did not like to say. 'I saw Father Hugh and decided to follow him, but he simply disappeared,' she murmured.

He frowned. 'He didn't approach you?'

'No.'

'Good.'

'But it's possible he saw us together,' said Beth.

He nodded thoughtfully. 'Anyhow, I did see Sam and he told me that the Cardinal has also returned.'

'You will seek an audience with him?' asked Beth eagerly.

'Aye. Pray that he will provide us with the answer we both want,' said Gawain.

When they returned to the house, Gawain excused himself and told Beth not to wait up for him. 'I could be some time.'

'You will be careful?'

He smiled faintly. 'You must not worry about me.'

She wanted to tell him that people who care for each other can't help but worry about the other's safety. 'I won't then!' she said lightly, closing the door on him.

Gawain hesitated a moment outside, wondering if he should have told her about his other destination, but he was short of time. He strode swiftly in the direction of the Bartholomew Inn where he had an appointment with one John Quedgeley. Earlier in the day he had rubbed shoulders with him at the sheep pens at Smithfield for a while before realising they had met before. He was an importer of wine and lived in Winchelsea just over the Kent border in Sussex. Master Quedgeley had mentioned having seen Mary in Winchelsea a month ago, but before Gawain could find out whether he knew where Mary and the children were staying, they were interrupted. Master Quedgeley had mentioned where he was lodging in London, so Gawain had decided to call on him that evening. He wanted to be as free of Mary as she did him, so he could not imagine she and the man she believed to be her husband not agreeing to his plan. As for the children, he was determined to bring them home with him as soon as possible.

Fortunately he found Master Quedgeley at the inn and he was able to provide Gawain with the information he needed. They talked for a while, but as soon as dusk fell, Gawain excused himself and returned to the house. He found the front door locked and, although exasperated, he knew that he should be grateful that Beth was taking all necessary precautions for her safety. He banged on the door and almost instantly heard the sound of footsteps hurrying to answer his summons.

The door opened and Beth stood in the doorway in her night attire, holding a candle. 'Did you see Wolsey?' she asked eagerly.

'I did not visit the Cardinal,' he replied, ushering her inside and closed the door behind him.

'Then where have you been?' she said, looking surprised, disappointed and a little suspicious.

'I will explain in a moment. Right now I am hungry and you should not have come to the door in your night attire,' he scolded.

She flushed. 'I thought that perhaps the Cardinal might have invited you to stay until morning and so I went to bed.'

'Well, go and get dressed. I have much to tell you,' said Gawain, stealing a brief kiss. 'And I will not be able to concentrate with you wearing so little.'

'If that is what you wish,' she said, smiling, and hurried upstairs.

Gawain fumbled his way to the kitchen where a fire still glowed in the fireplace. He lit a candle and placed it in a holder and took bread and cheese from the pantry and poured himself some ale. He had only begun to eat when he heard his name being called and feet on the stairs. He left the kitchen and collided into Beth. 'What is it?' he asked.

Her candle set shadows dancing about the walls. 'I deem there is a fire somewhere. There is a strange glow outside and I can hear the crackle of wood and a peculiar popping noise,' she replied.

'You stay here,' ordered Gawain, heading for the front door.

'No!' said Beth, clinging to his sleeve. 'I'm coming with you.'

He wasted no time arguing with her, but flung the door open. Instantly he knew that she was right because he could smell smoke and see that strange glow she had mentioned. He stepped outside and his heart began to thud in anticipation of what he might find; within moments he realised that it was Beth's business that was on fire. The instant that hit him, he spotted a gangly woman running away from the fire in the direction of St Paul's Cathedral. She was extremely tall for her sex and there was something odd about her gait. He would have gone after her if dousing the flames had not been his first priority.

He began to yell at the top of his voice, 'Fire, fire!'

Within moments doors opened and people hurried out into the street. Some were in night attire, but others were fully dressed. A ripple of sound passed through them.

'There'll be buckets of water in the yard,' cried Beth, seizing Gawain's arm. 'We always have some in hand in case there should be a fire. We'll need to fetch more water from the great conduit in Cheapside or from the River Fleet.'

He was about to tell her to rouse the servants when Jane, the cook and the maids appeared. 'What about the apprentices who sleep over the workshop?' panted Jane.

'We'll have to go through the back yard to wake them,' said Beth, gasping as the shutters at the front of the building fell apart and collapsed on to the ground in a burning mass.

They ran through the house and out of the back, followed by several neighbours. In no time at all the first buckets of water were being thrown into the flames, while Gawain forced his way into the print room and up the stairs. He was met halfway by the apprentices. One had still been awake and had heard the commotion. Gawain thought of all the paper inside the building and of the newly printed copies of *The Canterbury Tales* and was angry, thinking how quickly all would catch fire. He told them to help him save what they could.

News had swiftly spread and they were soon joined by the master printer and the bookbinder and their brothers. Somehow between them they managed to drag one of the presses into the yard before going back to try to save as many forms of lead type and paper and anything else they could lay their hands on. Some items of stationery and books had to be left to burn. Fortunately the shop had done brisk business in the sale of the new printing of Chaucer's *Tales* that day.

'The steel chests must be saved,' said Beth, her voice hoarse.

She would have gone inside herself if Gawain had not dragged her back and plunged into the building once more. Her heart was pounding in her breast, worried as she was for his safety. Really she should not have mentioned them. Then he appeared through the smoke with the bookbinder, dragging the chest, and she was filled with relief and gratitude that Gawain was safe.

He seized her hand and led her out of the yard, through her house and into the front. He had no doubt that the fire had been caused deliberately and felt heartsick for Beth. How would she recover from this terrible catastrophe?

Outside in the street, sparks had set fire to thatch, which was swiftly brought down by hooks on long handles. More people appeared with buckets and joined the gangs of people weaving a way to the great conduit, as well as the River Fleet. Gawain, Beth and her employees joined them. All worked tirelessly and without stopping to prevent the whole row of buildings from being destroyed. Despite all their efforts, Beth's business premises were destroyed, but at least the fire was contained and her home was still standing, although the windows were shattered from the heat.

She sank wearily to the ground and her tears formed rivulets on her blackened face. Gawain knelt and put his arm around her and tried to comfort her. She sobbed against his shoulder and only when she gained control of her emotions did she realise he was holding himself rigid. 'You are hurt?' she croaked.

'It could be worse.' His voice was hoarse. 'At least no lives have been lost.'

'I am grateful for that, but what am I to do now?' asked Beth in a despairing voice, gazing into his eyes that shone like steel in his filthy face. 'My business is destroyed.'

'We'll get the person who did this,' he said harshly. 'It was no accident. I saw a woman running away from the building.'

'A woman!'

'Aye, an extremely tall woman and I was reminded of the description of the figure who went into your father's tent in France.'

'I had almost forgotten about her,' said Beth, collecting her wits. 'Or had we decided that it was a him in disguise?'

'Whoever it was, for now they have escaped us,' said Gawain, helping her to her feet. She swayed against him and he lifted her high against his chest. 'You need to rest.'

'But I am filthy dirty and in no state to sleep between the sheets,' she muttered. 'Where are Jane and the other servants?'

'They're around somewhere,' said Gawain. 'Do not be worrying about others right now. Just rest against me.'

Beth obeyed him, closing her eyes but she could not ignore her senses as he carried her inside the house.

The air was hot and the smoke seemed to have permeated everything. 'We can't stay here,' said Gawain.

She lifted her head and stared into his face as she clung to him. 'But where can we go at this time of night?'

'We'll sleep in the open air.'

A throaty chuckle escaped her. 'You would take me into the country?'

'Aye, I will take you to my boat.'

She looked at him, surprised. 'I had almost forgotten we had travelled from Smallhythe in your boat. Will we not need blankets and pillows? And what about clean clothes and how will you find the way?'

'Questions, questions, Beth! Does that inquisitive mind of yours never stop?' he teased. 'Trust me.'

'All right, I will trust you,' she said, giving him a serious little smile. 'You do realise that it is unlikely that you will ever find a suitor for me now that I am without a dowry.'

'You sound almost pleased.'

'Every cloud has its silver lining. We're alive and while there's breath in me, I will rejoice that we both survived such a terrible calamity,' she said in a lilting voice.

He could only be glad that she felt like that right now. Of course, later she might feel differently.

More than two hours must have passed by the time they had sailed upstream by moonlight, passing the riverside residents of the bishops of Exeter and Bath and Wells that lay beyond the city walls until they had

left even the Palace of Westminster behind. The sun
was rising over the river in a ripple of apricot and gold
when Gawain furled the sail and used a weighted line
to test the depth of the water before dropping anchor.
Beth had dozed off in the stern of the boat, but now he
roused her before going over the side with a rope and
wading to the grassy bank where several trees provided
some shelter.

Beth stifled a yawn as she watched him from red-
rimmed eyes. 'Where are we?' she asked.

'Our own little paradise,' replied Gawain, his teeth
white against the dirt on his face as he smiled at her.
'You stay there and I'll come back for you.'

'It does not look very deep.' She clambered over the
side and after a moment's hesitation released her hold
on the boat. The chill of the water caused the breath to
catch in her throat, but as she waded towards him she
felt laughter bubbling up inside her. 'I never imagined
myself doing this a few hours ago and saying what I
am about to say. What a wonderful morning!'

Gawain's eyes flashed blue fire. 'We are both filthy,
our clothes are ruined and yet you are happy.' He threw
back his head and laughed joyously.

She twinkled up at him. 'Aye, because we are together and it does not matter if our garments are wet.'

'No, but they will be unpleasant against the skin if
we leave them on for any length of time,' he murmured,
holding her gaze.

The breath caught in her throat. 'Then I will take
mine off, although, I deem I will need help with my

fastenings.' She gazed down at her hands. 'I should have thought to put on gloves.'

Gawain paused in the process of unfastening his shirt and gently took her hands between his own. 'Why did you not say earlier how badly blistered they were? You should not have been passing pails with them in this condition.' He raised her palms to his lips and kissed them before dipping them into the water.

It was cool and soothing and a sigh escaped Beth. 'Do you swim?' she asked after several moments.

He nodded. 'I don't suppose you can?'

She shook her head. 'It would indeed have been a miracle if my father had thought it important that I should learn to swim, but I would like to float on the surface.'

'It would be a pleasure to help you do so,' said Gawain.

'You will not let me go?' she asked tentatively.

A laugh broke from him. 'What a question to ask! I will not let you go, love,' he said, his voice a caress.

He reached out and began to undo the fastenings on her gown. His fingers brushed against her bosom and he heard the breath catch in her throat. Should he be doing this when so many questions needed answers and their future hung in the balance? he asked himself as he eased her gown down over her hips, taking her chemise with it.

'You will wed me if you are able?' she whispered. 'Even though I would be content to be your lover if not?'

'I will have you for my wife,' he replied, tossing

aside the doubts that would assail him. They sank into the water and he brought her against him and kissed her sooty face.

'I do not like coming to you dirty,' she said, her eyes closed.

'The dirt will wash away.' He smiled and kissed her eyelids and then her throat and then his eyes took in the delicious curves of her breasts. Lowering his head, he caught one of her nipples between his lips and sucked. She gasped and her eyelids flew wide.

'What are you doing?'

'Do you not like it?'

'I did not say that.'

'No, you want us to be really clean.' Without more ado, Gawain released her, stripped and waded back into the water until it was deep enough to immerse himself fully.

Beth watched, enchanted by the sight of his muscular nakedness in all its comeliness before the water swallowed him up. She waded towards him, then suddenly the bottom fell away beneath her feet and she screamed. Instantly he was there beside her and lifting her against his chest. The next moment he was swimming on his back with her floating on top of him. She gasped as her chin touched his shoulder and then she swallowed a mouthful of water and coughed. Gawain begged her pardon and turned her over so that she was on her back. Beth's fear of the water abated and she closed her eyes, enjoying the silky feel of it against her skin, but more than anything, she loved the sensations roused within her by the feel of his body supporting her. But this first such experience of floating in the water did not last long and soon he swam with her towards the shore, until she was able to stand up and climb out of the water onto the grassy bank.

He had heaved himself into the boat, but after a few moments, he joined her on shore, carrying a couple of blankets and drying cloths. Neither could take their eyes from each other. He spread one of the blankets on the dew-sparkled grass and then brought her close to him and wrapped her in the drying cloth. He begun to rub her briskly until her skin tingled. She stilled his hands before placing her arms around him and kissing him on the mouth.

Afterwards, Beth could not remember how they came to be lying on the blanket, but she would never forget the strength of his arms or the hunger of his kisses that was savage in its intensity. Her desire for him to possess her spiralled out of her control as his touch roused in her sensations that demanded release. When he took her it was with a passion that swept her beyond all reason or resistance and she clung to him, her need for him as urgent as that which she felt in him for her.

'Gawain,' she gasped.

'Hush, Beth, this is no time for talking,' he groaned.

'I know. It is for lovemaking,' she whispered, allowing herself to be swept away on waves of such ecstasy that she thought she might die from the wonder of it.

She fell asleep in his arms with the blanket wrapped around them, all thought of the fire forgotten.

When Beth woke she had no notion of how long she had slept. Gawain's eyes were shuttered and he appeared perfectly relaxed. She broke off a blade of grass and tickled his face with it. He opened his eyes and gazed up at her and then at the sky before sitting bolt upright. 'You must get dressed,' he ordered.

'Of course I must, and so must you. You do have some clean garments for us?' she enquired. 'I have no idea what happened to our other clothes. I deem they must have floated away.'

He reached out a hand and closed it on her breast and brought himself against her. 'I care for you, Beth, more than I have the right to say at this moment. I should not have allowed what took place between us to happen until I could have called you wife.'

'It is too late for regrets now,' she murmured against his mouth.

He could not resist kissing her. Despite his words he was reluctant to break the spell that had bound them earlier. 'I only regret that you do not wear my ring and bear my name.' He sighed. 'We must go.'

'I know.' She gazed about her, all her senses alert in a way they had never been before. She could hear the plop of a fish and the breeze ruffling the grass and the chirp of a bird, smell the fragrance of a late-flowering wild rose and the smoke that still tainted her hair and part of her longed to stay in this place for ever. She wished that she could express the depth of her feelings for him, but the words stuck in her throat. She so hoped that he loved her. She was certain that she loved him, but perhaps it was best that she kept that to herself right now. With an abrupt movement she stood up and, with a blanket wrapped round her, waded out to the boat.

He followed her, thinking of what they must face when they arrived back in Pater Noster Row, wondering what to do that was best for her. 'You cannot stay in your house as it is, Beth. You must return to Raventon Hall.'

She glanced at him. 'I do not wish to be packed off to the country and leave everything for you to deal with here if that is your intention.'

'It is dangerous for you in London and I wouldn't be able to protect you all the time if you insisted on staying here,' rasped Gawain, frowning.

'Don't you believe that danger stalks you, as well?'

'Aye, but I am a man and can protect myself.'

'Can't I go with you wherever you go?' she pleaded.

He shook his head. 'I need to go to Winchelsea and I am best going alone.'

'Why do you go there?' she asked, unable to conceal her curiosity.

He told her about his conversation with Master Quedgeley and how he planned to speak with Mary and the man she claimed to be her husband. 'I must do this. If all goes the way I wish, then I will bring the children to you at Raventon, then visit the Cardinal and hopefully he will declare my marriage null and void and we can wed. Of course, it might take some time, but eventually I will marry you,' he said emphatically.

Beth believed he meant what he said, but she had other matters on her mind, as well. 'I understand what you are saying and I will be patient. But in the meantime, what about my business? We have one press, but to get it working we need to find somewhere to work from and I do not have the funds to rent another building and there are items we will have to buy and the men's wages to pay,' she said, almost despairing. 'I doubt I have enough money deposited with the bankers to deal with all of these things.'

'I will provide you with the necessary money,' assured Gawain, squeezing her hand.

She gnawed on her lip. 'I do not like taking money from you.'

'Then accept my offer to buy more shares in your business,' he said insistently.

She hesitated. 'In the circumstances I seem to have no choice. At least you will be able to buy them dirt cheap.' A wry smile twisted her mouth.

He frowned. 'I am not out to make money out of your misfortune, Beth. I will give you a good price for them. We could set up shop downstairs in your house until we can rebuild again. It is only a matter of cleaning the place up, finding a carpenter to get benches made and buying what else is needed after we've moved what we already have in.'

'You make it sound so simple, but I know it won't be.'

He nodded. 'But it will be done.'

'And the first printing will be of Nick Hurst's journal,' she said firmly.

'You're telling me that was not destroyed?'

'If Master Stanton did as I ordered and placed it and the manuscripts I gave him in the iron chest, then all is safe,' said Beth, smiling.

'Then the sooner we get back to Pater Noster Row and check that out the better,' said Gawain, his spirits lifting.

Beth's eyes were wet with tears as she surveyed the blackened ruin that yesterday had been a thriving business. 'I will arrange to have the site cleared in no time,' said Gawain, putting his arm around her shoulders.

'It just makes me so sad,' said Beth, easing the tightness in her throat. 'It would have broken my father's heart to see it so.'

'Look on the bright side, sweeting—the building we will raise will be a much better one. It will be of brick and with the latest glass windows and the roof will be of slate,' said Gawain.

Before she could comment they were interrupted by Jane saying, 'Mistress Beth, there you are! We did wonder what had happened to you?'

Beth wiped her eyes and smiled at her maid. 'I beg pardon if we have caused you concern, but I could not sleep in the house as it was so Sir Gawain and I removed somewhere else. Did you stay here, Jane?'

'Aye,' said the maid, 'I wasn't going to allow looters to get in whilst you were away, but it isn't suitable for you as it is, Mistress Beth. Cook and the girls went home, but Sam's been here, wishing to speak to Sir Gawain. He was real angry when he saw what had happened. He went away again, but said he'd be back shortly.'

'Good,' said Gawain. 'I have much to say to him. If you'll excuse me, Beth.' He strode on ahead into the house.

Beth and Jane followed him more slowly. 'We suspect it was arson, you know, Jane. I don't suppose you've had a chance to start tidying up?'

'Aye, I have made a start,' said Jane, 'but there's that much to do, Mistress Beth, and I don't know what you want to get rid of and what you want to be laundered and kept.'

They went indoors and Beth asked Jane if she could prepare some breakfast for them. Whilst the maid was busy in the kitchen, Beth went upstairs to her bedchamber. She was only there a few moments when she heard Gawain coming along the passage. She popped her head out of her door and instantly she knew there was something wrong.

'What is it?' she asked.

'Someone has been in my bedchamber,' he said grimly. 'They have rifled through my possessions and taken the dagger that I had stowed in the chest under my clothes.'

Beth gasped. 'You—you mean they've taken the murder weapon?'

'Aye! You know what this means, Beth—that the fire really was started deliberately not just to destroy your business, but to get us out of the house so as to search for the weapon?'

Beth paled. 'How did they know it was there?'

'They took a risk,' said Gawain, his eyes glinting with anger. 'You have to leave London without delay, Beth!'

She did not argue with him. 'Do you deem it possible that Cedric and the arsonist are in league together? That one caused the fire and the other stole the weapon?'

'I really don't know,' said Gawain, 'although I am of a mind that such a plan demands a ruthlessness and cunning that I do not believe he possesses.'

'But he is the only one who knows you had the dagger.'

'Unless he has already spoken to its owner,' said Gawain, his blue eyes darkening.

'Maybe Sam has discovered his whereabouts and that is why he wishes to speak to you,' said Beth.

Gawain agreed. 'I will await his return, but in the meantime, Beth, you must make your preparations to leave for Raventon Hall. Your servants will accompany you to Kent. I will hire a boatman for you as I might have need of mine. Once there you will stay put until you hear from me.'

Beth thought of the passion and conversation they had shared earlier that day and she was still not of a mind to be packed off into the country, but she could see that if she stayed, he would only worry about her and that could limit his activities. For now she had to obey him, pray that the murderer would be traced and she and Gawain would soon be together again.

## Chapter Ten

Beth was weary by the time they reached Raventon Hall. Yet she was glad to set eyes on the building that she now regarded as a second home. She only wished that Gawain was at her side. Sam helped her down from the saddle before turning to Jane.

As they walked towards the house the door opened and a woman dressed in black stood there with two young girls. 'Who are you?' she demanded.

Beth was stiff from the ride, but now her knees began to tremble. She did not need to ask that question of the pale haired woman in front of her. The taller of the girls was dark like Gawain and she had eyes the same colour as his, so she could only be his daughter, but the younger was similar in colouring to her mother.

With a sinking feeling in the pit of her stomach, Beth replied, 'I am Mistress Elizabeth Llewellyn. Sir Gawain is my guardian. Tell me, is Mistress Ashbourne at home?' She was amazed at how calm her voice sounded when she felt as if she might fall to pieces.

The woman's icy-blue eyes narrowed. 'So you are she! How is it that Gawain became your guardian? Aunt Catherine does not appear to know.'

Beth had no intention of telling this woman all her business. 'Sir Gawain was a trusted business acquaintance of my father. My half-brother, Jonathan, drowned and since my father feared he had not many more years left to live, he asked Sir Gawain to be my guardian if some ill fate should overtake him,' she replied coolly. 'Which it did. He was murdered in France.'

Mary's frown deepened. 'That is unfortunate and I can see why Gawain should want to help you. He always was a man ready to help lame dogs and beggars. Where is my husband now?'

Beth was tempted to say *Oh, so he is your husband now? Why is that?* Instead, she said, 'You must be Mary?' She'd be damned if she was going to say his wife.

'Of course! Lady Mary Raventon,' said Mary sharply. 'You have not answered my question.'

Beth decided that she would tell her as little as possible. 'I left Sir Gawain in London,' she said, removing a glove. 'He had business to attend to.'

Mary pouted. 'I heard from an acquaintance that he had met Gawain at Bartholomew Fair. I had hoped he would immediately come in search of us, but when he did not I decided to come home. Why can't Gawain get anything right?'

Beth's stomach clenched. 'From what I have heard, it is you who is in the wrong, madam!' she blurted out.

Mary's jaw dropped. 'How dare you speak to me so!' she hissed.

The words had hardly left her lips when Catherine appeared at her shoulder. 'Beth, you are back so soon! Is something wrong?'

'An arsonist set fire to my business, so Gawain insisted that I return here,' she replied, a tremor in her voice. 'He was concerned for my safety.'

'Oh, my dear!' cried Catherine, brushing past Mary and the girls and hurrying towards Beth with outstretched arms. She kissed her on both cheeks and hugged her to her bosom. 'Mary and the girls arrived but two hours ago,' she whispered in Beth's ear. 'And she has told me that her aunt is dead.'

Beth gave a startled gasp. 'But Gawain told me that there is no aunt, so why has she lied to you?'

'Because she met Matilda on the way here and she asked after her aunt,' whispered Catherine. 'Mary is no lackwit and realised instantly the tale that Gawain had spread to prevent folk from guessing the truth. She told Matilda that she is mourning for her and glad to return home to her wonderful patient husband.'

'By all that is holy, what are we to do?' muttered Beth. 'What of the man she told him was her true husband?'

'So you know about him, too,' murmured Catherine. 'My nephew obviously thinks much of you to be so honest with you. Mary has not mentioned him, but Lydia has told me that he has died of a fever and his family did not want them to stay. It seems to me that the children were never welcome there and he was not averse to hitting them or their mother for that matter. Anyway, Gawain will have the whole truth out of Mary.' She paused. 'Now tell me, how is my nephew?' she asked loudly.

Beth cleared her throat and said, 'Your nephew is unharmed, but the house is in a bad state. There is much to do to make it habitable again and he must visit Cardinal Wolsey, too.'

'I am relieved to hear that he is well but you, my dear Beth, look like you are in need of good country air,' said Catherine. 'I am so sorry about what has befallen you now. As if you had not suffered enough with losing your menfolk.'

'It is indeed a calamity,' said Beth, aware that Mary was listening. 'I would have remained in London if Sir Gawain had not insisted in my coming here.' She wondered if even now he was making his way to Winchelsea in the hope of finding Mary and the girls. What would he do when he found them missing? Come here or return to London?

A girl's voice said, 'Can we go to London, Mama? I want to see my real papa.'

'Do not bother me with such questions, Lydia,' said Mary, blinking down at her daughter. 'If your father has business to tend to, then he will have no time for you. Remember my telling you how the king and Cardinal Wolsey, who is the king's advisor, would often request his company? Besides, I am too exhausted to make such a journey. We will send a messenger telling him that we are home.'

'You said you would send a messenger when we first arrived at Winchelsea, but you never did,' said Lydia sullenly.

'Hush, daughter!' scolded Mary. 'Must you be forever arguing with me? You know how it brings on my megrim. I will go inside now and rest. You will stay with Aunt Catherine. Now we have returned home, you must learn not to be always clinging to me.' With a glance in Beth's direction she hurried inside the house.

The two girls looked at Beth and Lydia said, 'When do you deem that Papa will come home?'

'I cannot say. He has gone to Winchelsea in search of you after discovering your whereabouts. He spoke of you to me and told me he was concerned about you both and missed you very much,' said Beth, bringing down her head to the girls' level.

'Mama should never have taken us away,' said Lydia, shaking her dark head. 'When Papa did not come she told us that he didn't want us any more. She said that the man with the long fingers and sharp nails was our father.' Her eyes clouded and she shivered. 'I was glad when he died and we were told to leave and never come back. I didn't know what was going to happen to us, but Mama changed her mind about Papa and told me that he really was our father.'

Beth darted a glance at Catherine. 'It seems Mary is determined to worm her way back into Gawain's graces,' she said. 'But I deem she will find he is not prepared to take her back.'

'You could be right,' said Catherine. 'But come, Beth, you must be weary and in need of refreshment. Come inside.'

'May we have some refreshments, too?' asked the younger girl.

'Of course you may, Tabitha,' said Catherine, smiling down at her and taking both girls by the hand.

Beth followed them inside. Oh, why had Mary returned, obviously determined to resume her former position as his wife, making matters even more difficult than they were already? For the first time ever she felt an intruder in this house and she did not want to remain under this roof whilst Mary was there.

'Jane, take Mistress Beth's baggage up to her bedchamber,' said Catherine. 'Girls, you go to the kitchen and tell cook that Mistress Beth has arrived home and she is in need of refreshment. You may ask her to provide you with wafers and small ale, too.' She hugged them both and they hurried from the hall. Catherine bid Beth to sit down and sat opposite her.

Catherine took a deep breath, kneading the folds in her gown with unsteady fingers. 'It is possible that, although Gawain no longer cares for Mary, he will not rob the girls of their mother as she would their father. You must be prepared for that, Beth.'

Beth felt as if ice were forming about her heart. 'I would have been a mother to them if she were not here!' she said, placing a clenched hand against her breast.

Catherine nodded. 'I understand how you feel. What will you do?'

Beth stared at her for a long time before saying, 'I

cannot stay here right now. I will return to London and hopefully I will see Gawain and he can sort out this tangle. I will remain there until it is done.'

Catherine touched her hand. 'I would dearly love you to stay, but in these difficult circumstances you must do what you feel is right.'

'I am not as sure as I might sound,' said Beth. 'But I will leave early in the morning with Jane and Sam. I do not know when I will return.'

Two days later Beth arrived back in London and went straight to the house, to find not only that her master printer and her other employees had set up business on the ground floor, but that Gawain had gone to Hampton Court, the country home of Cardinal Wolsey, who had sent for him.

'He did not visit Winchelsea first?' asked Beth.

'No,' said the master printer, looking surprised by the question.

Beth wondered if she could get a message to Gawain, but decided that what she had to say would be so difficult to write that she would wait for a day or two. Perhaps he would return to London before going anywhere else and she could speak to him then. In the meantime there was plenty to be done sorting out the first floor of the house to be used as ordinary everyday living space. She also spent time in the printing workshop and went and spoke to the craftsman employed to do woodcuts for any illustrations. Fortunately, with Nicholas Hurst's journal having survived the fire and the work that she and his brother had done on it, there was much to think about. She presumed that Gawain would still be willing to buy shares in her business; it would not survive without his help and, without it or a dowry he would not be able to find a husband for her. If it was as his aunt believed and he would not rob his daughters of their mother, then her heart ached at the thought of relinquishing her dream of not only being his wife, but of being the owner of a successful business. Surely there must be a way for her to achieve both. In the meantime whilst she waited for him, she decided to write her thoughts down about the fire, intending to print it in her news sheet before Gawain returned.

But when he returned, one look at his grim visage was enough to cause her to fling down her quill and rise to her feet. 'What are you doing back here?' he asked, before she could get a word out.

'You are angry with me for returning here, but I had no choice,' she cried, stretching out a hand to him. 'Mary and the children have returned to Raventon Hall!'

'What!' Gawain was stunned.

She went over to the fire and placed a log on it. 'You look cold,' she said. 'Come and warm yourself by the fire.'

'In a moment.' He cleared his throat. 'I have to tell you that Cedric was found dead a week ago, killed with the dagger that was stolen from here the night of the fire.'

Beth gasped and sat down hastily. 'Is—is that why the Cardinal sent for you?'

'Aye. I should have spoken to him earlier about Cedric, but I explained my reasons and told him about the fire and how I believed it to be arson.'

'You told him of the theft of the dagger?'

'Aye, and we both agreed that he most likely did attempt blackmail and sealed his own fate.'

Beth said, 'He does not believe you to be the guilty party, then?'

'No.' He ran a hand through his hair. 'I mentioned Mary and an annulment to him and he gave me hope.'

'That is good, but what will he say now that Mary and the children have returned to Raventon Hall? She is saying now that you are her husband. Apparently this other man has died.' Beth could not control her voice, which shook with nerves. 'There is no doubt that she is expecting you to forgive her for the children's sake and to take her back.'

Gawain swore savagely before sinking on to a chair and washing his face with his hands. 'I will not have her back! I will not allow her to remain under my roof. She can go into a nunnery. My aunt will care for the children until we can wed.'

'If only Mary would go willingly,' cried Beth, kneeling in front of him. 'But I think you will find that she will dig in her heels. She knows that you told people that she had gone to tend her aunt and now she is pretending to mourn her.'

Gawain groaned. 'I should never have lied, but I wanted to protect the girls from scandal, as well as not have people know that she cuckolded me.' He lifted his head. 'The girls—they are well?'

'They have missed you, but they look well enough.' Beth hugged herself as she felt a shiver go through her.

He drew her into his arms. 'You must not fret. I showed the Cardinal the missive she sent me. I am certain he will take my side. I refuse to fall in with Mary's plan. We will be together, Beth.' He crushed her lips with his own.

She clung to him, but after a few moments drew away from him. 'There will be a terrible scandal if the truth comes out—how will it affect your daughters? Besides, the Cardinal might see matters differently if she is repentant and denies the truth of what she wrote in the missive.'

Gawain frowned. 'You are looking on the dark side. Why can't you have faith that I will make all well? I admit that there is bound to be a scandal, but I doubt folk will speak of it to the girls. As for myself, I no longer care what folk think of me. I do not doubt that when most know the truth, they will be sympathetic towards me and the children.'

'But perhaps not to me. All will depend on the tales she might spread. What if folk say that I have come between husband and wife and ruined your marriage? At the moment I cannot see how there can be a future for us together.' Beth's voice wobbled.

'Do not give up hope,' said Gawain roughly, bringing her against him once more and kissing her gently whilst stroking her hair with such tenderness that she thought she would die if she was never to be held by him again. Tears trickled down her cheeks, dampening his shoulder. 'Do not weep, love!' he said. 'I will speak to her and make her see that there is no chance that she and I will ever live together again as man and wife.' He wiped Beth's tears away with an unsteady hand and brushed her lips with his own before releasing her.

She fought for control of her emotions and managed to blink back her tears and tilted her chin. 'I will try to do as you say and hope and pray that all will come right for us.'

'Good lass,' he said.

Gawain's heart was heavy with anger and misery as he took his leave of Beth.

Later on the journey home to Raventon Hall, he tried to think of ways in which he could honourably be rid of Mary, yet keep the girls with him, and at the same time have Beth come and stay at Raventon Hall without creating a scandal. His mind was set on telling Mary how he felt in no uncertain terms. Yet as soon as he arrived home and Lydia came running towards him, he knew with a sinking heart that it was going to be more difficult to deprive the girls of their mother than he'd thought.

'Papa, you're home,' said Lydia, flinging herself at him. 'I have missed you so. Can I stay with you and never go away again?'

'That I cannot promise, Lydia sweeting,' he replied, hugging her tightly. 'But you must never go away again without my knowing where you're going.'

Suddenly he became aware that Mary was standing in the doorway with Tabitha clinging to her skirts.

She was clad in black. The colour did not suit her; it made her features look washed out. He remembered how he had once believed that Mary loved him. That was the biggest self-deception he had experienced in his whole life. Beth loved him. He was almost sure of that. The woman watching him had an expression in her eyes that caused rage to unfurl deep inside him, knowing she only wanted to use him. He longed to say *you should never have returned*, but knew that he couldn't say it in front of the girls. He yearned for Beth and wanted to see her smile again, to make her happy. But he realised that she had been much more perceptive than him when she had spoken her thoughts on how he would be bound by his love for his daughters. If he were to separate them from their mother, what effect would that have on their trust in him?

'The three of us have missed you, haven't we, girls?' said Mary, walking towards Gawain, her hips swaying and a smile glued to her features.

'Then you should not have kept the girls away from me so long,' retorted Gawain.

One of the stable boys came running and Gawain indicated that he tend his horse, then, with Lydia holding his hand, made for the house. Bending down in front of Tabitha, he smiled at her and then scooped her up with his other arm and carried her indoors. He was aware of the child's small soft hand curled about his neck and her round solemn eyes fixed on his profile. He thought of Beth and wished that this child was theirs and she could have borne him a son one day: the grandson her father had so wanted. He was seized by such a depth of longing for that to come true that he felt tears prick his eyes.

Catherine rose to her feet as he entered the hall with the children, followed by Mary. 'You have seen Beth?' she asked.

'Aye, she is in London and plans to remain there for now,' he answered.

'I would go to her if you wished it of me,' said Catherine.

'Not just yet,' said Gawain, pleased nevertheless by her thoughtfulness. 'I need you here to keep your eye on the children. Take them now, so I can speak to their mother.'

'Can't we stay with you a little longer, Papa?' asked Lydia, looking up at him anxiously.

'I will speak with you again shortly,' he said, kissing Tabitha before setting her down beside her sister and smiling at them both.

Lydia looked relieved.

Catherine took them by the hand and led them from the hall.

There was a long silence. A serving man entered the hall, welcomed Gawain home with a smile and asked if there was anything he could fetch him. He asked for ale and some bread and ham and the serving man hurried out.

'I—I suppose you expect me to beg for your forgiveness,' said Mary.

Gawain stared at her with a lack of expression on his face. 'It would be a start, but it will take a long time before I will be able to find it in my heart to forgive you for removing the children from my care. I have no illusions as to why you have returned. It was certainly not for love of me—it would be hypocritical for you to pretend differently. I have considered suggesting that you take yourself off to a nunnery for your safety—'

'I do not think the religious life would suit me,' interrupted Mary. 'Besides, I will miss the children and they will miss me.'

'You did not care about their feelings when you took them from me,' he said icily.

'I admit I was selfish,' cried Mary, gripping her hands tightly together. 'But let us make a fresh start. I will give you another son and we will be a happy family once more.'

Gawain stared at her in disbelief. 'You will never share my bed again. You have lived with another man as his wife. You said that he was your true husband and that I was not. I have that in writing. Do not think that this will be your home for very long. I plan to have our so-called marriage annulled.'

Mary flinched. 'Do you have to be so cold-hearted towards me? Have you no pity to spare for me? I was mistaken in Lionel. He beat me as did my father when he was in his cups. It was not easy for me to pluck up the courage to return here. Is it that you have used up all your love and compassion on that Beth Llewellyn?' she hissed.

Gawain's eyes narrowed. 'What do you mean by that? What has my aunt told you?'

'Catherine told me little, but I know that she now hates me,' said Mary petulantly, 'and that you and she have a fondness for Jonathan Llewellyn's half-sister. She loves you! I saw it in her eyes.'

Gawain stiffened, but he remained silent as the serving man re-entered the hall carrying a tray of food and drink. One of the trestle tables had not been put away and Gawain indicated that he place the tray there, then dismissed him. He sat down on a bench and poured himself some ale. He gulped half of it down before saying, 'How come you know of Jonathan Llewellyn? You're not going to tell me he was another young lover of yours that you forgot to mention?' he said sarcastically.

Mary's mouth tightened and she clenched her fists and flew at him and would have hit him, if he had not caught hold of her wrist. 'You insult me! How dare you accuse me of such a sin. I am hurting inside and out and you would hurt me more,' she panted.

Gawain had difficulty controlling his anger. 'I am hurting, too, but what do you really care about me?'

Mary's expression altered. 'I had thought to provide you with information about Jonathan if you were kind to me. Apparently you believe his death was no accident.'

He frowned and his grip tightened on her wrist. 'Who told you that? What is it you know?'

'Maybe I will tell you in the days to come if you are kind to me.' She pressed against him. 'Forgive me, Gawain! I will show you the scars where Lionel beat me and you will see how I have suffered. I should never have left you. People believe we are married and they need never know the truth about Lionel and I.'

Gawain wanted to throw Mary off him. He was sorry that she had been beaten, but she had brought it on herself. Right now it was a struggle for him not to hit out at her himself. He could not stay here or he might actually end up doing so. Beth's face swam before his eyes and he thought of her courage and strength and he knew he had to see her and regain his equilibrium. Besides, he was worried about having left her without a protector. He should return to London, but he would not go alone; he would take his aunt and the children with him. He would find an inn where they could stay whilst he visited Beth.

Several days later, he was almost ready to set out for London, having had to postpone his departure due to the autumnal rains. He had barely spoken to Mary in all that time especially after he had found her in his bedchamber. The first time he had found her making a search of his room apparently for the missive she had sent him. Fortunately he carried it on his person wherever he went. The second time she had been lying naked on the bed and he'd had to steel himself to roll her up in the counterpane and thrust her outside in the passage with her clothes. He would have departed earlier if he could, but he would not force the children or Catherine to suffer travelling in such inclement weather. He had kept his plans to himself until the last few hours, not trusting Mary to behave in a reasonable manner.

There came a knock on the door of his bedchamber. 'Who is it?' he called.

'It is I, Catherine,' said his aunt. 'Nephew, you have a visitor downstairs.'

'Who is it?'

Catherine smiled. 'Come down and see. He says that he has no intention of delaying our journey.'

'Where is Mary?'

'She has gone to visit Mildred Tyler.'

He frowned. 'I hope she did not take the children with her?'

Catherine shook her head. 'I made sure they were safe upstairs with me.'

Gawain wasted no time hurrying downstairs, curious to see this visitor whom his aunt was being secretive about. He entered the hall and his gaze went to the man rising from the settle in front of the fire.

'I hope that you don't mind my calling so unexpectedly, Gawain, but I felt I needed to see you before you left for London,' said his visitor.

'By St George, it's you, Nick!' Gawain walked towards him with an outstretched hand. 'When did you get back?'

'A few days ago,' said Nicholas Hurst, shaking his hand.

'Do sit down,' said Gawain. 'Can I offer you some refreshment?'

'No, I will not delay you long. In truth, if I had known you were also bound for London, I would have sought you out there.'

'Ah!' Gawain stared at him. 'You have seen your brothers, of course.'

'I have spoken to Chris,' he said shortly, sitting down

and placing his hands on his thighs. 'He must be mad, not only allowing Pip to go off with a troupe of travelling players, but also to decide to print my journal without a word to me.'

'It was meant to be a surprise,' said Gawain ruefully, scratching his jaw.

'The kind of surprise I can live without,' said Nick, scowling. 'My scribblings were not meant for other people to read. I believe that Pip and your ward have also altered my writing in an effort to improve it.'

'I can understand why you could feel vexed about that and Beth did have some reservations about printing without your permission,' said Gawain. 'But I have read the original and the other versions and was of the opinion that folk would enjoy reading it, too, but—'

'That is as it may be, but it still does not make it right that my brothers should go behind my back and do this,' interrupted Nick. 'I do not blame you and this ward of yours for seizing on it. Naturally, the pair of you only wanted to please my brothers.'

'No, that's not true,' said Gawain. 'Frankly, Beth persuaded me that there was money to be made out of your scribblings and I believed her.'

Nick stared at him fixedly. 'I have been told about Mistress Llewellyn and I'm surprised at you, Gawain, for allowing yourself to be influenced by a woman.'

'You have not seen or heard her yet,' said Gawain with a faint smile. 'I suggest, Nick, that you withhold judgement until you have met her. She will surprise you.'

'I am not as certain as you about that.'

'I would not expect you to be as you have not met her,' said Gawain. 'She will be very disappointed if you cancel the printing now. She's been through a difficult time.'

'I heard that her brother and father were killed. She has my sympathy,' said Nick.

'She has suffered more misfortune in that her business premises were deliberately set alight recently.'

Nick started forwards. 'My journal!'

Gawain smiled reassuringly. 'She had it safe in an iron chest. I tell you, Nick, she is a woman of good sense.'

'I will take your word for it and do as you suggest and speak to her. But I do not expect to be dissuaded from my decision.' He rose to his feet. 'Perhaps we can travel together, seeing as you are for London.'

'My aunt and my daughters are to accompany me,' said Gawain. 'You might prefer going on ahead.'

Nick smiled wryly. 'Thanks for the warning, but it is always good to have company on the road. I will travel with you as far as Smallhythe and then meet you in London.'

# Chapter Eleven

Beth was reading through the rough proof of some of the pages of Nicholas Hurst's journal when she heard the front door open and an unfamiliar voice enquire after the owner of the shop by name. She put down the sheets of paper and went through to the front of the building. A tall rangy figure of a man with sunburnt features and reddish-gold hair stood there. She thought he looked vaguely familiar and for a moment she was reminded of the king when he was a few years younger. Then she realised that she was being foolish to think that they could be kin for there was naught splendid about this man's attire. He was dressed neatly, but there was no touch of the peacock about him.

'You are Mistress Llewellyn?' he asked, meeting her gaze.

Beth noticed that his eyes were more green than hazel and they contained a hint of disapproval. She hoped that she did not have a smudge of ink on her nose. 'Aye, I am Beth Llewellyn,' she said warmly. 'Can I help you?'

'I have rather a large bone to pick with you,' said the stranger.

'I am sorry to hear it, sir,' she said, surprised. 'Will you explain what I have done to annoy you, Master—?'

'Nicholas Hurst,' he replied, 'and according to my brother, Christopher, you had the audacity to rewrite my words and plan to sell my journal in book form.'

Beth's face lit up and she held out her hand. 'It is a pleasure to meet you, Master Hurst! Your journal contained much that is fascinating and full of interest. It would be such a shame if you have come all this way to tell me that you are utterly against the notion of making it available to those who would wish to buy it. I believe it could make you a rich man one day.'

'If it is so fascinating and full of interest, why did you and my brother Phillip feel a need to rewrite it, Mistress Llewellyn?' he asked.

'Because, Master Hurst, even the most exciting adventures can appear dull if the writer seeps all the emotion out of events by writing about them as if he was simply walking along his own high street and they were commonplace.'

A flush darkened his cheekbones. 'I would not claim to possess the talents of Master Chaucer or Homer, Mistress Llewellyn,' he said stiffly. 'But I have only to read my own words and the memories come flooding back and I can feel the thrill and the fear.'

'But others do not possess those memories, Master

Hurst,' she said promptly. 'So that is why it was necessary for your brother and I to use our descriptive powers and fill in the gaps for your future readers.' She dropped her hand and said urgently, 'Surely you would not rob those who will never leave the security of their own hearth of the vicarious pleasure of sharing in your experiences?'

His brow knit. 'You really believe that there is a market for my ramblings?'

'Hardly ramblings, Master Hurst—that would mean your writing is all over the place, when it is set down in an orderly fashion,' said Beth. 'It just lacks—'

'There is no need for you to repeat your opinion of what it lacks, Mistress Llewellyn,' he responded. 'I must admit that I do find it difficult to accept that a young woman such as yourself is experienced enough to pass judgement in such matters.'

'That is a typical male remark,' said Beth sweetly. 'My guardian, Sir Gawain Raventon, was of a similar opinion when we first met, but if you were to speak with him now, I deem you would find that he has changed his mind concerning my abilities. I have grown up in this business, Master Hurst, and I have confidence that I know that your so-called *ramblings* could be a success.'

Nick Hurst hesitated. 'And if I refuse to permit you to use the material you have taken from my journal?'

'Then I and my guardian will miss out on recovering some of our losses and perhaps go out of business, Master Hurst,' said Beth.

He surprised her by smiling. 'You must have a lot

of faith in my ramblings if you believe they could help save your business, Mistress Llewellyn.'

'Indeed, I have,' she said firmly.

'Then I withdraw my objection and, if you are short of funds to achieve your plans, then I am prepared to invest in your company.'

She was taken aback. 'That is exceedingly generous of you, Master Hurst, but Master Christopher Hurst has already provided a sum of money for a special edition of your journal.'

'I am aware of Christopher's part in this, but my offer, Mistress Llewellyn, is more in the way of a business venture,' said Nick.

'Then you had best speak to my guardian. I am not allowed to make such decisions without his being consulted,' said Beth.

'I will certainly speak to Gawain about such an investment. It was he who suggested I visit you here.'

Beth stiffened. 'You have seen him?'

'Aye, he is on his way here now,' informed Nick. 'Is it permitted that I see your workshop?' he added, changing the subject.

'Of course you may,' said Beth, her emotions all in a whirl at the thought of seeing Gawain so soon after his last visit. What was it he had to tell her? Was it Nicholas Hurst's sudden arrival that had brought him hotfoot to London, or was it some other matter of a more worrying nature concerning Mary?

Nick cleared his throat. 'Mistress Llewellyn, you appear to have gone off into a trance.'

Beth collected herself. 'I beg your pardon! Do come

through to the back. Some pages of your journal were taken off the press a short while ago and I would be interested to see what you think of them. I may add that I am having woodcuts made of your drawings.'

He followed her through into the print room and she introduced him to her employees. As he asked questions she listened and decided that he was not only a man of adventure, but one of intelligence, and well educated if he had read Chaucer and Homer. He seemed impressed by all he saw, and afterwards she asked if he would care for some refreshments.

'I would like that,' he answered with a warm smile.

Later when they sat together, drinking wine and sharing a simple meal, she enquired after his latest adventures. So he regaled her with tales of Venice and Constantinople that held her enthralled. As he took his leave, he raised her hand to his lips and kissed it. 'It has been a pleasure making your acquaintance, Mistress Llewellyn, and I hope it will not be too long before we meet again.'

'You are welcome to call in at any time and see how your journal is progressing. I've enjoyed your visit, Master Hurst, and pray that Sir Gawain will agree to your proposal,' said Beth, seeing him out.

Once he had gone, she returned to what she was doing earlier, feeling all of a dither, wondering when she could expect Gawain.

Gawain stood in the doorway, watching Beth, who appeared completely absorbed in her task. There was no one else in the print room and for all he knew there was no one upstairs, either. What if he was their enemy? He or she could slit her throat in no time if they surprised her as they had done her father. The thought caused his blood to run cold and he realised just how much he cared for her. It was more than just a physical attraction or even the simple pleasure he found being in her company. If she were to die, then a light would go out of his life.

'Beth,' he called in a low voice.

Instantly she turned her head. Their eyes met and she saw something in his expression that caused her to rise from the stool and hurry towards him with her hands outstretched. He caught hold of them and drew her gently towards him. She rested her head against his chest. 'I know we should not be doing this, but I am so pleased to see you,' she said in a muffled voice.

'I am glad to see you, too, but you should lock the doors when you are here alone,' he chided. 'What if it had not been me, but someone who meant you harm?'

She looked up at him. 'But it is you and so I am not going to dwell on the worst that could happen to me when you hold me like this. You told me not to look on the dark side, but to have hope. What has brought you here? Was it Master Nicholas Hurst's visit?'

'So you have met him already?'

'Aye.'

'No, it was not his visit. I was already making ready to come when he arrived at the house.' His eyes darkened and then he forced a smile. 'What is your opinion of him?'

'I like him,' replied Beth, smiling. 'Although I think at first he was not prepared to like me.'

'No doubt you soon changed his mind,' said Gawain, feeling a twinge of jealousy.

'Aye, he wants to invest money in the business. I have told him he must discuss it with you.'

'He would make you a good husband,' blurted out Gawain.

A startled Beth said, 'You've changed your mind! I thought you disapproved of him as a husband. Besides, I hardly know him and I have little in the way of a dowry. As well, I thought that you and I—'

'I know. It is what I want, too, but what if—?' Gawain could not understand why he felt compelled to ask, 'What if you were to get to know him better and a dowry was of no importance to him?'

The colour rose in her cheeks. 'Why do you persist in asking me such questions? Am I and my business such a burden to you that you would prefer it if another man would take us both on? Is it that after all you realise that you love Mary despite the way she has treated you?'

'By St George, Beth, you are not a burden to me!' protested Gawain. 'It is that I do not wish to appear selfish. I want your happiness more than aught else in the world.'

'Aught else?' she asked swiftly, her heart leaping in her breast. 'What about your children's happiness? Is that not of more importance to you? And Mary—is she prepared to enter a nunnery? What did she have to say when you mentioned annulling your marriage? I mean…that is if you did speak of it to her.'

Gawain scowled. 'Of course I spoke of it to her. She is far from pleased, but I have every intention in proceeding with my plan however long it takes.'

Beth said in a voice that shook, 'Then I am prepared to be patient. Besides, I deem that Nick Hurst's life of travel is a lonely one at times, so it is only fair that he has a woman who can give her heart and soul to him.'

'You have already drawn such a conclusion after meeting him?' said Gawain, feeling that twinge of jealousy again.

Beth nodded. 'You are forgetting I have read his journal and as a woman I read between the lines. Now shall we not discuss Nick Hurst any further? How are your daughters? No doubt they were delighted to see you.'

His face softened. 'I have brought the girls to London with me. They are with Aunt Catherine as I had no intention of leaving them with Mary in case she should hide them from me with a view to blackmail me into doing what she wishes.' His expression was chilling. 'I took them to an inn and Aunt Catherine is showing them London whilst you and I talk. Mary told me something unexpected in conversation. It appears that she knew Jonathan.'

Beth started. 'What! How come? Tell me, what did she have to say about him?'

He took Beth's hand and led her towards the settle. 'Hardly anything, but she is holding something back. She says if I am kind to her then she will tell me what

it is, but so far I am none the wiser despite my allowing her to stay under my roof.' He kissed Beth's quiver-
ing fingers and then released her hand. 'What are your
thoughts on that?'

'She might have seen him at the boatyard when it
still belonged to her father?'

'Most likely, but who sent Jonathan there to have a
boat built?' said Gawain. 'Did he ever mention having
connections in Smallhythe?'

'No, but let me think,' said Beth, a difficult process
when Gawain was sitting so close to her. 'The only
connection I can think of is Father Hugh, but if that is
so, then why did he not send Jonathan to his brother
James's yard and give him the business?'

Gawain's dark brows formed a deep V as he considered her words. 'Perhaps he did, but for reasons of
his own James sent him to my father-in-law,' he said
slowly.

'I wonder what she knows that could be of help to
your investigations,' murmured Beth.

'That is what I aim to find out,' said Gawain.

He was silent for so long that Beth reached out and
touched his face with a gentle hand. 'Are you going to
tell me what you are thinking?'

'There are some things that a man should not speak
of to a lady,' he said, catching hold of her fingers and
pressing them to his lips again before getting to his feet.

She looked up at him. 'You will be careful!'

His face softened as he gazed down at her. 'I'll take
care, but it is you who needs a bodyguard and I can't
be here for you.'

'I have Sam,' said Beth.

'And where is Sam now?'

She pulled a face. 'He can't be here all the time, either.'

Gawain knew that to be true. 'I will provide you with another bodyguard.'

She raised her eyebrows. 'And where will you get him from? You have need of Tom.'

He grinned. 'You will see. In the meantime, I am hungry, so shall we go and dine at the inn where I left my aunt and my daughters?'

She did not need asking twice. She was looking forward to seeing Catherine again and the girls, too, although it would not do to get too fond of them just yet.

As it was, Gawain's aunt and daughters were not to be found at the inn, so over their meal Beth and Gawain discussed the business and the rebuilding that needed to go ahead next door now that the charred remains of the shop and print room had been cleared. The oncoming winter might cause delays, but nevertheless, come next summer, hopefully all would be completed.

When they returned to the print room it was to find Nick Hurst there, talking to the master printer. He smiled as he caught sight of them. 'I am glad I have not missed you both because I have received an urgent message from the captain whose ship I travelled on when I went to the New World and must visit him in Portsmouth.'

'Does that mean you will be off on your travels again soon?' asked Beth.

'Possibly. It all depends on what he has to say.' said Nick, his eyes warm as they rested on her face. 'But I still wish to invest money in your business, Mistress Llewellyn.'

'Oh, please, do call me Beth,' she said, smiling up at him.

He cocked an eye in Gawain's direction. 'I believe I have to deal with you.'

Gawain was filled with conflicting emotions, but knew he must trust Beth as she must trust him. Even so he still hesitated about having Nick as a partner in the business. 'Are you sure about this, Nick?' he asked.

'Aye,' he said firmly.

'Then I suppose I could take you to meet the lawyer and sort this matter out.'

As the two men headed for the door, Beth called, 'Will I see you again, Gawain, before you return to Kent?'

'Aye, after I have visited an old friend,' he replied, turning and meeting her gaze. For a moment they stared at each other, then he left.

It was two hours later that Beth heard a commotion in the shop above the sound of the printing presses and, instantly fearing the worst, she reached for the blade she had taken to keeping nearby and crept towards the door. Before she could open it, she heard a dog barking and the next moment the door was pushed open and she saw a man wearing an eye patch with a huge hound straining at the leash.

'Holy Mary, Mother of God!' exclaimed Beth. 'Who are you and why have you brought that monster on to my premises?'

'He's not a monster,' said the man, looking affronted. 'At least only to those whom I set him on. Sir Gawain sent me. Told me yer needed a protector.'

Beth stared at the dog from whose chest issued a low rumbling. 'Am I to presume that it is the dog who is to be my bodyguard? For if that is so, then you'd best tell him that I am a friend, not a foe.'

The man snorted. 'Of course, that goes without saying, Mistress Llewellyn. Although Sir Gawain sez that I'm to hang around for a while and make meself available if yer in need of a messenger or want someone followed.'

'That is generous of him,' said Beth, touched by Gawain's thoughtfulness. 'I presume you have a place you call home that you can return to when necessary?'

'Of course! I have me Adam's rib and she'd get real vexed if I didn't turn up regular. Although, having said that, she understands the nature of me work so knows I have to put me clients first.'

Beth nodded. 'I think you'd best put the monster in the yard for now or he might break something.'

'Aye, I will, but yer'd best come with us so yer can make friends with him.'

Beth opened the door that led to the yard and he forced the dog through the opening and followed after them. 'I presume the monster has a name,' she said, watching the hound as it began to explore its surroundings.

'Cerberus.'

Beth stared at him, finding it incredible that this man should know the name of the dog that guarded the entrance to Hades in Greek mythology. 'How did you come by that name for him?'

'Sir Gawain! He said that even as a puppy he was such a good guard dog that he deserved a name that was fitting.'

Beth smiled as all was made clear. 'And what is your name?'

'Benjamin,' he replied.

'Then, Benjamin, I suppose I will have to provide food for this monster of a guard dog.'

'Sir Gawain has given me coin for some good red meat, although sometimes it's best to leave him a bit hungry, but I wouldn't say no to a jug of ale and some bread and cheese,' he said, scratching his chin. 'I gets peckish handling ol' Cerberus here.'

'Well, introduce me to him and then my employees will need to be made known to him, as well, as I do not want him tearing them apart,' said Beth, hoping she would not find it too difficult handling this hound when his master was not around.

When Gawain returned later in the day it was obvious that he and Cerberus were old friends and also that Benjamin felt easy in his company. She wondered how the two men had met; as if he had read her mind, Gawain told her that Benjamin had once worked for his father, but after his sudden tragic death, he left Kent and came to London to seek his fortune. Here he met a widow who was comfortably off and married her.

'So presumably whenever you have need of someone tough and strong in London, you call upon him?' asked Beth, smiling.

'Aye, and in this case it is useful that he also remembers Father Hugh in his youth and reckons he would still recognise him. My main aim is your safety and happiness, Beth,' Gawain said, his handsome face serious.

'I know and I appreciate your concern,' she murmured, thinking how much she wanted his love and companionship. 'It has been a short visit.'

'I felt I had to talk to you face-to-face.'

'You will be careful!' she burst out, reaching out a hand to him. 'And let me know when you find out anything more?'

'Of course!' For a few precious moments he hugged her, then let her go and strode from the building.

Beth had the most horrid feeling that she might be seeing him for the last time and she wanted to run after him and tell him to stay. Then she told herself that she was being foolish. He knew to be on his guard and would have the good sense not to go out alone after dark. She wondered when she could expect to see him again.

The following week passed slowly and so did the next one. She heard naught from Gawain and wondered if he had spoken to Mary about Jonathan and if she had anything to say that was of help to him. No doubt he would have been careful about how he voiced his questions if he mentioned Father Hugh. She tried not to dwell on the thought of Gawain being at home with Mary. Beth was not sleeping well and had been feeling queasy lately and often she would lay awake, tortured by the thought that he might after all share a bed with Mary.

'You have been with her, haven't you?' Mary had accused as soon as Gawain entered his hall. She stared at him, her nostrils flaring, her fair hair untidy about her black-clad shoulders.

'If you are asking if I have been to visit my ward, then I would not deny it,' he replied, looking at her with exasperation. 'I am her guardian and there are decisions only I can make about the business.'

'I don't believe you. You are in love with her, aren't you?' cried Mary, flying at him and poking him in the chest. 'Well, she will not have you!'

'Keep your voice down,' ordered Gawain, seizing hold of her wrists. 'You forget yourself and I will not have you upsetting the girls.' He turned to Catherine. 'Aunt, take my daughters to their bedchamber.'

His aunt nodded and hurried the children away.

'You should not have taken them with you! They are my daughters!' panted Mary. 'As God is my witness, you will be punished for your wrongdoing!'

'My wrongdoing!' exclaimed Gawain, exasperated almost beyond bearing. 'I deem you are confused, Mary.

Perhaps it would be good for you to go and stay somewhere quiet where you can rest and regain your wits.'

'So you can bring her here?'

'She would not come,' retorted Gawain, hanging on to his temper. 'She has her business to oversee.'

There was the sound of a throat being cleared. 'Sir Gawain, a messenger arrived for you from the king whilst you were away. He requests your company at Eltham Palace.'

Gawain experienced a surge of relief and, releasing Mary, turned to face the manservant. 'Have me a fresh horse saddled. I will leave straight away.'

The man nodded and hurried out.

Mary stared at Gawain. 'Can I go with you?'

'No!' he replied firmly. 'You know that only at the king's invitation can you attend.'

She pouted. 'Do you not fear what I might do whilst you are away?'

He frowned. 'You would threaten me?'

She hesitated. 'What if I were to tell you that I might be able to help you find her brother's murderer?'

Gawain stilled. 'What do you know?'

'I know who sent him to Smallhythe.'

'Jonathan Llewellyn told you?'

'Aye, but not only that—I saw them together a few days later and they were…' She paused and her colour was suddenly high and she moistened her lips. 'I will say only that if Jonathan Llewellyn was to have exposed the other man for what he was as he threatened, it would have ruined him.'

Gawain's eyes narrowed. 'Who was this other man?'

'I will tell you only if you promise to have naught else to do with Mistress Llewellyn and to be a proper husband to me.'

Gawain stared at her for a long moment, thinking that the word she had hesitated to use could be *unnatural* and an almost-forgotten memory from his childhood surfaced. He felt certain the person she had seen with Jonathan was Father Hugh, as Beth had suspected. If Father Hugh had been responsible for Jonathan's death, then it was likely he had also killed Beth's father and Monsieur Le Brun. He had certainly been in France at the time.

'Well, what are you thinking?' demanded Mary, rousing him from his reverie.

'Of murder!'

'I meant about giving *her* up!' cried Mary.

Gawain's face darkened and his eyes glinted. 'I made a promise to her father that I intend to keep. As for this other matter, I would not speak of it to anyone else if I were you. I have a fair idea of whom it is you refer to.'

She paled. 'I don't see how you can. But never mind that now! Why can't you keep the promise you made to me at the altar?'

'You mean just as you did?' he said scornfully. 'Besides, you have admitted in writing that our marriage was bigamous.'

She licked her lips. 'You will regret it if you don't do what I ask.'

'You are a fool to threaten me. I give you fair warning—if you were to attempt to hurt the girls or take them away from me again, then it will be you who will be sorry,' said Gawain softly.

Mary stared at him, then turned on her heel and rushed from the hall.

Gawain wasted no more time, but prepared to leave to join the king's court. As he headed north he was considering exactly what he would tell Beth about her half-brother and Father Hugh when next he saw her, which regrettably might not be for some time.

Beth was thinking of Gawain when she had a visit from Nick Hurst, who called to see how the printing of his journal was progressing. His arrival was greeted by a flurry of barking from Cerberus and she had to make him known to the hound. She had thought Nick would be off on his travels again, but he told her that he was not planning to leave England before spring and until then he would be staying in Greenwich. He asked after Gawain and she told him that she had not heard from him. He looked surprised, but did not comment.

A week later Nick called again and could not conceal his delight when he held the first complete copy of his original journal, beautifully bound in vellum, in his hand. 'I cannot wait to see Christopher's face when he sees this,' he said.

'I am glad you are pleased with it,' said a wan-faced Beth.

'More than pleased,' he said, turning over a page and admiring a woodcut of one of his drawings. 'I must tell you that I saw Gawain in Greenwich village,' he added casually, glancing at her.

Her heart seemed to flip over. 'How—how did he appear?' she asked. 'Was he well?'

'I would say he has much on his mind. He would have walked past me if I had not hailed him.'

'Did he say what he was doing in Greenwich?'

'Apparently the king had sent for him and he is staying at Eltham Palace nearby.'

'I—I see. That must be why I have not heard from him.'

'If I see him again, do you have a message for him?' Nick's eyes were intent on her face.

She hesitated. 'You can tell him that I hope all is well with him.'

'You do not look well,' said Nick with concern. 'You have no roses in your cheeks.'

'I am little off my food, but it is naught to worry about,' she answered easily. 'No doubt you could tell him how the work is progressing next door and naturally you will show him your printed journal.'

'Of course, I will show everyone I know and tell them that soon they will be able to buy a much cheaper version of it for themselves and their friends,' he said, smiling.

'That is good. They should be ready in a few days' time.'

'November, then,' said Nick. 'I look forward to seeing you again and perhaps I will have another proposal to put before you.'

Beth caught her breath and for a moment she thought

that perhaps the proposal would be one of marriage. Then she told herself that was unlikely when they scarcely knew each other, even though his brothers had probably mentioned she was in the market for a husband. She prayed that she would hear from Gawain before Nick's next visit.

A few days later she was surprised to have a visit from Phillip Hurst. His arrival, too, was greeted by barking from her watchdog. After making sure Cerberus knew him to be a friend, Phillip told her that he had returned home to visit his family. Having heard that the stirring tale of his brother's adventures could be in print any day now, he could not wait to see a copy. She handed him one and, despite the worry and indecision that was nagging her, could not prevent smiling at the expression on his face as he gingerly turned a page.

'It's marvellous,' he said. 'I cannot wait to show it to my friends. I am immensely proud of it. By the way, I saw Gawain yesterday down by the river at Greenwich.'

She stiffened. 'He is still at court?'

'Was. The king had given him leave to return home that day.'

Beth clasped her hands tightly together. 'Did you tell him that you planned to come here?'

'I did mention it. He asked whether Nick would be accompanying me. I told him not this time, but that no doubt he would be visiting you shortly.' Phillip smiled, but said no more.

'Gawain did not give you a message for me?' she asked.

'No.'

Beth was hurt and wondered if Gawain believed that Nick's visits to her were more than purely business. Did he deem her to be so fickle? Suddenly she came to a decision. After Phillip had left, she went upstairs and, before she could change her mind, took a sheet of paper and wrote swiftly to Gawain that something had happened that made it vital that she see him. Then she sealed the missive and called Sam and asked him to deliver it into only Sir Gawain's hands at Raventon Hall.

When Gawain came out of the boatyard at Smallhythe after having visited James, he was deep in thought as he walked along the river. He was surprised to be hailed by Sam, but was glad to see him. He wasted no time greeting him. 'You have news for me from your mistress?' he asked eagerly.

'Aye, Sir Gawain. Glad I am to see you here. It will save me the journey to Raventon Hall,' said Sam, taking the missive from a pouch and handing it to him.

'You will come into the yard and partake of a drink of beer and a hot pasty? Your mistress will surely want a reply to this message, although I would prefer to visit her myself,' said Gawain. After giving an order for refreshments for Sam, Gawain broke the seal and, spreading the paper on the table, began to read:

My dear Gawain,
Something momentous has happened and it is urgent that I see you before making any decisions

that will change both our lives irretrievably. Do not keep me waiting for time is of the essence.
Yours, Beth

Gawain wished she had written more. Had this to do with Nick Hurst? Had he proposed marriage? He clenched and unclenched his fists. He must see her. He went and spoke to Sam. 'I will have to go to London. I would appreciate it, Sam, if you would make the journey to Raventon and inform my aunt that an urgent message has arrived for me that needs my immediate attention. You will stay there until my return.'

'Aye, sir,' said Sam.

Gawain gave orders to those in the boatyard and then, taking a couple of men with him, set sail for London.

## Chapter Twelve

Gawain arrived the following evening and, leaving the men in charge of the boat, made his way to Pater Noster Row. He was fortunate to find Beth upstairs partaking of supper in the room that had once been her father's bedchamber. She looked so relieved to see him that he wondered how he could have doubted her and would have kissed her there and then if it had not been for Jane's presence, but the maid instantly made herself scarce.

Then Gawain was unable to resist taking Beth in his arms. Only for a moment did she succumb to his embrace, then she held him off. 'There is something important I must tell you, Gawain.'

He released her abruptly. 'Has it to do with Nick Hurst? Has he asked you to marry him?'

'No, but I suspect he might do so.' She wrapped her arms around herself and gazed at him. 'Phillip was here and he told me that you knew he was coming to see me. Yet you sent no message for me. Why?'

'Because he told me that Nick had been to see you. I thought that perhaps you should have the opportunity to get to know Nick better,' said Gawain, removing his hat and running a hand over his dark curls.

'Why the change in you? Have you spoken to the Cardinal about Mary and he has told you her return means that your marriage cannot be annulled?'

Gawain frowned. 'It is not as certain as it was before.'

Her bottom lip quivered. 'So you decided that I could be happy married to Nick, knowing I have strong feelings for you. Are you happy living with Mary whilst you have such feelings for me? That is, if you still have them.'

He frowned. 'Of course I still care for you. You must know I'm not happy with Mary.'

'I know nothing of the sort. I can only imagine what is happening between you and her,' said Beth.

His frown deepened. 'What is this about, Beth? Surely you don't believe that I am sleeping with Mary?'

'Why not? You are a man and have needs!'

'I am not sleeping with her,' said Gawain, grabbing Beth by the arms. 'I do not want her! I no longer regard her as my wife.'

'Your mistress, then?'

He swore. 'What is this about, Beth?' he demanded for the second time. 'This is not like you.'

'No.' She gazed up into his worried face and tears

filled her eyes. 'But then I have never been with child before. Your child, Gawain.'

He stared at her and there came such a light into his eyes that a thrill of delight went through her. Then the light in his eyes died and he released her. 'What do you want me to do?'

'Do not suggest that I marry Nick to legitimise our child,' she warned.

'I would not. It would be dishonest if you were to make a cuckold of him.'

'I agree. You might say that even the king has foisted a bastard child on his mistress's husband, but—'

'But I am no king and I admire and like Nick Hurst,' said Gawain.

'Then I must make it obvious to him that I am not in the market for a husband, despite what his brothers might have said to him,' said Beth. 'I must face the wagging tongues of my employees and neighbours alone. No doubt the scandal will be a five-day wonder and most probably I will lose the respect of some of our customers, but what does that matter?' she cried. 'I always planned to remain a spinster.'

Gawain seized hold of her again and pressed a kiss on her lips. 'Do you really believe that I would let you face the future alone? You do not have to live here for the business to prosper. I will buy you a house where you and our child can live and—'

'Visit me when you can?' retorted Beth. 'I will not be your mistress! Besides it being immoral, it is not a position I wish to fill. I love you and I want to be your wife and for us to live like a proper family. I do not wish for our son to be called a bastard child. He is worth more than that and is entitled to your name.' Her voice cracked and she could not go on.

Gawain wrapped his arms around her trembling body with his head in a whirl. Beth loved him—how could he fail her in this? 'I will speak to Wolsey again and tell him that you are carrying my child and that we are desperate to provide it with a proper family home.'

'Mary will fight against it tooth and nail,' warned Beth.

'It will avail her nothing, even if she were to go to Father Hugh and try to persuade him to help her prevent the dissolution of our so-called marriage.'

'You have spoken to her about him?'

'No, but she told me that she saw Jonathan with the man she suspects could be our murderer, but she laid conditions on naming him to me. I refused to do what she asked, but I told her that I had a fair idea of the person responsible and that did not please her at all.'

'You mentioned none of this to Wolsey?'

'I saw him only for a short time and was more concerned with terminating my relationship to Mary. Besides, I still have no proof that Father Hugh is our murderer.'

Beth nodded. 'So what will you do next?'

Gawain hesitated. 'I must return home and see that the children are safe and I will send Catherine with Sam to be with you. She knows how we feel about each other and I am certain will be of support to you in this time of your great need until we can be together as husband and wife.'

'I would like that,' said Beth with a sigh. 'Yet I cannot help wondering how your children will feel about it all—they will miss your aunt and she them.'

Gawain touched Beth's cheek with a gentle hand. 'You're always considering others, but now you must think of yourself and our child. You must not worry. I will ensure that all will be well.'

Beth could only accept his word. They talked for a while until he had to take his leave of her. Only after he had gone did she wonder how long it would be before she would see him again. Yet whilst she hated being parted from him, she looked forward to welcoming Catherine to London.

Several days passed and still there was no sign of Sam or Catherine. Then she had a visit from Nick Hurst. At any other time she would have welcomed him, but her nerves were like tightly coiled springs, wondering how she could prevent him from proposing marriage to her without spoiling the friendship she felt towards him. But his first words took her aback as they were not at all what she expected.

'Is Gawain here?'

'He was here a few days ago, but he returned home. Why do you ask? Have you seen him again?'

Nick frowned. 'Obviously, you have not heard the news from Raventon Hall?'

She was filled with apprehension. 'What news? Tell me!' she urged.

'Perhaps after all it is only a rumour, but it was brought to us by a ship's captain from Smallhythe and he seemed very certain that what he told us was true,' said Nick.

'What is true?' demanded Beth. 'Please tell me.'

'Gawain's wife is dead.'

'What?' gasped Beth, shocked to the core. 'How?'

'She was found at the foot of the stairs. Mistress Ashbourne is abed, as it appears she also fell, and I was told that she was still unconscious.'

Beth wrung her hands. 'But that is terrible. She was supposed to be coming to visit me. I must go to her.' She turned and would have hurried upstairs to pack when Nick stayed her with a hand.

'Do you really think you should?'

She stared at him and what she saw in his face frightened her. 'Why do you say that? What is on your mind?'

He hesitated. 'It is possible that Gawain might come here to bring you the news himself.'

'He would not leave his aunt.'

'But he has done so because he was not to be found at home and the children are also missing.'

Fear gripped Beth's heart like a steely hand. 'What are you suggesting? That he has something to do with his wife's death?'

'Why should you think that?'

'I didn't say I did, but do you?'

'It seems strange that he and the children are missing,' he said slowly. 'It was known that he was extremely fond of his aunt and there have been rumours lately, during the months his wife was away, supposedly tending a dying aunt, that in truth she was living with another man who has since died.'

Beth took a step back. 'Who started such a rumour?'

'Who can say? But it's also being said that during her absence you and Gawain grew fond of each other. Is this the truth, Beth?'

'He is my guardian, so it is natural that we grew close during that time,' said Beth in a low voice. 'My father and brother had both been murdered and I needed a man's protection.'

'Pip and Chris both believe it to be more than that between the pair of you. I need to know the truth, Beth.'

She was silent, wondering how much she could trust Nick. She had a great respect and liking for him, but if she told him the truth then it would give him a reason to believe that Gawain might have possibly murdered Mary. She did not believe it for one moment. If Mary had made it her business to seek out Father Hugh and tell him of her conversation with Gawain, then the priest might have killed her.

'It is true that Gawain and I care for each other. Mary told him that the man for whom she left him was her true husband, their having made vows when they were children. Then Mary returned and Gawain was determined to have the marriage annulled, believing her to have committed bigamy. He had a missive that she sent him and this he showed to Cardinal Wolsey. There is no reason for him to murder her. I deem the person guilty is the one who killed my half-brother Jonathan and my father because they knew something about him that would ruin him.'

'Do you have proof of this?'

'Not yet, but Mary told Gawain that she had seen

the suspect with my brother and they were quarrel-
ling. Surely someone must have seen what happened
at Raventon Hall?' added Beth.

'One would think so, but people seem to believe
there were no witnesses to what happened.'

'Were there any visitors to Raventon Hall that day?'

Before Nick could answer there came the sound of
barking and an angry voice outside. Beth and Nick
turned and stared at the door as it was thrust open.

'That dog should be destroyed,' said Father Hugh
in a furious voice, entering the room, clutching a torn
sleeve. He ripped off the strip of dangling cloth and
flung it on the floor.

He was the last person Beth expected to see and she
was glad that she did not have to face him alone. Yet
what was he doing here? Surely it could be no coin-
cidence that he should call here on the day she had
received the news that Mary was dead and Gawain and
the girls missing.

Father Hugh stared at Nick. 'Do I know you?'

'I saw you recently at Greenwich,' replied Nick.
'And, if I rightly recall, the experience was not a happy
one.'

Father Hugh's lips tightened. 'You're one of the Hurst
brothers. What are you doing here?'

'I deem that to be none of your business,' drawled
Nick.

'If you're part of this plot, I could make it my business,' blustered the priest. 'When did you last see Sir
Gawain?'

'That I cannot remember,' said Nick, giving him a contemptuous look.

Father Hugh glared at him and then turned his attention to Beth. 'And you, Mistress Llewellyn?'

Beth's heart was beating so heavily that she felt a need to place her hand over her breast. 'I have not seen him for several days,' she said breathlessly. 'I don't believe Sir Gawain is involved in any plot.'

'The king has issued a warrant for his arrest.'

The colour drained from Beth's face and she reached out and clutched Nick's sleeve and his arm went round her. 'For what reason?' he asked.

'The murder of his wife,' said Father Hugh, his eyes narrowing as he stared at the pair of them.

'I don't believe it,' said Beth, recovering herself. 'What proof have you?'

'You think I would tell you so you can run off and warn him in order for him to try to overset what I have to say,' he sneered. 'The pair of you want to get married so he would rid himself of his wife. Now tell me where he is or you will be arrested too.'

'Mistress Llewellyn does not know where Sir Gawain is so that could prove difficult,' said Nick.

'And how do you know that?' asked Father Hugh, turning on him.

'Because she had no knowledge of what happened at Raventon Hall when I arrived here,' said Nick. 'And let us be honest, I did not witness what happened—all I have heard are rumours. So tell us, how do you know of them?'

'I will not tell you anything,' said the priest, clenching a fist. 'But I warn you, Master Hurst, if you try to get in my way by protecting this young woman and concealing Sir Gawain's whereabouts from me, then he will not be the only man to go to the gallows.' He turned on his heel and the skirts of his robes whirled about his ankles as he hurried from the room.

Beth released her grip on Nick's sleeve. 'I have to find Gawain and warn him!'

'That is exactly what that priest wants you to do,' said Nick, his brow furrowed in thought. 'If the king has truly issued a warrant for Gawain's arrest, then he would not have sent Father Hugh without a couple of yeomen to accompany him and assist with the arrest.'

Relief flooded Beth's face. 'You are saying that the king knows nothing of this and that Father Hugh is trying to set a trap for Gawain?'

'It is possible that his Majesty has been informed, but who would take the news to him? If he does know, then I do not doubt he will want Gawain to be found to prove his innocence. After all, he was still at court a short while ago.'

Beth knew this to be true and, feeling a little better but still weak at the knees, she sat down. 'Where can he be? And where is my servant, Sam? He took a message for me to Raventon Hall and was supposed to be escorting Mistress Ashbourne here. Is it possible that he saw what happened and is with Gawain and the children?'

'It's no good our trying to piece together what happened,' said Nick. 'If Gawain and the children are with your servant, then no doubt they will come here eventually.'

'And I will be waiting for them,' said Beth, tilting her chin.

'Would you like me to stay with you?' asked Nick.

She shook her head. 'I have appreciated your support, but I would not keep you from whatever other business you might have in the city.'

Nick gave a wry smile and, taking her by the shoulders, kissed her on both cheeks. 'If they do not arrive, then I suggest you come and stay at our family home in Greenwich. You can inform those in the printing workshop of your whereabouts. If Gawain does send Sam to you with a message, they will tell him where you can be found. I do not like leaving you alone in such circumstances.'

'You are kind, but I must stay here,' said Beth, her voice softening. 'Besides, I am not alone. I have Jane and the hound and, if needs must, I can send one of the men when they return from the dinner to fetch Benjamin.'

Nick nodded and stepped away from her. 'I bear you a great affection, Beth, but I can see that the death of Gawain's wife has changed everything. But my offer still holds. If you are in need and others cannot help you, come to Greenwich and I and my brothers will certainly do what we can to support you.'

She blinked back tears and thanked him warmly and saw him out before going back inside, thinking that it was going to be a very long worrying day if she did not have news of Gawain soon.

* * *

Gawain had left his boat moored at the quayside and had strode up with Sam from the Thames when he noticed Father Hugh hurrying along in front of them. His lips tightened and he laid a hand on Sam's sleeve and indicated the priest with a nod of his head. Sam nodded and a few moments later they watched him enter Beth's premises by the front door. The next moment it sounded as if all hell had broken loose and, even from where he stood, Gawain could hear the priest's shouts of complaint. He grinned, thinking that at least Beth's other protector was performing his duties satisfactorily. He told Sam to stay where he was and follow the priest when he emerged from the house whilst he went round the back. To his exasperation, he discovered the gates to the yard locked, but at least it told him that Beth was being careful to watch her back. He guessed that he was going to have to climb over the wall.

Beth noticed Cerberus's head tilt to one side and she tensed. Until then he had been growling and tearing with his sharp teeth at the fabric from Father Hugh's sleeve. Now he whined and went over to the door that led to the yard. Obviously a friend, she thought, relieved. Perhaps one of the men was returning early from his dinner. She went over to unlock the door and relief flooded her as she recognised the tall strong figure standing there.

'Beth, love, are you all right? Or is that damned priest hiding somewhere?'

She threw herself into Gawain's arms and he hugged

her close and kissed her. That kiss seemed to go on for ever and then his mouth lifted from hers and he smiled down at her. 'That is the kind of welcome I have dreamed of.'

'I am so glad to see you. I have been hearing such rumours that I have been frightened for you,' she said huskily.

His expression altered and his mouth was set grim. 'What did Father Hugh have to say?'

'Not just him, but Nick Hurst who arrived before him. He told me that he had heard rumours that Mary was dead and your aunt was unconscious and that you and the children were missing.'

'It's true that Mary is dead,' said Gawain with a sigh. 'And, God forgive me, when I heard the news, all I could think of was that now I'd be able to marry you without further difficulty.'

She gave him a luminous smile, her arms looping about his neck. 'So what do we do next?'

'We can marry this day secretly. I want you to bear my name just in case aught should happen to me,' said Gawain.

She clutched him tightly. 'Do not say that! As soon as Nick Hurst informed me of your wife's death and told of the rumours that she had left you for another man and that we had become fond of each other in her absence, I have feared for your safety.'

Gawain swore.

'There is more,' said Beth. 'Father Hugh told me that the king has issued a warrant for your arrest.'

Gawain's eyes glinted. 'He said it to frighten you.'

A shadow crossed his handsome face. 'I was nowhere near the house when Mary died. I was on my way back from the Weald and found Tom in the stables. He was making ready the horses to escort my aunt to London. We were met at the front door by the girls, who were almost speechless with shock. They had seen their mother die.'

'So Mary's death was an accident?'

'No!' His expression was suddenly fierce. 'Lydia managed to tell me that she saw a woman hit Mary on the head and send her crashing to the floor. Apparently she was hit again whilst she was down. The children were upstairs with my aunt and they saw what happened. Catherine immediately went to Mary's aid, only to end up wrestling with the woman. Lydia swore that she was wearing a wig and it slipped. My aunt came off the worst of it and I found her unconscious near Mary's body. I sent one of the servants to fetch the physician and Tom and I carried my aunt to her bed. I would not have left her without making sure she was well taken care of.' He made no mention of Mary's body, which had been placed in the family vault.

'Where are the children now? Were they able to describe the woman?'

'Aye, and interestingly her description fits the one seen going into your father's tent in France and on the night of the fire,' he said grimly. 'Lydia said she was as strong as a man and naturally that set me thinking.'

Beth nodded. 'You mean it was a man in disguise and that was the reason for the wig, not that a woman might not have lost her hair due to some foul disease.'

'Aye! If only I had arrived back earlier, I would have caught him in the act and known for certain his identity. As it is, I cannot prove it was Father Hugh.'

Beth said slowly, 'Yet it seems extremely likely. At least you have witnesses to prove that you could not have killed Mary,' she added.

Gawain's expression hardened. 'I want him to pay for these murders and for making you suffer and terrifying the girls.'

'But how can we prove he is guilty?' she asked. 'You must admit he is crafty.'

'Not crafty enough. How is it he managed to get here before I did with the news that Mary was dead and the king had issued a warrant for my arrest? The king has moved his court to Westminster. He will return to Greenwich for the twelve days of Christmas. I deem Father Hugh was unaware of the king's movements, so I doubt even Wolsey knows aught of this, never mind Henry. The only way Father Hugh could have known of Mary's death was if he was in the vicinity at the time. Possibly Mary wrote to him. We can only guess. I have thought that he might have murdered Mary not only to silence her, but to implicate me. The same with Cedric and the dagger, only his plans didn't work out the way he wanted. I deem he panicked when he heard mine and the men's voices outside the hall before he could do anything about the girls.'

'He must have scurried out by another door and instantly begun to spread rumours,' said Beth, 'so providing people with a motive for why you should want

Mary dead. Yet he must have known you had an alibi and the children witnessed Mary's murder?'

'Aye,' he rasped. 'We have to start a counter-rumour, but must be prepared for him reacting by spreading another to counter ours—maybe that Tom and my children and the servants would cover up the crime because they are in my power.'

Fear trickled down her spine. 'People can be so easily convinced that a falsehood is truth if it is repeated often enough. We must catch him before he can react,' she said swiftly.

Gawain said, 'You must not worry for yours and the child's sake.' He kissed her tenderly. 'I have set Sam to watch him. I will know where he goes this day.'

'Good. I have one more question. Where are the children?'

'I wanted them in a safe place, so I took them to the convent of the order of St Clare at Aldgate. The chaplain to the Sisters is a kinsman of mine. He used to be a priest, but is now a Franciscan friar—he is licensed to perform the sacraments. He will marry us this day.'

'Without banns?'

'Aye.' He chucked her under the chin.

'He can be trusted?'

'You doubt my judgement?' said Gawain, raising an eyebrow. 'Not all priests are corrupt and live in sin and luxury.'

'Of course not! I have always admired the Franciscans for their way of life,' she said.

He released her at the sound of footsteps outside. 'There are matters I must see to now, but I will return at dusk. Wear your prettiest gown and don't forget a warm cloak and to pack extra clothing.'

Gawain exchanged greetings with a couple of the men as they entered and slipped past them, hurrying down the yard. Beth prayed he would be careful and watch his back. After a few words with her employees, she hurried upstairs to speak to Jane. Her heart was aflutter at the thought that tonight would be her wedding night and that her child would bear Gawain's name.

Beth had been pacing the floor for the last half-hour. She felt as tense as a coiled spring despite her trust in Gawain to keep his word that they would wed that day. She had told the men to go early and soon it would be dusk. Jane was sitting in front of the fire, stirring a pan of pottage, her eye half on the hound. Both women knew that he would alert them to any visitors, welcome or not.

'You will be all right here?' asked Beth.

'I'll be fine, Mistress Beth. I just wish I could come with you and see you wed,' said Jane, sniffing back a tear.

'We shall see what Sir Gawain has to say when he arrives,' said Beth.

Not for one moment had she considered keeping the truth from Jane, knowing that she would support her in whatever way was needful. The maid had helped Beth into a gown of saffron linsey-woolsey with a low square neckline, trimmed with lace. The removable sleeves were full and attached at the elbow with ribbons. There were also ribbons in her chestnut hair that she had left loose. She was wearing stout boots because she did not want her fine leather shoes spoilt if she went and stepped in something nasty in the dark, so she had placed the latter in a drawstring cloth bag. She also had a blade in a leather sheath attached to her belt from which also hung her purse. Her hooded thick winter cloak was ready at hand for her to snatch up the moment Gawain came for her.

Suddenly Cerberus's head shot up and he stood up and whined. Instantly Jane removed the pot from the fire and looked at her mistress. Beth picked up her cloak with a hand that quivered and wrapped it around her. She told Jane to wait at the top of the stairs. Then she hurried downstairs with the dog at her heels. 'Who is there?' she called.

'It is I, Gawain.'

Hastily Beth opened the door to his shadowy cloaked figure and instantly Cerberus pushed past her and went out into the yard. Gawain smiled at her. 'I am glad to see that you are ready.'

'Aye, but Jane wishes to come. Is that acceptable to you?'

'Of course she can come,' said Gawain. 'Benjamin is also accompanying us.'

Beth called up to Jane, who instantly seized her cloak and came running down the stairs. The three of them stepped outside and Jane made a grab for Cerberus's collar, but the hound dodged her. 'Bad dog,' scolded Jane. 'You must go back inside.'

'Leave him be, Jane,' murmured Beth. 'Is he not my guard dog?'

'Indeed, he is,' said Gawain. 'Let him come with us.'

Beth drew her cloak tightly about her against the cold wind. Gawain took her hand and drew it through his arm. 'Benjamin, you have your orders.'

Benjamin slipped away and the hound followed him. Jane clutched her mistress's cloak. 'Don't want to lose you in the darkness,' she whispered.

'Just let us not draw attention to ourselves,' murmured Gawain. 'Don't talk unless it is needful.'

So they did not speak as they made their way through the dark narrow streets. Beth was aware of the sound their footsteps and their breathing, as well of the hound growling in his throat every now and then when close by there came a slithering or a scurrying of feet. Several times she was tempted to glance over her shoulder, knowing there was always the chance of attack by footpads if one was out after dusk. She was glad of Gawain's muscular arm beneath her fingers and remembered that time in France when she had been tense with nerves and shock and depended on the strength of this man to protect her. She thought of her father and hoped he could see her from heaven and be pleased that she was marrying the man to whom he had entrusted her future.

If the evening had not already taken on an air of unreality, it would have done so when they came to a door set in a wall. Gawain lifted the large handle and banged it. He was obviously expected because the door was opened almost immediately by a religious. Smiling, she ushered them inside and they were led across a courtyard to a building that loomed up dark against the starlit sky. At the door they were greeted by a man dressed in the brown habit of a Franciscan friar.

'Beth, this is my kinsman, Brother Thomas,' said Gawain easily.

The friar took Beth's hand and held it a moment. 'I am pleased to welcome you here, Mistress Llewellyn. Please, follow me.'

Gawain took Beth's hand and she gripped it tightly as they hurried after the friar. They, in their turn, were trailed by Jane. The interior felt damp and was lit by just a few candles. The musky smell of incense hung in the air and a vase of autumn leaves and berries stood at the foot of a statue of St Clare.

The service did not take long and Beth and Gawain's eyes never left the other's face as they plighted their troth, taking each other for better and for worse, for richer and for poorer, in sickness and in health, till death parted them. Unfortunately, Gawain had forgotten to buy a ring, so with a teasing smile, Beth tugged the one that had belonged to her mother from a finger and gave it to him. With a wry smile he pushed it on the third finger of her left hand before raising it to his lips and kissing it.

Beth heard a sob escape Jane as Brother Thomas pronounced them man and wife. She remembered how she had made a list of those traits in a husband that she considered most desirable. Now she knew that which was most needful in a marriage: a companion whom you could love without reservation and who would love you for yourself. Although Gawain had yet to say he loved her—but how could she doubt him when he had done so much in order for them to marry? Even so, she experienced a little ache inside her, wanting to hear him say those words. They left the chapel as they had entered it, hand in hand. As they walked through the darkness to the guest house attached to the abbey, Gawain told Beth that in the morning he would return with her and the children to Raventon Hall.

'I deem it likely that going back there could give them bad dreams, but sooner or later they will have to return home, so best they do so in our company. Lydia is also worried about my aunt.'

'You will not tell them yet that we are married?' she asked, gazing up into his shadowy features. 'That would be too much for them to cope with so soon after losing their mother.'

'I would not dispute that and, knowing that your return so soon to Raventon Hall might set tongues wagging, it is perhaps sensible that we keep it quiet for a while,' he said. 'Still, I deem it best for us to behave boldly and face up to people and speak the truth about what the children saw. We must let our local people have a description of the murderer and that will make them sit up and think. Besides, I must talk to my aunt if she has gained consciousness. The servants and our neighbours surely know how fond you were of each other when you stayed there during the summer and that should be reason enough to explain your presence at Raventon.'

'Obviously you believe it will be safer there than if we remain in London?'

'Aye,' said Gawain. 'Sam sent a boy with a message, telling me that Father Hugh did not go to York Place as I expected, but to a house a short distance away from Pater Noster Row in Cheapside. It is possible that he plans to remain nearby so as to keep an eye on your home. I have sent Benjamin to relieve Sam so he can have some rest. It is possible that during the night hours Father Hugh might decide that it is safe for him to slip away unnoticed.'

He fell silent as they reached the lodging house and were ushered inside, followed by Jane. 'We are staying here tonight?' whispered Beth, gazing about the dimly lit entrance hall.

Gawain brought his head close to hers. 'I know it is our wedding night and it is my dearest wish to spend it with you, but—'

'We will be sleeping in cells,' said Beth, unable to conceal her regret.

'Alas, but I promise you I will make that first night we spend together as man and wife unforgettable,' he whispered in her ear.

She could feel herself blushing. 'I already deem that this evening has been unforgettable. Now you must reassure your children that you are here for them.'

'You will come with me now?' said Gawain, drawing a little away from her.

She shook her head. 'It is you that they need, not me.

Pray God there will be time enough in the future for them to get to know me and become used to the idea that I am to be their new mother.'

He gazed down at her and squeezed her hand. 'You are right. At the moment they could be a little jealous of you. I do not think all women would understand that.'

Two of the nuns suddenly appeared and Beth knew it was time for her and her husband to take their leave of each other. 'Until the morrow,' she said.

He nodded, regret in his dark blue eyes.

Beth sighed and went with one of the nuns to her solitary cell. It was not the wedding night she had imagined earlier in the day but she looked forward to Gawain keeping his promise.

## Chapter Thirteen

Beth ran through the swirling sleet towards the entrance of Raventon Hall with her arm held protectively around a struggling Lydia, whom she had covered with a fold of her own cloak, and Cerberus was at her heels. Jane followed Beth, carrying Tabitha. It was only three in the afternoon, but it seemed much later. To her dismay Beth found the front door barred to them and had need to hammer on it and shout to be let in.

It seemed an age before she heard dragging footsteps approach the door and quavering tones asked who it was demanding entry. 'Sir Gawain is not at home, so if you wish to speak to him, please go away.'

With a flood of relief Beth recognised the voice and obviously so did Lydia, for she cried out, 'Aunt Catherine, please let us in or we will die of the cold out here!'

'Child, is that you or someone pretending to be you?' asked Catherine.

'It really is me,' shrilled Lydia, 'and Tabitha and Mistress Llewellyn and her Jane are with me whilst Papa and Benjamin have taken the horses to the stables.'

Then came Tom's voice from inside. 'Mistress Ashbourne, you should have stayed in your bedchamber and left this to me or one of the servants,' he scolded, drawing back the bolts.

'Don't fuss, Tom. A miracle has happened and they are returned to me. I—I cannot believe it,' said Catherine, as the door opened. 'But what was my nephew thinking of travelling on—on such a cruel bitter day?' she gasped as a flurry of sleet hit her in the face.

Beth and Lydia almost fell inside. The hound slunk past them, followed by Jane and Tabitha. As soon as Beth recovered her balance, she put her arms around the older woman and hugged her. 'I feared the worst and I am so pleased to see you on your feet.'

'It was no thanks to that devil in skirts,' said Catherine fiercely, who had a bandage tied round her head.

Lydia tugged on her skirt and Catherine place a hand on her head.

'You remember?' said Beth.

Catherine snorted. 'Not immediately. I woke up, but then I heard his voice in my ear and I knew it was him come back to haunt me.'

For a moment Beth wondered if the knock on the head had affected the older woman's wits. 'I don't understand,' she said.

Catherine freed herself from Beth's embrace and said, 'Remember my telling you how during the twelve days of Christmas, we'd have the mummers come dressed up in costumes and some would wear masks and one in particular frightened me? I'll never forget that hissing voice. It reminded me of a serpent. I am now convinced it was Hugh Tyler!'

'You are certain?' asked Beth, her eyes alight.

'I'd swear it on holy writ that it was him then and now. And him a priest, too,' she said with a sniff. 'He's not a man to be trusted and I was a fool to have not seen his true colours earlier.'

Lydia tugged hard on Catherine's skirts. 'Why must you speak to her? You are *my* aunt and you should be heeding me!'

Catherine looked down at Lydia. 'Oh, by the virgin, you look like a drowned rat! Now over to the fire with you. Where is Tabitha?'

'I have her here, Mistress Ashbourne,' panted Jane, setting the little girl down.

'Well, take her over to the fire quickly, too,' said Catherine. 'Then, off with their clothes and into dry night rails. They can go into my bed, which will be warmer for them than their own.'

'I'll see it's done,' said Tom, hurrying from the hall.

Beth would have placed her arm around Lydia and ushered her over to the fire, but the girl shrugged it off and clung to Catherine. Beth sighed, recalling how Gawain's elder daughter had resented any attention that her father had given to her on the journey. She guessed that it was going to be more difficult for Lydia to accept her than she had thought.

The older woman let out a yelp at the sight of the

hound stretched out in front of the hearth. 'Where did that monster come from?' she cried.

'He belongs to Benjamin, who is in Papa's employ, and is here to protect us if Papa is out on the Weald or at the shipyard,' said Lydia. 'He can bark very loudly.'

'My nephew has dogs. I only hope this hound does not eat them alive,' said Catherine.

'I should not think so once Ben or Gawain introduces them to Cerberus,' said Beth, following them over to the fire.

Catherine gazed at the hound doubtfully. 'That is an unusual name for a hound.'

Beth would have explained if Lydia had not said, 'My fingers are frozen, Aunt Catherine. Will you help me remove my cloak and hat?'

'Of course, my little chick. You know I will do anything for you. Now here comes Tabitha, we must not neglect her. Beth, perhaps you can help her.'

Tabitha shot a glance at her sister and then pressed her face against Jane's stomach. 'Don't want her. Jane will help me.'

Jane glanced at her mistress. Beth found herself blinking back unwelcome tears. 'Go ahead, Jane,' she said gruffly. 'I will see if Sir Gawain is on his way.'

Beth hurried away before Lydia decided to change her mind and follow her to demand her father's immediate attention instead of that of his aunt. Beth left the hall by the rear entrance and sped along a passage and out of a side door that led into the stable yard. She stood in the doorway, gazing towards the stables and thinking about the actions that Gawain had taken on the way here. He had spoken to several people of his acquaintance, telling them of the mysterious woman whom it was suspected was a man in disguise and responsible for murdering his wife and leaving his aunt unconscious. He had given a description of the suspect and said that he planned to give a reward to anyone who might have seen this person and had information that could lead to an arrest. He did not doubt he would get some folk coming, saying they'd had sighting of the murderer just to gain a reward, but maybe amongst them there would be someone who had seen the culprit. Gawain also hoped that his action would help to quash the earlier rumours implicating himself. Beth did not have long to wait before her husband appeared. Thinking of him in such a way still felt unreal in the circumstances, she thought, watching him come striding across the yard.

'What are you doing standing here, Beth?' he demanded, ushering her inside and kissing her swiftly. 'You should be by the fire,' he added, holding her tightly for a moment. 'You must take care of yourself and not forget the babe you carry. Or is it that you had bad news for me?' he added anxiously.

'No, no, not that,' she said. 'I was not needed and I wanted to speak to you alone.'

He gazed intently into her face that was flushed with the cold. 'What do you mean, you are not needed? I need you.'

'And I need you,' she said softly, her hurt being replaced by the warmth of his response. 'I wanted to tell you what your aunt said without the children listening.'

Swiftly she repeated her conversation with Catherine and when she had finished he said, 'I certainly believe her, but will a court of law? They might say she is an old woman who had a knock on the head and was imagining things.'

'You're saying that we need someone who has naught to gain and is regarded as reliable,' said Beth.

'Aye,' he said grimly. 'But that is easier said than done.'

'We must hope and pray, nevertheless that such a person will turn up,' said Beth.

Gawain agreed. 'I need to speak to Wolsey, but I don't want to leave you,' he said, brushing her cheek with the back of his hand.

'Can you not send a message to Wolsey?' asked Beth, who was also reluctant to be parted from Gawain. 'The sooner he knows the truth the better.'

'I agree,' he murmured. 'Although some matters are best discussed face-to-face.'

'Then what will you do?'

'I will send Tom to London and he can see if Sam has any further news of our quarry. Then hopefully he will be able to gain an audience with Wolsey at York Place. If not, he must try Westminster Palace. I will write down all the information I have so far and Tom can take it to him. With luck the weather will have improved by morning and he can leave then.'

'And in the meantime we must hope that Father Hugh stays put,' said Beth.

'As we will stay put,' murmured Gawain. 'I only wish that we did not need to keep our marriage a secret.'

'I, too,' said Beth. 'I hear footsteps. Perhaps you should take your arm away,' she added with a sigh.

He grimaced and began to walk with her towards the hall, saying loudly, 'It will be interesting to see what response comes from my offer of a reward.'

'What is this about a reward, nephew?' asked Catherine, appearing in front of them.

'Aunt Catherine!' He smiled and kissed her on both cheeks. 'I am so glad to see you up and about and was very interested in what Beth has told me.'

'Hugh Tyler always was a strange young man. He had a beguiling way with him at times. Very fond of your father, though. Hopefully he will soon be apprehended, but I feel sorry for James and Mildred because his arrest will create a scandal.'

'Then let us keep names out of this for now,' said Gawain. 'You must not speak of it to anyone. We will play a waiting game.'

'And hopefully the king won't be sending for you for a while,' said Catherine.

'Now that I had not thought of,' said Beth, dismayed.

'If he does, then he will not want me until the twelve days of Christmas,' reassured Gawain.

Beth had said no more on that matter and after supper they all retired to their bedchambers. As she undressed, Beth half-hoped that Gawain would come to her during the night and she left her door unlocked, but as the moments passed and there was no sign of him, she drifted into sleep, guessing he was being sensible for both of them, knowing there must be no gossip amongst the servants.

She was woken by a shift in the change of temperature as the bedcovers lifted and the next moment she felt an arm go around her waist and the long line of Gawain's muscular body press against her through the fabric of her night rail. 'I could not keep away,' he murmured, caressing her ear with his tongue.

'I am glad you have come, but you must be careful not to be seen,' she whispered, turning in his hold to face him.

'Stop worrying and let us make the most of this time together.'

'But you are wearing your nightshirt,' she rebuked, wanting his flesh against hers.

'Alas, I thought I might have to leave you in haste if the girls should wake and demand my attention.'

She understood his reasoning and swallowed a sigh as he kissed her ardently whilst removing her night rail. She caught her breath as he began to kiss and caress her exposed skin, arousing in her feelings that reminded her of that dawn when they had made love for the first time. Instinctively her hands dived down and found the hem of his garment and delved beneath it. She felt him jerk away from her as she touched him tentatively.

'Careful, wife,' he gasped, 'or it will be over too soon for both of us.'

'Aye, husband,' she said meekly and heard him chuckle.

'It is what I wanted to be to you from that first moment I kissed you,' he said, nuzzling her breast.

'So soon?' she asked.

'I wanted not only to possess you, but to have the taming of you,' he admitted with a chuckle.

'The taming?' she said with mock indignity.

'Aye! Now shush, wife, for who knows how much time we have before we could be disturbed,' he said, taking a moment from kissing her belly where he hoped their son lay, to kiss her lips with a sensuous sweetness that caused her expectancy of approaching bliss to soar.

'It is not I who is doing all the talking,' she said, once she had breath again.

'Then I will say no more,' he whispered.

She felt so full of love for him that she could not keep silent, especially when he caused her such delight and took her to heights beyond even that which he had taken her that glorious first time. Afterwards she had fallen asleep in his arms.

When she woke, it was only to find him gone. It was no more than she had expected and it caused her a momentary sadness, but at least he had kept the promise he had given her on their wedding day. If only he had spoken words of love to her. Yet she had much to be thankful for and pray to God that she could look forward to many mornings when she would turn and see his beloved face on the pillow beside her.

They did not have to wait long before the first informer arrived at the house, intent on gaining some reward. A couple of days after Tom had left for London a boatman arrived, but he had little of real interest to give them; even so, Gawain did not send him away empty-handed. There were other men who came and he doubted the truth of what they also had to say. It seemed that Father Hugh had the ability to disappear like a wraith. In the meantime Beth was trying to make friends with Lydia and Tabitha, but it was an uphill task. Lydia was careful not to be impolite to her when her father was present, but when he was not there, for a girl of her age, she was surprisingly able, without a word, to make Beth know that she did not ever intend to accept her as a loving member of the family. Beth did not speak of it to Gawain, believing he had enough on his mind, and tried to be as patient and as kind to the two girls as she could.

It was December before Tom returned, bearing the news that not only that Father Hugh had returned to York Place, but also that he had seen Nick Hurst, who was pleased that the sales of his book were going well. He had also asked after the health of Gawain and Beth and wished them well.

'It was almost as if he knew we were wed,' murmured Gawain.

'I told him nothing, sir,' said Tom.

Gawain nodded. 'Carry on.'

Tom spoke of how he had also had an audience with Cardinal Wolsey, who wished to see Gawain, as did King Henry, who was also in possession of all the information that Gawain had sent. Preparations were already in motion for the move to Greenwich for the twelve days of Christmas, so Gawain was expected to attend the king there immediately.

'He made no mention of Father Hugh being summoned into the royal presence?' asked Gawain.

Tom shook his head. 'But if he has any sense the Cardinal will be having a watch kept on him.'

Gawain thanked him and then dismissed him before going to tell Beth what Tom had told him. After he had finished he said moodily, 'I don't want to go to court. I would be happier staying here with you.'

'But you have no choice,' she said.

'I wish you could come with me,' said Gawain, wrapping his arms around her.

'I am not invited,' she murmured forlornly. 'I deem the king has forgotten the friendship between his father and mine since his death.'

'No, I am sure he hasn't.' Gawain kissed her.

There came the sound of a drawn-in breath that caused them to separate. Beth thought she caught a whisk of skirt from the corner of her eye but they were too late to see who was there, although she suspected it was Lydia and her heart sank.

After Gawain left, the days dragged and Beth spent time in Catherine's company discussing the preparations for the Christmas festivities. She tried to involve the girls; although Tabitha seemed willing, Lydia always dragged her sister away, saying she wanted to show her something.

\* \* \*

It was a week after Gawain had departed that a girl arrived at the house, saying that she had information for him. Beth told her that Sir Gawain was away from home, but welcomed her into the house, offering her refreshment and a place by the fire.

'Thank you, Mistress Llewellyn,' she said, removing her gloves and holding her hands out to the blaze.

'You recognise me,' said Beth, taken aback.

She smiled. 'I saw you at James and Mildred's wedding, but obviously you were unaware of my presence.'

Beth gazed at her intently and was surprised that she had failed to notice her because she was really quite pretty with unusual slate-grey eyes and dimples in her cheeks. She was plainly dressed and spoke well. 'I beg pardon, but I knew scarcely anyone at the wedding. I suppose you only recognised me because I was a stranger.'

'You were pointed out to me by my brother, who was a protégée at one time to Father Hugh. David is a musician, you see. He composes, as well as plays the viol and harp. We are not an influential rich family and so it was greatly appreciated when the priest took an interest in him.'

'I should imagine it would be,' said Beth, alert to her mention of Father Hugh. 'And your name is?'

'Rebecca Mortimer.'

'Was your brother one of the musicians at the wedding?'

'Aye, my father used to work at the Tylers' shipyard amongst others. We are not natives of Kent, but my father travels from shipyard to shipyard wherever there is work. He is a skilled carpenter.'

'I see,' said Beth, remembering Gawain telling her of such craftsmen. 'Then most likely you have heard of the Hurst family who have a shipyard at Greenwich?'

'Aye.' She paused. 'But no doubt you are wondering when I will come to the point.'

Beth smiled. 'I have found all what you have to say of interest but, aye, I would like to know what you came here to tell Sir Gawain.'

Rebecca squared her shoulders. 'I was lodging in Smallhythe with my father not so long ago and was walking down by the river when I saw what I presumed to be a woman in a boat.'

'Presumed?' asked Beth swiftly.

'Aye, because it was not a woman, but a man,' said Rebecca, leaning towards Beth. 'I thought I recognised him as Father Hugh, but could hardly believe my eyes.'

Beth was thrilled by this news. 'I presume that you did not speak of this to anyone at the time?'

'Only my brother and his face took on a thunderous expression and he said that he was not in the least bit surprised. He remembered the priest appearing suddenly one evening, clad in woman's clothing. He told David that he had been taking part in a play, but my brother said he was a man not to be trusted and left his lodgings straight away. I am sure there is more my brother could tell Sir Gawain about him if he were to seek him out,' said Rebecca, her brow knitting.

Beth thought of Jonathan and his passion for play-acting and she grieved afresh for him. 'I wonder if your brother ever met my half-brother, Jonathan Llewellyn?'

'Aye, he was sorry to hear of his death and spoke of Jonathan having an excellent singing voice.'

Beth nodded. 'Tell me, what did you do after you spoke to your brother about Father Hugh?'

Rebecca said seriously, 'My father took ill and I had to return with him to our home in Oxfordshire where I nursed him. Sadly he died a short while ago and my brother suggested I keep house for him as he has been hired as one of the court musicians. It was at Greenwich that I heard that a reward had been offered for any information concerning a woman whom it was suspected was a man in disguise.'

'And instantly you remembered seeing Father Hugh in disguise,' said Beth.

Rebecca nodded.

'You are prepared to swear to this to Cardinal Wolsey and perhaps even King Henry himself?' asked Beth.

'Of course.'

Beth heaved a sigh of relief. 'If only Gawain had known of this earlier, he could have told this to Cardinal Wolsey and the king, but it is not too late. I would ask you to stay here the night and in the morning I will return with you to Greenwich.'

'Certainly,' said Rebecca.

It was at that moment that Catherine came hurrying across the hall in an agitated state. 'Beth, the girls are missing and I cannot think where they have gone.

Perhaps that devil in skirts has returned and carried them off!'

Beth's heart sank. 'Let us hope not! I fear Lydia does not like me and maybe she is just hiding to be difficult.'

'I deem you mistake the case,' said Catherine, frowning. 'Certainly she is jealous of the attention my nephew pays you, but you must not forget that she has had a tremendous shock and is dreadfully insecure.'

'I understand that,' said Beth, her voice softening. 'But let us hope that they are simply playing a game. Is there a favourite place where the children like to hide?'

'I could not say,' replied Catherine. 'Is not the point of a hiding place to keep it secret so no one can find you?'

Beth smiled wryly. 'True. I presume you've had a search made of the house?'

'Of course! Otherwise I would not have come to you.'

'Then a search must be made outside,' said Beth, getting to her feet. 'I will take Cerberus and see if he can nose them out. Have you one of the children's shoes?'

'I will send a servant to fetch one,' said Catherine, and bustled off.

Rebecca said, 'Can I help?'

'That is kind of you to offer, but unless you know the area, I fear you could get lost.' Beth smiled. 'You've had a long journey. It is probably best that you rest here and keep Mistress Ashbourne company.'

'If that is what you prefer me to do, then certainly I will do so,' replied Rebecca.

It was at that moment there came a knock on the

door. Instantly Beth hurried over to it and called out asking who is there. The name given reassured her and she opened the door to a young weaver from Tenderden.

'Jed, what are you doing here?' she asked, surprised.

'I've come about what I just seen earlier on, Mistress Llewellyn,' he said. 'A tall figure dressed as a woman, but walking like a man and muttering to himself. I kept my distance, knowing the terrible deeds he has done.'

Apprehension seized her. 'Where was he?' she asked, a quiver in her voice.

'The wood! He was coming from the wood where there is the haunted tower.'

'Haunted tower?'

'Aye, strange sounds come from it and we young 'uns believed it was haunted by demons in years gone by.'

'You must take me there,' said Beth despite the shiver that ran down her spine.

He hesitated. 'What if he returns and we has to face him?'

'Don't be such a coward, Jed! Besides, we'll take the hound.'

She found the dog's lead and fastened it to his collar. At that moment a servant appeared, carrying a small shoe. For good measure Beth placed it beneath Cerberus's nose and said, 'Seek and find!'

The hound sniffed it and then began nosing about the hall. Beth seized her cloak from a hook by the door and donned it before picking up one of the stout sticks that were there.

'Hopefully, I will return soon with the girls, Mistress Mortimer! Explain to Mistress Ashbourne when she returns where I have gone,' said Beth, before turning to the lad. 'Hurry, Jed!'

Beth was glad the day was fine as Cerberus led them away from the house, past the stables and then beyond the gardens and across a field towards the woods in the distance.

'If that hound is taking us to the haunted tower, it's not easy to get to these days,' said Jed. 'Once there was a path that led to it, but now it's overgrown with brambles.'

'Then it is good that I thought to bring a stick with me, so I will be able to bash them down,' said Beth, thinking that at least if Father Hugh was to return then she had a weapon.

The hound led them to the woods and they did not have as troublesome a time going along the path as she had feared as someone had obviously beaten back the brambles and nettles recently. Did that mean that Jed had guessed aright and the children had been taken this way? She prayed that she would find Gawain's daughters alive.

Cerberus led them straight to the tower and began to bark and scratch at the rickety door. Jed refused to go into the building, so Beth had to go alone. The thought of demons was enough to cause her to clutch the crucifix about her neck as she unlatched the door and called out the girls' names.

There came no answer, but she caught the sound of shifting on the floor like the sinuous movement of a serpent. Setting aside her fear of the supernatural, she entered the tower. It took several moments before her eyes grew accustomed to the dimness inside and then she saw the girls as the hound bounded forwards. Cerberus licked their faces, then he turned away and began to sniff around.

Beth hurried over to the children, who were trussed and gagged and lying on a truckle bed. Their faces were dirty and tear-stained, but their eyes lit up at the sight of her. She fell on her knees besides them and removed the gags. Instantly Lydia began to babble about rats, going to join her papa and the horrible woman-man who had caught them. Beth soothed her with comforting words as she struggled with the knots in the cord that bound them. At last the girls were free. Then she heard a shout that caused her to seize their hands, 'Come, let us away from this horrible place before he returns,' she whispered.

There was no sign of Jed outside, but there was a figure coming towards them through the trees that she recognised. 'Run, girls! Hide so he cannot find you,' she said in a low voice, pushing them away.

They scuttled into the undergrowth and were out of sight in moments. Fear seized Beth by the throat as she saw the evil intent in the face of the man who now appeared in front of her. At the same time she realised that she had left her stick inside the tower. She needed Cerberus, but where was the hound?

'You will insist in interfering with my plans, Mistress Llewellyn,' said the priest.

Beth eased her throat and said fiercely, 'What harm have those girls ever done to you, Father Hugh?'

'What a foolish question to ask?' he sneered. 'They can identify me and I fear you know more about me than I find acceptable. It's only due to the fact that I used to meet their grandfather here when we were boys that I did not kill the girls earlier.' A reminiscent smile played round his lips for a moment and then his expression changed and his eyes were cold as he drew a dagger from his skirts.

Beth thought of Gawain and their child and screamed as loud as she could, hoping that Jed would find his courage and come to her aid. The priest lunged towards her, but she managed to avoid him and darted inside the tower and slammed the door shut.

Her scream was heard a short distance away by Gawain and the group of men with him. Instantly, he began to run, leaving them behind in his fear and haste. If Beth were to die, he would not be able to bear life without her. He burst into the clearing with his sword in his hand. Instantly his gaze fell on the peculiar figure presented by Father Hugh in a woman's gown and with his wig askew. He was trying to force open the door to the tower with his shoulder and slashing at the wood with a dagger.

With a mixture of relief and fury, Gawain yelled, 'It's over, Hugh Tyler, you are not worthy to be a priest. Turn and face me like a man. I will not stab you in the back as you did others or kill you by cunning as you did Mary and Jonathan Llewellyn!'

Father Hugh turned and there was a mad expression in his eyes. 'I loved Cedric as I had once loved Jonathan, but both rejected me in the end for each other. I pleaded with Jonathan to leave Cedric for me, but he refused and threatened to expose me in that news sheet of his. I could not allow him to do that, so regretfully I had to kill him.'

'But why did you have to kill my father?' demanded Beth angrily, emerging from the tower.

The priest spun round.

'Beth, get back!' shouted Gawain.

'No, leave her be,' said Father Hugh, glancing over his shoulder at him and smirking. 'I want to tell her what a fool her father was. He suspected Cedric of killing Jonathan and asked me to help bring him to justice. Too late he realised his mistake, just the same as Cedric—he thought he could get the better of me.'

'But why kill Monsieur Le Brun?' whispered Beth.

'In an attempt to put Gawain off the scent,' replied Father Hugh.

'And Mary?' asked Gawain.

The priest turned to face him. 'She really was unworthy of you, Gawain. Such a foolish woman—I couldn't resist getting rid of her, especially as it gave me the opportunity to implicate you in her death. Now, it's your turn to die.' He launched himself at Gawain.

The dagger slashed his sleeve, but even as Father Hugh drew back his arm to attack again Beth, who had recovered her stick, struck him on the back with it. He cursed and turned to face her. Blood seeped through the sleeve of Gawain's doublet, but he ignored it and shouted the priest's name.

Father Hugh turned and Gawain ran him through

with his sword. As Father Hugh staggered and made another attempt to kill Gawain, Cerberus came at him from the side and knocked him off his feet.

Beth raced over to Gawain. 'You are hurt,' she cried in distress and placed an arm around him.

He gazed into her lovely eyes with a faint smile and placed his sound arm about her shoulders. 'And you? You are unharmed?'

'Aye!' She kissed him.

At that moment those who had accompanied Gawain arrived on the scene, as did the girls. Hearing the commotion, Beth nudged her husband, but he paid no heed to her and continued to kiss her. Then she felt him sag against her and she called for assistance.

Tom and Nick came hurrying forwards, as did a younger man whom Beth did not recognise. They hoisted Gawain upright and for a brief moment her eyes met Nick's. 'Thank you! We must get him home,' she said earnestly.

He nodded, and without further ado the three men hoisted Gawain up on to their shoulders and set off through the woods. Beth felt a tug on her skirts and looked down at Lydia and Tabitha. 'Is Papa going to be all right?' asked the elder girl.

'Of course, he is,' said Beth stoutly. 'Your father is one of the strongest and mightiest men I have ever met. Come, let us go and tend him. I will need your help.'

'Wh-what of *him*?' asked Lydia, jerking her head in the direction of Father Hugh, lying on the ground still held in Cerberus's powerful jaws.

Beth looked a question at Benjamin. 'Don't you be

worrying about this nasty fiend, me dears,' he said. 'The Almighty will deal with his black soul now my hound has finished with him,' he said, dragging Cerberus away.

Beth decided there was no more to be said on that score and hurried with the children after her husband, rejoicing that he had arrived in the nick of time and praying that he would soon recover from his wound.

Gawain was propped up with several pillows in bed. Beth was perched on the side of it, holding his hand. 'So,' she said, 'it was the king who insisted that you rush straight home?'

'Aye, but not until after Master Mortimer met Nick Hurst and mentioned what his sister had told him and suggested that he speak to Wolsey of it. The Cardinal spoke to the king. Until then, Henry had found it difficult to accept that a priest could willy-nilly murder several people. Henry is extremely religious, you know!'

'What happened next?'

Gawain's eyes darkened. 'Father Hugh vanished from the quarters where he had been confined. I tell you, when I heard that news I was almost beside myself with fear for you and the girls. And rightly so. He was completely mad.'

Beth said thoughtfully, 'Master Mortimer deems it likely that Father Hugh saw Jonathan acting in a play and pursued him, even to following him everywhere he went. He must have come disguised that time Cedric visited the shop and I overheard them talking, for I remember there being a strangely dressed woman there who stared at them in such a way that if looks could kill, then they'd have both died on the spot. If only I'd made the connection with the priest earlier on.' She sighed. 'As it was, I remembered him coming into the print room another time as himself and talking to my father. I couldn't hear what they were saying, but perhaps it was about Jonathan.'

'I remember my mother didn't like him trying to monopolise my father,' said Gawain, squeezing her hand.

'He mentioned your father back at the tower,' said Beth. 'He said something about having memories of meeting your father there when they were boys. If he hadn't, he would have killed the girls immediately.' She shuddered.

Gawain held her hand all the tighter. 'Apparently they had been great friends before Father married. It was as if Hugh couldn't accept all that had changed once my mother came on the scene. I sympathised with my mother's feelings because I would have liked more of my father's attention. As it was, my father loved my mother so much that sometimes I felt that there wasn't any love left over for me. When Mother died I thought then there would be an opportunity for Father and I to grow closer together and comfort each other in our grief, but it never happened. He couldn't live without her and I think he set his mind on joining her in death and was careless for his safety. I felt as if he had rejected me and I determined when I had children that I would always be there for them and never shut them out. It was only when I fell in love with you that I began to understand how my father must have felt when my mother died. I wouldn't want to live without you, darling Beth.'

'You really love me?' she said with stars in her eyes.

'Of course I do.'

They kissed long and sweetly.

When they drew apart she rested her head on his shoulder and said, 'Thank God it is all over and that Father Hugh is no longer a threat to us and we can finally look to the future.'

'Aye,' he said. 'And that means you sharing my bed. I do not intend remaining quiet about your being my wife any longer. When I heard you scream in the wood, I knew then that I loved you so much that I would give my life for you. I wouldn't want to live without you, Beth.'

'You really do love me then?' asked Beth, her eyes moist.

'Have I not just told you so?' He brought her against him and kissed her soundly.

Eventually they drew apart and Beth sighed. 'You must not put too much strain on your arm or shoulder or it will delay your recovery.'

He grimaced. 'And that is something I cannot afford to do. The king commanded me to return to Greenwich once this matter was sorted out and you and the children are to accompany me. He has not forgotten your father and would like to meet you again. He also considered the girls could be playmates for the Princess Mary, who is four years old.'

Beth said, 'You have told him we are married?'

'Aye, I thought it best. Soon we will be unable to hide that you are carrying our son.'

Beth placed her hand on her belly. 'You are very certain I am carrying a boy. What if it is another daughter for you?'

He covered her hand and laced his fingers through hers. 'Then I will still give thanks to God because, if she is aught like her mother, then I will be doubly blessed.'

Beth squeezed his hand, touched by his words. They were extra-precious to her, knowing how much he wanted a son. She prayed that she would give birth to the boy that he and her father had so wanted. In the meantime, there was much else to look forward to before then. 'So when will I meet the king if all goes well?' she asked.

'The eve of the Nativity. Pip Hurst and his troupe of players are to entertain the court and David Mortimer has composed music specially for the occasion.'

Beth's face lit up. 'You must not forget to reward his sister, Rebecca.'

'No, I will not,' said Gawain, smiling. 'And what will be your reward for rescuing my daughters?'

'I have all that I need here,' she replied, caressing his strong jaw. 'Although I would welcome a new gown for the occasion and a new quill, ink and paper would not come amiss. Imagine the copies of my news sheet I could sell if I wrote about the celebrations at court.'

'Beth, you would not dare!'

She chuckled and silenced him with a kiss.

# *Epilogue*

*August 1521*

Beth hummed softly to herself as she and Rebecca Mortimer pegged sheets of newly printed pages on lines in the print room. They had risen early and she prayed that they would finish their task before Gawain and the printers made an appearance. He had been against her coming to the city after the birth of their son, but three months had passed since then and Jerome Gawain Llewellyn Raventon was thriving and so her husband had agreed to the family attending Bartholomew's Fair. He had refused her little since their marriage, but she was taking no chances of having him forbid her from printing herself the tales she had spun whilst living quietly in the country awaiting her lying in.

'What are you doing?' enquired a male voice.

Beth almost jumped out of her skin and, guilty, she

turned to meet her husband's eyes. In his arms he carried a grizzling baby. 'Our son is hungry,' he said.

'I'll be with you both in an instant,' she replied hastily. 'Just give me a moment to finish what I'm doing.'

'What is so important that you rose so early?' asked Gawain curiously, coming over to the two women. 'Couldn't one of the men do what you are doing?'

'Aye, but I wanted to do it myself,' said Beth cheerfully, pegging the last page on the line to dry.

'When are you going to accept, love, that as a wife and mother you have more important work to do these days and leave the printing to one of the men,' teased Gawain.

'Or Rebecca,' said Beth, flashing him a saucy smile before turning to her friend. 'I do not see why she should not take my place here now I have a different role to fill.'

'You are ahead of your time, love,' said Gawain. 'The men might accept you as you are their employer, but not—'

'I know what you are going to say,' said Beth with a sigh.

Rebecca said, 'I have told her so, Sir Gawain—besides, I must return to Oxford soon, but I have benefited from my time here.' She smiled at husband and wife. 'I will leave you now and see you at the fair.'

Beth thanked her for her help and saw her out before turning to face Gawain. He handed their son to her. 'The girls were asking where you had gone. They want your help to get ready. It will be the first time for us as a family watching the procession.'

She reached up and kissed him. 'Then let us go.'

Gawain placed his arm around her shoulders and as they left the print room, he said, 'So what were you printing?'

'Tales of romance and adventure, but you don't have to worry about their content. They all end happily ever after just like ours,' said Beth.

\* \* \* \* \*

*A sneaky peek at next month...*

# HISTORICAL

IGNITE YOUR IMAGINATION, STEP INTO THE PAST...

*My wish list for next month's titles...*

In stores from 3rd February 2012:

❑ The Disappearing Duchess – Anne Herries

❑ The Surgeon's Lady – Carla Kelly

❑ Improper Miss Darling – Gail Whitiker

❑ Beauty and the Scarred Hero – Emily May

❑ Butterfly Swords – Jeannie Lin

❑ Gold Rush Groom – Jenna Kernan

Available at WHSmith, Tesco, Asda, Eason, Amazon and Apple

*Just can't wait?*

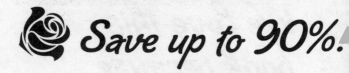

# Have Your Say

*You've just finished your book.*
*So what did you think?*

We'd love to hear your thoughts on our
'Have your say' online panel
**www.millsandboon.co.uk/haveyoursay**

- Easy to use
- Short questionnaire
- Chance to win Mills & Boon® goodies

*Visit us online*

Tell us what you thought of this book now at
**www.millsandboon.co.uk/haveyoursay**

YOUR_SAY